The Silence of the Sand

A Jake Horn Mystery

Gregory Payette

8 Flags Publishing

For my son, James.

THE SILENCE OF THE SAND

Danny's Womack's .38
We're Not Down (summer 2026)

CHAPTER 1

NANCY AND I HAD driven to Kennebunkport, Maine, late Friday afternoon, getting stuck in Boston traffic on Route 1 that added an extra hour to the trip. I should've known better than to leave so late. But it'd been a busy summer for my business and Nancy worked part time at a pool club in Canton.

The house where we were heading belonged to my cousin Raymond's wife, Beth. Beth's family owned the summer house, and Raymond and Beth somehow always got the tail end of the summer—the nicest part of the season. They'd invited us up to spend the weekend with them before Nancy had to go back to school in New Hampshire at the end of the month.

After a couple of beers and a decent night's sleep, I got up early to go for a run on Goose Rocks Beach. Tiptoeing through the house, I tried not to wake anyone.

The screen door from the porch creaked when I opened it, easing it closed so it didn't slam behind me. I headed toward the driveway and had just started to stretch my legs when I heard my name.

Nancy was standing on the porch, on the other side of the screen door. "Can I come?" she said.

"For a run?" I nodded, waving for her to come outside. "You ready to go?"

It was already warm outside with a fair amount of humidity in the air. I looked at my watch. "It's supposed to be warm today."

"Well, it *is* August," she said, stepping outside. She was already dressed in the shorts and T-shirt she wore to bed, sneakers in her hand. She smiled. "Ready."

"Did you at least brush your teeth?" I said, half joking.

She rolled her eyes and didn't answer.

We started down the driveway.

I said, "Did I wake you up?"

"I heard you sneaking out. But I was already up," she said. "I think I ate too much last night."

"How many did you have?" I said, laughing.

"Lobsters? Two. But I've been eating like a pig all summer. When I get back to school, everyone's going to think I'm a whale."

"You don't look like you even gained a pound," I said.

Nancy was always tall, even as a little girl. And she was always thin. I didn't think she had to worry about being called a whale.

"You wouldn't say anything if I did get fat," she said. "You didn't even mention the freshman fifteen."

"The freshman *what*?" I said.

"They say everyone in college gains fifteen pounds their freshman year. It's called the freshman fifteen."

"From drinking all that beer?" I said, giving her the side-eye and a crooked grin.

Nancy said, "They have mashed potatoes in the food hall every night. It's hard to pass that up. And the gravy's pretty good."

I just looked at her.

She said, "Did you know they're raising the drinking age to twenty?"

I rolled my eyes. "I'm sure that'll stop all the drinking in college."

She leaned into me as we walked. "In two and a half months, *I'll* be twenty." She took off ahead of me and started to jog.

"Don't remind me," I said, under my breath.

She was still my little girl.

Nancy stopped and waited for me at the end of the driveway and we turned right, onto King's Highway, which wasn't actually a highway at all. It was the road in Kennebunkport that ran along Goose Rocks Beach.

We waited for a car to pass and ran across the street to the other side, then took the worn path through the tall grass over the dunes.

We both stopped when our shoes hit the sand and looked south in the direction of Cape Porpoise. There was a group of maybe ten people standing around an older pickup truck parked on the beach, although I couldn't see exactly what they were doing or why the truck was there.

Nancy jogged toward them. "Let's go this way."

I started into a light jog but picked up my pace to keep up with her. "Are you getting faster?" I said, my breathing already heavy.

She laughed, looking back at me over her shoulder. "You're just getting slower."

She wasn't wrong.

We slowed to a walk once we got closer to the group and went over to see what the story was. The truck was a black Ford F-100, a 1971 or '72, or in that range of being a model at least six or seven years old. There was some rust on the roof and along the lower parts of the door.

We were close enough to see that the group standing around was made up of mostly all women. In fact it was all women, and there were nine of them. In front of the women stood one tall and lanky police officer with a boyish face, who looked to be no more than Nancy's age.

The young officer was talking to the women with his arms out wide as if trying to corral them. "Please step back, ladies. Come on, give us some room."

Nancy and I stood in back behind everyone, and couldn't get a good look at what all the excitement was around the truck.

I noticed another officer. He had snow-white hair under his hat. Crouched down near the front end of the truck, a gentle wave rolled up behind him, only to recede as soon as it touched the heel of his boot. From where I stood and with the way the truck was angled, I couldn't see what was in front of him.

The tall young officer continued pleading with the women who seemed to keep trying to get closer. "I'm not going to ask you again to step back."

I stepped to my left to get a better look at the officer crouched in front of the truck. And when I saw what he was doing, I pulled Nancy back. "Don't look."

But she couldn't help herself. She pushed my arm away and went around me. She turned to me, a blank look on her face after seeing what I'd hoped she wouldn't.

A body was covered with a blanket. It was apparently a female. I could see her dark, wet hair under the blanket.

None of the women standing around seemed to shy away from watching. Nancy wasn't the least bit bothered by the body either. She leaned in toward me and whispered, "Do you think she drowned?"

I said, "This doesn't bother you?"

She gave me a look like she didn't know why I'd ask such a foolish question. "Not at all."

An older woman in front of us turned and looked me over, then glanced at Nancy. She gave us a look like she didn't think we belonged there.

"What happened?" Nancy said, never one to be shy about asking questions.

I had no doubt where she got *that* from.

The woman kept her voice low, almost in a whisper. "Well, that's Ron Tompkins' truck, so..."

"Ron Tompkins?" I said. "Who's he?"

She turned all the way around this time, facing me. "You're not from around here?"

"We're from the Boston area."

She reacted with a look like she couldn't care less where we were from. It wasn't likely interesting enough, since most people vacationing in Maine were from some part of New England. The woman pointed with her thumb over her shoulder toward the other women in the group. "We saw her first," she said, like she was bragging. "We were out for our morning walk. It's the last thing you'd expect on my beautiful beach."

Like she owned it.

I glanced past her, at the body. "Do you know who she is?"

The woman shook her head. "None of us got close enough to look." She pointed toward a yellow, Cape Cod-style home less than a few hundred feet from where we stood, the fence along the grassy backyard meeting the sand. "That's my house. We had some coffee on the deck and only made it halfway down when we all saw Ron's truck." She pointed to a woman who looked younger than the others. "Alice was the one who walked around the truck, nearly stepping on the poor girl's body."

The woman she was referring to, Alice, looked back at us when she heard her name.

The older woman continued, "I ran to the house and called Thomas right away."

"Thomas?" I said.

She nodded toward the young officer. "That's him. Thomas Silva. I've known him since he was a little boy."

I tried not to stare at the body but couldn't help noticing all the footprints around the truck and in the sand. I found it odd, the way the cops seemed careless with the way they moved around. I couldn't understand why they wouldn't tape off the area.

I noticed footprints in the sand, coming away from the truck and toward the water. But most of them had washed away with the rising tide. It looked as if whoever was driving the truck had gone in the water and never came back out.

I suppose it was possible.

I said, "Who did you say owns the truck? Ron Tompkins?"

The woman glanced at me with a curious look on her face. "You ask a lot of questions, my dear."

Nancy smiled, like she was proud. "Dad's a private investigator."

The woman looked somewhat impressed, her eyebrows raised. "Is that so? I *love* Jim Rockford." She looked me over. "I've never met a real private investigator."

She was a tall woman, somewhere in her late sixties, if I had to guess. "What's your name?" she said.

"Jake. And this is Nancy."

"I'm Mary. Mary Potter." She glanced at the other women in the group, some who had already started to walk away in the direction of the yellow house.

The young policeman, Officer Thomas Silva, as I'd been told, was leaning in over the seat on the driver's side of the truck looking around the interior. The other officer, no longer crouched over the body, was at the truck's bed picking through what looked like scraps of wood and wet cardboard. He had a paint can in his hand and tossed it back into the pile, then grabbed the wooden handle from some kind of yard tool.

Mary Potter finally answered my previous question, her voice again slightly hushed. "It doesn't surprise me to see Ron in some kind of trouble again."

Officer Thomas Silva got out of the truck and turned to Mary, as if he'd been listening to her every word. "Mrs. Potter! I told you Mr. Tompkins reported this truck stolen last night, before any of this happened." He cleared his throat, like a nervous kid talking back to an adult. "We don't need rumors being spread around town at such an early stage of the investigation."

I wondered what kind of rumors he was referring to, and if the way he'd said it meant whatever rumors there were, were already out there.

Mrs. Potter gave him a thumbs-up. "Sure thing, Thomas." She rolled her eyes.

One of the women yelled from off in the distance, "Come on, Mary. Haven't you seen enough?"

She looked toward the covered body and sighed. "It was nice meeting you both." She turned and followed her friends.

A large, white, truck-like vehicle with red lights flashing on top drove onto the beach, heading toward us.

I pulled at Nancy's arm. "Come on, let's get out of here." I glanced back at the officers and the one I knew as Thomas was watching me, but turned away as Nancy and I started in the other direction.

***

My cousin Raymond was out on the screened-in porch with his feet on a white wicker ottoman, hiding behind the *Boston Globe* he held up in front of him. There was a cup of coffee on the small table next to him. He pulled the paper down to his lap when Nancy and I walked in through the screen door.

Raymond said, "What'd you, already go to the beach?"

"Tried to go for a run," I said. I could smell whatever Beth must have been cooking in the kitchen through the open door from the house.

"Tried?" Raymond said.

"Yeah, we only got as far as the body on the beach."

Raymond folded the paper over and straightened out in the chair with both feet on the floor. "Are you making a joke?"

"Not at all," I said.

He leaned toward the door and yelled into the house. "Beth, come out here! There was a body on the beach!"

Beth hurried out, wiping her hands on a flowered kitchen towel. "Was it a seal? One washed up on the shore earlier in the summer, when my sister was here with her family."

Raymond laughed, turning to me. "Oh, I thought you meant a *human* body," He opened the newspaper and leaned back in his chair.

"That *is* what I meant," I said. "It was a woman."

Beth gasped, her eyes wide open, covering her mouth with both hands.

Raymond dropped the paper again to the floor, looking at Beth, holding his surprised gaze, before turning to me and Nancy. "What happened?"

"I don't know. It appears the woman was hit by a truck. But it was hard to say for sure. The whole scene was strange, from the group of women watching like it was a show, to the two officers who didn't appear to've ever dealt with a dead body before."

"I'm guessing you spoke with the officers?" Raymond said. "Asking a hundred questions?"

"No. They looked like they had their hands full. And I don't think they would've been able to answer me anyway. One of the officers—a young kid—apparently knew who owned the truck. And so did the woman we spoke to."

"Someone local?" Beth said, a look of pure shock plastered on her blood-drained face.

"The victim?" I said. "I have no idea."

Beth said, "I meant the truck."

"Well, if the two knew him, I'd have to guess the answer's yes. But the officer mentioned something about the truck being reported stolen the night before, so if that's the case..."

Raymond said, "Did they tell you his name?"

I looked at Nancy, sitting in a folding lawn chair in the corner of the porch. I said, "Ron Tompkins, right?"

Nancy nodded. "And the woman we talked to... Her name was Miss Potter."

"She wore a wedding ring," I said.

"Oh, right; *Mrs.* Potter... didn't seem to like this guy, Ron."

"Well, I don't know if it's that she didn't *like* him," I said. "But she did make a comment about not being surprised he was in trouble."

"I know who Mary Potter is," Beth said. "She's the one who lives in that big yellow Cape Cod home on the beach?"

I nodded. "That's her."

"What about Ron Tompkins," I said. "You know the name?"

Beth shook her head, staring out through the screen in the direction of the beach. She took a deep breath and let out a sigh. "Last thing you'd ever expect at Goose Rocks Beach." She started for the open doorway into the house, but stopped with what looked like a forced grin. "Well, I made pancakes, assuming you all still have an appetite."

Beth wasn't the best cook around. And she'd be the first to admit that. Actually, she'd be second, after Raymond. But when it came to baking, or making pancakes, it was a different story.

Nancy headed into the house behind her.

Raymond said, "Fresh pot of coffee in there, if you want a cup."

I nodded, but that was it. I was having a hard time getting the picture of the dead woman's covered body out of my head. "One thing I wondered, the way the footprints from around the truck kind of disappeared into the ocean, what if there's a chance this woman could've been the one driving the truck."

Raymond said, "I hope you're not going to spend the short time you're up here trying to figure out what happened."

I stared back at him, thinking, but walked into the house without responding.

CHAPTER 2

BETH, RAYMOND, NANCY, AND I sat in a booth at Bartlett's Dockside—a popular restaurant just over the bridge in Kennebunk—after waiting almost thirty minutes for the table. The place was busy, as most of the restaurants were in Maine during tourist season. It looked to be a packed house, with every booth and table and the stools at the counter taken.

I got the fish and chips, Nancy got baked stuffed shrimp, and Raymond and Beth each ordered a lobster roll.

The waitress had just brought over our meals when I looked through the window at the front of the restaurant and watched a police vehicle stop short on Western Avenue, beacon lights spinning. Two officers stepped from the car and walked toward the entrance.

Raymond had his back to the door, but followed my gaze and turned to look as the two officers walked in. He said, "They don't look like they're here for takeout."

"That's the two cops from this morning," I said, looking at Nancy nodding.

"That's just about the entire force," Raymond said.

11

The older one, the one with the white hair under his hat, was met at the entrance by the restaurant's owner, Mrs. Bartlett.

Raymond looked over his shoulder, watching them move toward the counter. "That's the new chief of police. His name's Chief Hanley, from Portland."

I watched Mrs. Bartlett, who appeared animated, talking to the officers, but keeping her voice low at first. But then I could hear her: "Chief Hanley, please! He's a good man. He wouldn't do something like this." She tried to step in their way and stop them from going around the counter.

But they both went past her, around the other side and through the swinging door into the kitchen.

Mrs. Bartlett followed, pleading as the door swung closed behind her. Her voice grew louder from in the kitchen, but muffled. "Thomas, please. Tell him he didn't do it. You know he wouldn't hurt anyone." There was a pause. "Chief Hanley, please. Don't do this."

Everyone in the busy restaurant was quiet. The only sound came from Raymond chewing his food, shifting his plate in position as he took a bite of his lobster roll. He dipped a french fry in the spreading circle of ketchup on his plate.

Beth, seated next to him in the booth, watched him stick another fry in his mouth. "Aren't you paying attention to what's going on?" she said, her voice hushed.

He glanced at her with a shrug, nodding. "Yeah, but what do you want me to do?"

Mrs. Bartlett yelled, "Stop! You're hurting him!"

Someone was in trouble.

Beth tugged at Raymond's arm. "Do you hear this?"

He rolled his eyes, nodding his head. He wiped his mouth with a napkin. "I haven't eaten all day. I'm hungry."

Beth leaned on the table, looking at me and Nancy. "Do you think it has something to do with that woman's body on the beach?"

Raymond put down his sandwich and looked toward the swinging door. "I highly doubt it," he said.

Beth said, "How do *you* know?"

Ray took another bite of his lobster roll. "It hasn't even been twenty-four hours." He picked up his can of Black Label and took a sip.

Three waitresses stood behind the counter and appeared unsure what to do. There wasn't much they could do, including getting food for customers who were waiting to eat. They didn't look like they were willing to walk into the kitchen.

The door swung open and all three waitresses scurried in different directions.

The young officer from the beach, Thomas Silva, walked out of the kitchen. He had a man in custody who wore his long gray hair in a ponytail, and a tie-dyed T-shirt with shorts underneath. A dirty, stained apron was tied at his waist.

The man didn't say a word, trying to bury his face in the crux of his arm.

Nobody in the restaurant said a word. Just gasps as Officer Silva led the man away from the counter. I looked around, and it was clear by the expressions on their faces that most knew the man from the kitchen now in custody.

Chief Hanley emerged from the kitchen with Mrs. Bartlett behind him, still pleading as the swinging door closed.

I noticed a young man's face, looking out through the round window in the door, but then he disappeared.

The two officers left the restaurant with the man in custody, neither saying a word. I watched through the window, like everyone else, but then lost sight of the three until they came back into view, moving through the crowd waiting outside.

The young officer put the man in the back of the cruiser and closed the door. He turned to Mrs. Bartlett and she grabbed him by the arm, but the chief pulled her away. He appeared upset, perhaps losing his cool, until she finally hung her head, wiping her tears.

The two officers got back in the vehicle and drove away, back over the bridge and into Kennebunkport.

***

By the time we finished our dinner, the atmosphere inside the restaurant had gotten somewhat back to normal, although conversations were mostly loud whispers.

The waitress came back to our table and appeared frazzled.

Raymond said, "Who was that? The man they arrested?"

She looked toward the kitchen, holding our empty plates in her hand. "That's Ron. Mrs. Bartlett's brother."

"Ron Tompkins?" I said.

The waitress nodded, but walked away when a male voice from the kitchen called for her.

"That's the man from the beach," I said. "The truck, I mean. It was Ron Tompkins' truck."

"I had no idea it was Mrs. Bartlett's brother," Raymond said.

The four of us got up and headed for the cash register at the counter where we paid the bill and headed out the door.

Beth grabbed Raymond's arm once we were outside. "Aren't you going to admit you were wrong?"

"About what?" he said, although of course he knew exactly what she meant.

She said, "You said it had nothing to do with the body on the beach."

Raymond shrugged. "I told you I didn't know what was going on."

Nancy walked side by side with Beth and said, "The younger officer, the one who led him out the door... He was the one who said the truck had been reported stolen last night, like he was defending this guy, Ron."

"Well, something clearly changed since this morning," I said.

With the sun just about down, it had gotten cooler outside, compared to when we first showed up at the restaurant. Even though it was fairly dark, there was a good amount of light from the lamps casting an orange-tinged glow onto the parking lot. The crowd outside waiting to get into the restaurant had thinned, but there were still plenty of tourists walking the sidewalks between Kennebunk and Kennebunkport.

We walked to the side of the building where I'd parked the Nova, and got a whiff of cigarette smoke as soon as we turned the corner.

An orange glow floated in the darkness. Someone was smoking, almost hiding in the shadows a few feet away from the screen door into the kitchen.

I unlocked the Nova's passenger door but stopped with the door open when a woman's voice said, "Sorry about all the commotion in there."

I couldn't see the person, but walked closer.

Mrs. Bartlett stepped out to where we could see her. She took a drag from her cigarette, the glow lighting up her face.

"Is everything all right?" I said. I looked through the screen door and could see someone cooking in the kitchen.

"I wish I could answer that," she said. "They arrested my brother."

Beth and Nancy stayed by the car, but Raymond followed me over toward Mrs. Bartlett.

"Hello," she said, smiling at Raymond. "You're the Boston cop, aren't you?"

"Formerly," Raymond said with a proud grin. "Retired."

Mrs. Bartlett said, "You and your wife have been coming here for years, haven't you?"

Raymond nodded.

She dropped her cigarette and crushed it out with her sneaker. "I don't know what you heard in there, I'm sure there were plenty of whispers. But Ron... He's innocent. I know he is. His truck was stolen last night, right from this parking lot."

Raymond said, "They tell you what they have on him?"

"Besides that it was his truck?" She shrugged. "That new chief, Chief Hanley, he wouldn't tell me anything." She pulled a pack of cigarettes from her pocket and stuck a fresh one in her mouth.

Raymond pointed at me with his thumb. "Jake here's a private investigator. Maybe he can help."

I gave Raymond a look, like I'd wished he hadn't mentioned it. I was heading back to Boston with plenty of work on my plate. The last thing I needed was a case in a different state, an hour and a half from the office.

"A private investigator, huh?" She lit her cigarette and drew from it. "I bet that doesn't come cheap, hiring someone like you?"

A young woman, one of the waitresses I recognized, stood on the other side of the screen door. "Marilyn? Do you want us to lock the front door?"

Mrs. Bartlett crushed the cigarette she'd just lit against the side of the building. "First pack I've bought in three years, since my husband passed. I should've gotten that cigarette machine out of here, for my own sake." She opened the screen door and started to go inside, but stopped before she did. "Do you have a business card?"

I hesitated, then reached into my pocket, pulled one out and handed it to her. "I don't normally take cases up this way, but if I can help in any way..."

She looked the card over and tucked it in her shirt pocket. "Hopefully the cops will come to their senses and Ron'll have nothing to worry about." She continued inside, letting the screen door slam shut behind her.

I watched Mrs. Bartlett walk across the kitchen and disappear through the swinging door I assumed came out behind the counter inside.

Raymond and I headed back to the Nova, but I stopped to look when I heard the screen door slam.

A young man I couldn't quite see in the darkness walked away from the building with a large, full garbage bag slung over his shoulder. He continued to a dumpster at the back of the lot, threw the bag inside and started back toward the building. But first he stopped to light a cigarette of his own.

"Quite a night," I said to the young man.

He looked at me, exhaling a stream of smoke. I couldn't quite make out his face, but it looked like the same person I'd seen through the window in the door, when Ron was arrested.

"Can't say I'm surprised," the young man said. He took another drag from his cigarette, then went with it inside without another word.

Raymond looked at me across the roof. "Not surprised? What's that supposed to mean?"

I thought about it, then slid in behind the wheel.

Nancy was in the back seat with Beth and leaned forward. "Did that kid say he wasn't surprised about that man who was arrested?"

I looked at her through the rearview. "I don't know." I expected more questions from her—she always had plenty—but she'd already leaned back again, looking toward the screen door.

I started the engine and commenced backing out of the parking space. I said, "Raymond, I appreciate you trying to get me business, but I really hope she works it out with the cops. I can't drive up to Maine to work a case."

CHAPTER 3

NANCY AND I LEFT Kennebunkport around six thirty Monday morning and stopped off Route 1 for breakfast at the Maine Diner. We would have stayed with Beth and Raymond longer, but Nancy had to work at the pool club. And I had work I had to deal with.

One of the cases had dragged on longer than it was supposed to, and if I didn't wrap it up soon I'd be losing money just thinking about it.

My client was the owner of an insurance agency on the North Shore. She gave me a decent amount of work, although I found it somewhat boring. It did, however, put food on the table. My Uncle Pat, the man who started Horn Investigations after his brief career as a Boston cop, always believed in two types of work he liked to have coming in the door for the agency: The kind of work we wanted, and the kind of work we needed.

The client I *needed* was the one that had me on contract, investigating insurance fraud. It had been keeping me busy and paid the bills. Most of them, at least.

Nancy had been quiet for a good part of the ride back while listening to the new Talking Heads 8-track she'd bought at a record store in Wells.

"What's this?" I said, nodding toward the radio.

"Talking Heads: *More Songs About Buildings and Food*."

I said, "Did you know David Byrne went to the Rhode Island School of Design?"

She nodded. "I heard he dropped out."

"I believe that's true," I said. "That's where his first band was—in Providence—before he started the Talking Heads. They were called the Artistics. But they weren't around very long."

Nancy laughed. "I didn't know you were a Talking Heads aficionado."

"I only know because I had a friend, lived in Providence a few years ago. He was into the local music scene, about a year before David Byrne went to New York and started the Talking Heads."

Nancy turned up the volume, when a song came on that I recognized.

"I know this song," I said. "It's a cover."

Nancy looked at me like I was crazy, shaking her head. "It's brand new."

I listened, the sun to the left of us getting brighter. I could feel the warmth coming through the window, and slipped on my sunglasses. "'Take Me to the River' is an Al Green song, from a few years back."

She said, "Really? I never heard it before."

For the most part, I liked the music she listened to. I was glad she hadn't really gotten into disco, especially since it had taken over the radio. Disco clubs had taken over the city over the past couple of years. It just wasn't my thing. Maybe it was all the dancing I didn't like. Give me a small bar with a guy playing guitar...

We had our windows down and spent a good part of the ride with nothing but the sound from the wind and the 8-track playing.

Nancy reached for the knob and turned off the music. "Do you know her name? That woman... the one on the beach?"

I paused for a moment before answering. "Her name was Casey. Casey Jilson."

Nancy remained quiet. I could tell she was thinking it through, her eyes on the highway ahead. "It's just so strange," she said, turning to me. "I mean, besides the fact her body was on Goose Rocks Beach. But, I mean, if Mrs. Bartlett's brother really hit her with his truck, why would he just leave her there?"

I didn't have an answer.

Nancy said, "You think maybe they just wanted to clear their desks? You said that's what the cops do sometimes."

"I didn't say that, did I?"

She nodded. "More than once."

I looked ahead at the highway, watching as the traffic got heavier approaching the Massachusetts line.

I said, "There's always pressure to find answers as quickly as possible, but most people don't want to take the extra steps to avoid mistakes. And that goes for anyone. Not just the cops."

Nancy looked out the passenger side before turning to me. "How come you got mad at Raymond? You said you didn't want him to tell Mrs. Bartlett you're a private investigator?"

I reached for the radio and switched it back on. "I don't know. I guess... If she decided to hire me—I doubt she would—but I wouldn't be able to take a case in Maine."

"Even if she asked for your help?"

I didn't want to get into it, but Nancy was the type of kid who wouldn't let up until she got the answer she was looking for.

"Do you think he did it?" she said.

I paused before answering. "I have no idea."

Nancy got the hint, folded her arms, and looked out the open passenger window, her hair blowing straight back from the wind.

We spent the next few miles without another word, leaving New Hampshire, and into Massachusetts. The traffic had gotten heavier, but at least we were still moving at fifty-five.

"Wouldn't you want another murder case?" she said.

"Who said it was murder?"

"Don't you think it was?" she said. "You're the one who said you hate doing the insurance work," she said.

"When did I say that?"

"I heard you say it to Raymond."

It was hard having a daughter who not only asked a lot of questions, but also rarely missed a beat.

"It's not that I hate the work," I said. "Work is work. I take what comes to me, so I can put food on the table. And to pay your tuition."

She said, "But wouldn't you rather be investigating *real* crimes?"

"Real crimes?" I said. "What are real crimes?"

Of course, I knew what she meant. But I wasn't going to give in to what I knew she was fishing for.

"You know. Murders. Kidnappings. Missing people. *Real* crimes."

I laughed. "It's a business, Nancy. I'm in it to get paid. There's nothing more to it."

Nancy could be pushy when she wanted something. But I also raised her to know she could tell me whatever was on her mind. And she usually did. The relationship we had together was different from what most father-daughter relationships were like. It had been just the two of us for two-thirds of her life.

I took the first exit after we crossed over the Merrimack River. "I have to call Maggie," I said.

"What about?"

"She was going to look into something for me."

"Do you think she knows about Casey Jilson?"

"I have no idea," I said.

"Can you ask her?"

"Probably not. I have other things I need to worry about right now. My client's likely been calling the office all weekend."

"Sorry," Nancy said, turning toward her window.

I said, "You don't have to be sorry. But I just can't worry about what happened up there. Not right now. I have enough on my plate."

She said, "How come Maggie didn't come up to Maine with us?"

I cut the wheel and pulled into Mac's Food and Fuel. "Well, somebody's gotta keep Boston safe." I gave Nancy a small grin and parked next to the pay phone at the front corner of the lot. I opened the ashtray looking for change, but other than a few sticky pennies and crinkled gum wrappers, it was empty. I got out of the Nova and checked deep in my pockets. I had nothing. I said to Nancy, "Do you have a dime?"

She reached into her pocket and came out with a nickel in the palm of her hand. "This is all I've got."

I pulled out my wallet and checked to make sure I had a couple of bills. "I gotta run in and get some change. You all right out here for a minute?"

Nancy nodded, looking at me like I had two heads. "Why wouldn't I be all right?"

I smiled and closed the door, heading into Mac's for some change.

The old man behind the counter had his back turned when I walked inside, facing a black-and-white TV on a small table behind the counter. He was adjusting the rabbit ears.

"Can I get some change?" I said. "For the phone?"

He turned, nodding, but didn't seem to want to take his eyes from the TV. He was watching the Channel 4 morning news with Jack Williams.

I said, "Anything exciting going on?"

He pressed the button on the cash register and the bell dinged. The drawer slid open. He counted out some change in his hand and dropped three quarters, two dimes, and a nickel on the counter. He said, "What was that?"

I swiped the change from the counter and dropped it in my pocket. "I was just asking if there's anything exciting going on in the news?" I wasn't even sure why I'd asked.

But the man nodded. "Some kid from Cambridge is missing."

"A kid? How old?" I envisioned a child.

"Well, *I* say he's a kid. But, I don't know, whatever you want to call a twenty-eight-year-old. I guess his girlfriend was killed over the weekend, up in Maine. Now nobody knows where he is."

I stared at the TV, but it had switched over to a commercial for Riverside Park. "Did they say anything else?"

The old man looked at me and shrugged, taking down a brand-new pack of Lucky Strikes from the case over his head. "I have no idea, buddy. I'm sure it'll be back on the news sometime later." He peeled off the plastic from his pack, took out a cigarette and stuck it in his mouth.

I turned for the door. The bell above it dinged when I opened it. "Thanks for the change."

Nancy had the music up loud, slouched down in the passenger seat with her bare feet up on the dash.

She straightened up and looked out at me. "What time will we be home?"

I looked at my watch. "Half an hour. I'll be two minutes." I walked into the phone booth and dropped a dime in the slot. It rang twice before Maggie picked up.

"Hello?" Her voice was scratchy and almost in a whisper.

"Sorry," I said. "Were you sleeping?"

There was a brief pause. I pictured her nodding. "I'm on the late shift now."

"Oh, right," I said. "Maybe we can meet later?"

"Yeah, but I didn't have a chance to get what you needed. Streets were busy. You know how it is. August in Boston."

I thought for a moment. "Do you know anything about this missing man? A kid from Cambridge?"

"Logan Reed?" she said.

"I don't know. Is that his name? I just heard about it. I'm sure you know about the woman they found in Kennebunkport?"

"Yeah, it's the kid's girlfriend? But I don't know any specifics. Boston PD hasn't been involved." She paused. "Did you hear anything about it when you were up there?"

I watched a Chevy Nova—the same model as mine, but black—pull up to the gas pump. "Actually, yeah. Nancy and I saw the woman's body."

"Are you serious? You called it in?" Maggie said.

"No, we were out for a morning run on Goose Rocks. The cops were already there, dealing with the scene. And, get this," I said. "We go to dinner that evening, and the owner's brother gets arrested. Cops went in, pulled him from the kitchen in handcuffs."

"Honestly," she said, "I hadn't even heard they found her in Kennebunkport. I would have tried to reach you if I knew."

"You don't have any word on the boyfriend?" I said.

"Not now. Cambridge PD is leading the search."

I looked at Nancy in the passenger seat. Her eyes were closed. I said to Maggie, "I have to get Nancy home so she can get to work. Can you meet? Maybe we can grab lunch?" Even with the door closed on the phone booth, I could hear the music coming from the car.

Maggie said. "I can meet around one o'clock, if that's not too late? That'll give me a chance to go into the station, see what I can pull for you."

When my uncle was still alive, he always had friends in the Boston PD who would help him with his cases, pulling files and reports he otherwise couldn't get his hands on. Maggie was that person for me. Of course, there was risk for her. But she didn't seem to mind. I think she enjoyed it.

CHAPTER 4

I DROPPED NANCY OFF at the pool and made it back to Boston by ten, but had a tough time finding a place to park on East Broadway. August brought too many people into Beantown. Some of it was the usual crowd, but others—I could tell just by looking at them—were tourists thinking August might be fun in Boston, not expecting the heat wave that had enveloped the city.

I parked two blocks away and, by the time I got to my office, I was soaked with sweat, wishing I'd gotten some window units to keep the office cool. I turned on the two box fans I had, but all they did was blow the warm, sticky air in circles.

By the time I finally sat at my desk, I was tired from the weekend and needed caffeine. But a hot cup of coffee in ninety-something-degree heat didn't sound too appealing.

I tried to ignore my discomfort, looking through some of the folders I'd had piling up. Although work had been busy for most of the summer, I knew it could turn on a dime. It happened before, going at it twenty-four seven without a break, until a dry spell hit and the phone didn't ring.

I'd hoped with my steady insurance client and a new Yellow Pages ad I got talked into by the cheesy salesman, business would keep me going into the winter.

I called Beth's family's house in Maine and leaned back in the chair, using a piece of paper towel to wipe the sweat from my face.

It rang three times before Raymond picked up. "Hello?"

"Hey, it's me."

"You miss me already?" he said.

I wanted to laugh, but didn't. "Listen, you hear anything about this kid who's missing from Cambridge?"

"Don't know anything about it."

"Well, you know Casey Jilson, the woman from the beach? Apparently, it's her boyfriend. He's disappeared, and nobody knows where he is."

He said, "No kidding, huh? Well, Beth left for the store, said she'd grab the *Globe* for me. They didn't deliver this morning for some reason. I didn't hear anything on the radio."

"Something doesn't add up," I said. "Makes me wonder if they had all the information they needed to go in the restaurant and arrest that man."

"Probably not," Raymond said, always a bit skeptical. "Did she call you?"

"*Who*?" I said.

"Mrs. Bartlett. About her brother."

"No." I swiveled in the chair and looked at the Devil's ivy on top of the beige metal filing cabinet behind me. I stuck my finger into the dry soil.

The plant was a gift my wife Barbara had given me for the office a few weeks before she was killed. And I'd somehow managed to keep it alive for all these years since.

"So why are you asking about it?" Raymond said.

"I'm just curious if you heard anything. There's obviously more to the story now, with the boyfriend missing."

"Was he here in Maine with her?"

"I don't know much about it," I said. "I'm meeting Maggie at the diner, although it's about something else. She doesn't know much about it either."

Raymond cleared his throat. "You two have been hanging out a bit more lately, huh?"

"Me and Maggie? She's helping me with a case. Nothing more to it than that."

"No?"

I let it hang.

"We'll catch up later," I said, and hung up. I didn't need to hear Raymond go down a road he seemed to want to be on a lot lately, when it came to me and Maggie.

***

I sat on the bench in a shaded area in front of First Street Diner waiting for Maggie, looking back and forth. I finally spotted her coming toward me from a block away. She stood out in a crowd, as she always did, not only because of her height—she was close to six feet—but also because of her red hair that almost glowed under the bright morning sun. She walked with a sense of urgency, weaving in and out of the others clearly in her way on the sidewalk.

Maggie was dressed for the summer heat wearing shorts and a buttoned shirt tied at her stomach. She looked like a different person from the one in uniform.

I met her halfway and we hugged. I'm not even sure when the hugs had started, but our relationship had changed over the past few months, ever since we'd gotten back in touch with each other.

I said, "Did you get any sleep?"

She shrugged, showing me the manila envelope she had in her hand. "I went by and got what I could. Sergeant O'Roarke is out this morning, so it was a good time for me to get in fast and get out of there."

"Nobody asked what you were doing?"

Maggie shook her head. "I often end up in there on my days off, especially when I have filing to catch up on." She handed me the envelope. "He doesn't have any convictions, but I wouldn't say he's squeaky-clean."

I opened the flap and pulled out the papers inside.

Teddy Nolan was in the auto-body repair business, suspected of padding accident insurance claims, through my client's business, by damaging cars beyond what had actually occurred in an accident. It was a fairly common practice by body repair shops looking to increase the amount they'd be paid for repairs covered under insurance claims.

All I had to do was find my client the proof she needed to take it to the next step. That meant either somehow catching the body mechanic in the act—which was nearly impossible—or finding suitable evidence.

Not as easy as it sounds, the way these places were locked up outside of business hours. You had your barbed-wire fences, your dobermans or pit bulls, alarms, friends of the owners who were cops—often on the take—or, in some cases, someone living in an apartment above or next to the body shop's garage.

Part of the evidence would often include whatever I could dig up as a criminal past or prior convictions. It wasn't always technically considered evidence, but helped the insurance company lawyers bring down the hammer in front of the judge.

If the work wasn't some small business owner trying to pad his pockets, it was someone, usually in a crummy job, claiming to be too injured to work.

The fact was, most of these people weren't too bright, and usually wouldn't get very far in their game because of their own stupidity. When it came to injury claims, all it took was a few photographs of the claimant riding a bike or chopping wood or competing in a weight-lifting contest... and my job was done.

Maggie and I walked into the diner and toward the booth to the far left on the end. It was *our* table.

We sat and I asked her about Logan Reed, the missing kid from Cambridge.

"He's not exactly a kid, you know. He's twenty-eight. According to reports, the last time his parents spoke with him was Thursday."

"And his fiancée was dead Saturday morning," I said. "Any word he was in Maine with her?"

Maggie said, "The parents said he was supposed to meet her there. They were engaged to be married next year."

"Nobody knows if he showed up?" I said. "Sounds a little suspicious."

Maggie shrugged. "I don't think anyone's ready to make any assumptions at this stage."

Our waitress came over, put two glasses of water on the table and flipped over her pad. "You guys ready to order?"

We hadn't even taken the menus out of the rack behind the napkin dispenser. It didn't matter, I knew the bill of fare by heart. I said to Maggie, "You know what you want?"

She ordered a cheeseburger, medium-well.

"I'll have the same," I said. "Medium-rare."

The waitress scribbled on her pad, then looked from me to Maggie. "Fries?"

We both nodded and she walked away, to another table.

Maggie sipped her water. "Why are you so interested in what happened?"

I leaned back with my arm straight along the top of the booth behind me. "I've just been thinking about it. After seeing that body, and talking to the suspect's sister..."

Maggie said, "How did Nancy react to seeing the body?"

I smiled. "She wasn't the least bit bothered by it. The whole ride home from Maine she just kept peppering me, asking if I'm going to get involved."

"Involved in *what*?"

"I don't know, investigating the young woman's death."

Maggie had a curious look on her face.

I told her how we ran into Mrs. Bartlett outside the restaurant, and how Raymond offered my help. I said, "I had to at least give her my business card. But I don't *want* to be involved."

Maggie said, "Then why are you so interested?"

I had to think about it. "Well, it's grabbed my curiosity. I'd be lying if I said it didn't... especially now that the boyfriend has disappeared." I picked up my glass, thinking. "The only reason they arrested this guy, Ron Tompkins, as far as I know, is because it was his truck on the beach where the body was found. Looks to me like a good old-fashioned setup."

"Do they even have an official cause of death?" Maggie said.

"I don't think so. Which is another reason why it just seems so odd they went ahead and arrested him. Not to mention his truck was reported stolen Friday night."

Maggie looked surprised to hear that one.

She said, "Why don't you call her? See if she needs your help?"

"Who? Mrs. Bartlett?" I shook my head. "She has my card if she needs me."

Maggie leaned on the table, getting closer like she was studying my face. "You have that look in your eye. I can see the wheels turning."

I laughed. "If it was a local case, I'd be all over it."

Someone called my name and I looked toward the counter. The owner, Dennis, was holding up the phone, the cord stretched from the wall. "Jake, someone's on the phone for you."

Sliding out of the booth, I couldn't think of who would call me there. I walked around to the other side of the counter and Dennis handed me the phone. He held up the cord to keep it over the waitresses' heads as they hurried in and out of the kitchen.

Dennis pointed with his thumb over his shoulder. "Why don't you take it in the kitchen, stand by the phone back there so you're out of the girls' way."

I followed him through the swinging door to the other side, where the phone's base was hung on the wall behind the door. I stretched the cord as far as it would go to get out of the way, raising the handset to my ear. "Hello?"

It was Raymond. "Hey, sorry to interrupt your lunch, but I thought you'd like to hear some news, assuming you haven't already?"

"I haven't heard anything," I said.

"About Mrs. Bartlett?"

33

"No."

"She confessed to murdering that woman on the beach."

"Is she serious?" I said.

"I have no idea. Sounds like it."

I watched the owner, Dennis, and the other cooks moving on the line, yelling at each other, dishes clattering. "Who'd you hear this from?"

Raymond said, "Beth and I drove by Bartlett's. Saw the lot was empty, and pulled in to read the sign on the door. There was a kid outside, one of the cooks, sitting on the steps. He's the one who told us what happened."

"What else did he say? And what about Ron Tompkins? Is he still in custody?"

"I have no idea," Raymond said. "I'd guess they've released him."

CHAPTER 5

WE WERE BACK AT my office where Maggie called the Kennebunkport police station trying to get some information on what exactly had happened with Mrs. Bartlett, but was told there were no available officers to take her call.

When she hung up we tried calling Raymond back, but nobody answered at the house.

"Who else can we call up?" I said. "There's got to be someone up there who can tell us what's going on?"

Maggie stood in front of the fan by the window, her hair blowing straight back from her face. "I don't know how you can work in here like this. It must be a hundred degrees."

I looked at the thermostat. "It's supposed to cool off in a few days," I said.

"Didn't you used to have an air conditioner in the window?" Maggie said.

"I had one," I said. "But it was stolen, right out of the window."

The rent I paid for the office was cheap. Part of the reason was a friend of mine bought it from my uncle when my uncle died, and part of the deal was Horn Investigations would always get the first-floor space, for as long as I wanted it.

The other reason it was cheap was because the building was so old.

The carpet was worn. The tiles on the ceiling were stained. When it was humid outside, the smell of mildew would hang in the air. Air-conditioning helped, but window units disappeared as fast as we could get them installed. And my friend and landlord, Nick, wasn't about to outfit the whole building with a new HVAC system.

The only positive was a decent Boston location.

The truth was, I hadn't done much to it at all since my uncle left me the business. I never even thought about taking down the framed photos he had up on the walls, mostly of my uncle with clients, some of them famous. At least in Boston.

The only thing I had done was get rid of the extra desks and moved mine so it was in the middle of the office. I even kept the paneled partition up that separated me from the client area on the other side.

I went over to the refrigerator I had tucked in the corner by the coffee machine. It was a mini fridge, like the kind you'd see in a hotel room. But there was barely enough space inside it for a six-pack and a leftover sandwich. And that's usually what you'd find if you looked inside it.

I asked Maggie if she wanted a beer. "It's all I've got that's cold enough, unless you want tap water from the bathroom."

She turned to me from the window. "Not now, thanks."

I didn't normally drink during the day. Not when I was working. But I went ahead and opened a 'Gansette. I said, "You sure you don't want one?" I took a sip of beer and grabbed my Red Sox mug, filled it with water from the bathroom and watered the Devil's ivy.

I sat behind my desk and Maggie walked over and sat across from me in one of the chairs. "I can't believe you've kept that plant alive all these years. I didn't even know they lived that long." She grinned. "I can't have plants in my place. Max eats whatever I bring in the house, then throws it up on the carpet."

Max, her cat, weighed over twenty pounds. The plant was far from the only thing he ate.

I glanced at the framed photo of me with Barbara, holding Nancy when she was just a little girl. "I heard Devil's ivy'll live for ten years. But we've got that beat by a few. Nancy says I have a green thumb."

The phone rang loud enough it startled me a bit. I'd turned up the bell a couple of days ago when I was taking a nap on the couch and forgot to lower it.

I lifted the handset. "Horn Investigations."

"Hello. Is this, uh, Jake Horn?"

"This is Jake. Who's this?"

The line was quiet for a beat.

"My name's Ron. Ron Tompkins."

I straightened up, my eyes on Maggie. "Ron?"

"Is this the private investigator?" he said.

I nodded. "It is." I pulled my yellow legal pad from the drawer. I wrote RON TOMPKINS on the top sheet and turned it so Maggie could see it. "I'm glad you called," I said. "I heard about your sister."

"You know Marilyn?"

"I know her as Mrs. Bartlett, but only from going to the restaurant over the past few summers. I don't know her personally, but..." I thought for a moment. "Did she ask you to call me?"

"No. I'm at the restaurant right now."

"I thought it was closed?" I said.

"It is. But I have the keys. I saw your business card on the desk in her office."

"Oh, okay. I gave it to her the night you were arrested. I was there, eating dinner. We saw the two officers take you into custody, and when we were leaving, it was mentioned to her I was a PI. I gave her my card, but I had no idea she..." I paused. "She didn't kill that woman, did she?"

"No! Of course not," Ron said. "She had nothing to do with it."

"Have you spoken to her?" I said.

"No, not yet. I was just released a couple of hours ago. They didn't even tell me why at first, just said I was free to go. They told me Marilyn confessed to the murder."

I wrote on the pad RELEASED and underlined it, turning the pad once again to Maggie.

"If she didn't do it," I said, "why would she confess?"

"The only thing I can think of is she's trying to protect me. That's how she is." Ron's voice cracked. "Marilyn would give the shirt off her back to anyone."

"But confessing to killing someone is more than giving the shirt off her back," I said. "Unless maybe she thinks you're guilty, and there's no other way out for you?"

"No!" Ron said. "I did not kill Casey!"

I thought for a moment. "Casey?" I said. "The way you say her name... Did you know her?"

There wasn't an immediate response. "Casey was... She was a student. My student."

"You're a teacher?" I said. "I didn't know that."

Ron didn't respond. And I wasn't sure why. "What are your fees?" he said. "If we were to hire you?"

"Hire me?" I said. I leaned back in the chair, looking up at a brown stain on the ceiling tile. "I mean, I'm not sure I'm available right now but... I charge two hundred a day. Plus expenses."

"That's a lot of money," Ron said. "Private Investigators do all right I guess?"

"Not exactly," I said.

"What do you mean by expenses?" he said. "Gas? Food? There can't be much else, right?"

I said, "Well, if I were to have to travel out of town—which I don't typically do—it would mean paying for the hotel room. I don't charge for meals or drinks or much else like that. I don't want to have to worry about all that record keeping. So, yeah, hotel and gas. Some other things come up here and there. If I have to pay for copies of police records or reports I'd need, or..." I listened for a second, but the line sounded as if he wasn't there. "Mr. Tompkins? Are you still there?"

"Call me Ron," he said. "Yeah, I'm here. It's just... I'd have to see if I can come up with that kind of money."

I looked down at the pad, circling his name with my pen. "Well, as I mentioned, I can't promise I can take on work that's out of my geographic area."

"Then why did you give Marilyn your card if you wouldn't be able to help her?"

I pulled at my unshaved chin. "Well, that's a good question. It's a long drive, back and forth for me. But here's what I'll do: Why don't you talk to your sister and see what the story is. I don't have any information right now, so it's hard for me to say one way or the other. Sometimes these things have a way of working themselves out. And I assure you they're not going to put your sister away based solely on her midnight confession." I flipped through my Rolodex for my client at the insurance agency. If she had anything else lined up for me, it would be almost impossible for me to even entertain the thought of taking on a client in Maine.

I said, "Where are they holding her? Is she at the station, in Kennebunkport?"

Ron said, "No, they moved her up to Skowhegan."

"Skowhegan? Are you kidding me? They put her in *prison*? They wouldn't just..." I tried to think it through. It was almost unheard of. "They must have some other kind of evidence, then. I mean, I find it kind of hard to believe they'd even accept her confession in the first place, without some evidence. Especially... How old is your sister?"

"She's sixty-nine."

"And what about you?" I said.

"You want to know how old I am?" He paused. "Forty-eight."

I did the math. There was a twenty-one year difference. All I could think was how Ron was closer to the age he'd be if he were her child, which would perhaps explain her going to the extremes to help him.

"She practically raised me," Ron said. "That's why she treats me like I'm one of her own kids."

I said, "Are your parents still around?"

"No."

"Does she have any kids of her own?"

"A son. He lives out in California. They don't really talk much anymore though."

I looked at my watch. I hadn't touched the full can of beer in front of me. "Ron, listen, I... I'd like to help you. But, I'm afraid between the expense of hiring a private investigator, and..."

"What if I can come up with the money?" he said.

40

I didn't answer, because there was more to it than just the money. I didn't want to leave Ron or his sister hanging, but I had to think some things through before I made any promises.

Ron said, "Before you say no, let me talk to Marilyn. I'll tell her I called you. Please. She didn't kill anyone, Mr. Horn. Neither did I."

"When you talk to her," I said, "why don't you tell her to retract her confession? That might be the best route right now, to at least get her out of jail. And if there's no other evidence..."

Ron took a moment, then said, "So, after I go see her, I can call you back?"

"I'll do whatever I can to help you and your sister, but I can't make any promises." He obviously already had my office number, but I also gave him the number at the house.

"I appreciate that," he said.

"Just call me after you talk to your sister. We'll worry about everything else later." I placed the phone down on the hook, grabbed the can of beer and took a sip. It had already gotten warm, and I'd changed my mind anyway. I didn't need a beer, so I went in the bathroom and poured it down the sink.

Maggie walked up behind me. "So what did he say?"

"He found my business card in her office, at the restaurant."

"She didn't ask him to call you?"

I walked past my desk toward the window with the fan in front of it, blowing in nothing but hot, humid air from outside. "I can't understand how they could put her in prison like that."

"Well, it's just for holding," she said. "But maybe they're trying to scare her, call her bluff?"

I said, "Assuming the police didn't intimidate her into confessing, and she just walked in off the streets? It's over the top, especially for a sixty-nine-year-old woman."

41

"Sixty-nine-year-olds kill people too," Maggie said.

I stayed quiet, thinking about it.

She said, "You really don't want to take a case in Maine? Or is there something more to it? You make it sound like Kennebunkport is on the other side of the earth."

"It could tie me up for months," I said. "And I'm not sure I can afford to do that, not when Nancy goes back to school in a couple of weeks. Am I going to just leave her in Milton for the rest of the summer and go live in Maine?"

Maggie said, "You're overthinking it."

"It's an hour and a half each way," I said. "I can't spend three hours on the road every day, going back and forth, with gas prices the way they are."

Maggie nodded, like she understood. "How come you didn't mention the victim's boyfriend to him?"

"I didn't want to get into it too much over the phone."

We stood in the warm office and both looked toward the front door when a horn blew outside on East Broadway.

I said, "Ron was Casey Jilson's teacher."

Maggie nodded. "I heard that part. You asked him about it, but did he answer?"

"It could be high school?" I said.

Maggie said, "If he's a teacher or, whatever he is... why is he working in his sister's restaurant?"

"Maybe it's just a summer thing?" I picked up my pad. I hadn't written much down, other than his name. "Is there anyone you can call over at Cambridge PD to ask about Logan Reed?"

Maggie nodded. "I can call right now." She picked up the phone.

I wiped sweat from my forehead. "After that, let's get out of here, go somewhere cooler."

Maggie held the phone to her ear. After a couple of moments, she said, "Hi, this is Officer Maggie Donovan, with the Boston PD. Is Officer Kelly in today?" She glanced over at me and grinned. "Sure, I'll hold."

"Who's Officer Kelly?" I said, my voice low.

She covered the mouthpiece on the handset. "A friend of mine." She held her index finger up toward me to wait, turning her back to me. "Hey Eddie. It's me." She nodded. "Yeah, I'm good," then smiled. "No, I didn't get it. I'm not home." She listened. "Sorry, but I might be tied up tonight, but... Okay, yeah. I'll let you know." She paused. "Eddie, listen, I was just wondering if there've been any updates on that missing man, Logan Reed?" She leaned back against the desk. "New Hampshire?" She squinted her eyes. "Any-where else?" She listened. "Right. Okay. Thanks." After another brief pause, she smiled. "Sure, call me at the apartment. I'll be off for a couple of days." She hung up and said, "Logan Reed may have been spotted in Portsmouth over the weekend."

"About forty minutes from Kennebunkport," I said. "Did he say what day?"

Maggie nodded. "Saturday night."

I said, "When Casey was killed."

Chapter 6

I'D SPENT SOME OF the afternoon at the library doing research inside, in the comfort of air-conditioning, and was happy when I walked outside to rain coming down. Cooler air followed when the sun finally came back out. It was nice enough that I rolled the windows down on the Nova on the drive to Canton.

I pulled into the parking lot ten minutes before Nancy got off work, and walked to the pay phone on the side of the building.

I dropped three quarters into the slot and the phone rang six times before Raymond finally answered.

His voice was raspy and deeper than usual. "Hello?"

"Did I wake you?" I said.

"Me?" Raymond paused. "I don't know. I must've dozed off. I was watching the Sox." He cleared his throat. "They're still losing, of course. Another promising baseball season going down the drain."

"What's the score?" I said.

"Milwaukee's up, two-one. Lee's on the mound, so you'd think they'd want to win this one. But the way they've been losing the last couple of weeks..."

"So, listen," I said. "I got a call from Ron Tompkins today. He called me at the office."

"Yeah? What'd he say?"

"His sister's up in Skowhegan."

"Prison? Are you kidding? What else do they have on her?"

"That's what I've been wondering. Makes no sense a confession's enough to send her up there without some kind of trial, don't you think? Maggie thought maybe they've tried to scare her, see if she'd retract her confession."

Raymond said, "I can't imagine they'd send her up there, just to try and see if she'd tell them if she knew what happened."

I looked at the chain-link fence surrounding the pool. I said, "But if they think her confession's false, and she won't budge, then I don't know. I guess if they're trying to get her to admit the truth..."

Raymond said, "So what are you doing now?"

"Right now? I'm at the pool club, waiting for Nancy to get off work."

"No, what I'm asking is, you're talking to me like you're involved in a case you said you didn't want to get involved in. And now you've got Maggie pulled into it?"

"Well, after Ron Tompkins called..."

I shared most of the details of Ron's call with Raymond, watching the gated entrance to the walkway for the pool.

"It's not that I don't want to help them," I said. "If I could afford to take a month or two without putting a dime in my pocket, I'd drive up to Maine and do whatever it takes. But I'm not in that kind of position right now. Nancy's tuition bill is sitting on the table at home, waiting for me. If I don't wrap up this insurance case I'm supposed to be working on, it's a thousand-dollar bill I won't be able to pay."

"A grand, huh? I'm glad I don't have kids to put through college."

I watched a station wagon full of kids drive past me and out of the parking lot. "So, I did some research at the library, found out Casey Jilson's parents were both killed in a car accident the year she was supposed to graduate from college."

Raymond said, "For someone who wants nothing to do with investigating what happened on that beach, you're doing a lot of digging."

"I was just curious," I said. "Besides, Ron Tompkins told me he knew her."

"He knew who, the woman on the beach?"

"Casy Jilson. Yes." I told Raymond how Tompkins told me she was his student, but that he didn't elaborate. I said, "I wonder if that has something to do with why the police moved so fast, arresting him. But it wasn't like he was trying to hide the fact from me that he knew her."

I could hear the sound from the baseball game on his TV in the background.

Raymond said, "Didn't you say that woman, Mrs. Potter, said she wasn't surprised Tompkins had something to do with it?"

"Yes. And so did the kid working in the kitchen with him. That's two people, both suspicious of him."

We were both quiet until Raymond yelled into the phone. "Dammit! Milwaukee just scored again. Sox'll drop out of first, they lose any more games. And the damn Yankees are coming right up behind Milwaukee." He sighed into the phone. "These bums are ruining my summer."

Nancy left the pool and came out through the gate, still in her orange bathing suit with a whistle around her neck, and her Plymouth State duffel bag hung over her shoulder.

I said to Raymond, "Listen, I gotta run. But, do me a favor: if you hear anything else, call me at the house."

"Okay, but I'm still confused about what you're up to. First, you say you want nothing to do with this case. But here you are. You just can't help yourself?"

***

It was 8:41 when the Red Sox finally lost to the Brewers, four-to-three. Maggie had come over to watch the game and stayed for pizza with me and Nancy. But she got up as soon as the game was over and grabbed her keys. "I have to get home," she said. "Max needs to eat."

"Don't most people just leave a bowl of food out for their cats?" I said.

Maggie nodded, smiling. "Why do you think I call him Fat Max? If I leave too much food, he'd devour the whole bowl. I just leave enough to get through the day. He's probably screaming at the door, annoying the neighbors, waiting for me."

Nancy said, "We should get a cat."

I laughed, shaking my head. "While you're in school? I have enough trouble taking care of myself. Maybe when you graduate you can get a cat."

Nancy got up and followed Maggie to the door. She said, "Are you sure you can't stay and watch *One Day at a Time* with us?"

Maggie shook her head and gave Nancy a hug. "Maybe next week." She looked at her watch, then over at me. "I guess he never called?"

I was carrying the empty pizza box into the kitchen but stopped at the doorway. "Ron?" I shook my head.

Nancy said. "Ron? From Maine?"

I hadn't gone into it much with Nancy. And even though I'd been thinking about it all evening, I didn't mention the fact that the phone never rang. I said, "Mrs. Bartlett's brother."

Nancy looked from me to Maggie, like she was waiting for one of us to tell her what was going on.

I went ahead and told her what had happened, how Mrs. Bartlett was being held in the women's prison up in Skowhegan, Maine, because she'd confessed to a crime.

"Do you really think she did it?" she said.

"I don't think so," I said. "I'd have to believe she didn't."

"Can't you help her?" she said.

"Ron Tompkins was supposed to call me back." I looked toward the clock on the wall in the kitchen. "I thought I would've heard from him by now."

Nancy looked concerned. "Does he want to hire you?"

"Maybe," I said. "But it doesn't sound like he's in any kind of position, financially, to hire a private investigator."

Nancy stared back at me. "But aren't you the one who always says not to do things just for the money?"

She was right. I *had* said that. More than once. But as much as I felt it was true, the reality of life didn't always make it possible for me, or anyone else, to help everyone who needed it, as if money wasn't a necessity in life. "I think you know what I meant," I said. "When you're running a business, you—"

"But what if you're the only one who can help them?" She said. "You can't just turn your back on them."

I looked at Maggie standing by the door, hoping she could throw me a lifeline and say something to Nancy.

"Nance," Maggie said, "Your dad has clients down here he has to take care of. As much as he wants to help Mrs. Bartlett and her brother..."

Nancy looked at me. "But you told him to call you? And he didn't?"

I nodded. "It's very possible he and his sister decided to go in another direction. Maybe she knows someone local up there who can help them. There's also a chance Mrs. Bartlett withdrew her confession. I don't know, Nance. I don't have any information right now."

The phone rang. Nancy would normally try to beat me to answer it but this time she let me take the call. I leaned through the doorway into the kitchen and grabbed the receiver off the wall. "Hello?"

I expected to hear Ron Tompkins on the other end.

"Hi, is this Jake?"

"It is," I said.

I didn't recognize the voice.

"I'm sorry if I'm calling too late. This is Eddie Kelly. Maggie gave me this number, said I could reach her there if I needed to. Is she there, by any chance?"

"Oh, uh..." I nodded. "You just caught her on the way out. Hang on." I held the phone toward Maggie standing by the front door. "Eddie Kelly."

She took the phone from my hand, covering the mouthpiece with her palm. "I hope it's okay I gave him your number?"

I nodded and walked over to the TV. It was still on Channel 38, and *Hogan's Heroes* had started.

Nancy sat on the couch. "Who's Eddie Kelly?"

Maggie went in the kitchen with the phone.

I said, "A friend of Maggie's, with the Cambridge Police."

Nancy stared at me as I sat down next to her. "Is it about that man who's missing?"

I shrugged. "I have no idea. I didn't ask."

"Is it personal?"

I cracked a smile. She was itching to ask more questions. I said, "I'm sure she'll tell us what it's about when she gets off."

Maggie hung up the phone and came back over toward the couch. "Logan Reed has been found."

"Alive?" I said, standing from the couch.

She shook her head. "He was in a parked car, in a parking lot up at Acadia National Park. Killed by gunshot."

I said, "Did he say anything else?"

"There's a strong possibility it's a suicide. But they don't know yet. There was a twenty-two pistol in his hand. The police up there aren't saying much."

I said, "Is Eddie involved in the case?"

Maggie said, "It sounds like Maine state police are heading the investigation."

I looked at the TV, seeing Bob Crane, the actor in Hogan's Heroes who had been murdered barely two months earlier, in June, inside his Arizona apartment. I said, "This takes a little gas out of Marilyn Bartlett's confession."

"It's a little early to jump to any conclusions," Maggie said.

"Yeah, of course," I said, walking toward a window at the front of the house. I stared outside, into the darkness. "How far is Skowhegan from Bar Harbor?"

Maggie said, "Two hours. But if you're trying to say Tompkins could've somehow tracked down Logan Reed in Acadia National

50

Park, and potentially killed him?" She shook her head. "That's a bit of speculation, don't you think?"

Nancy said, "And why would he call you in the first place?"

I looked at my watch and asked Nancy what time she had to be to work in the morning.

"Eight thirty."

I said to Maggie, "You want to take a ride up to Maine?"

She paused, staring back at me. "Are you serious?"

I nodded. "I'd like to go see Mrs. Bartlett."

CHAPTER 7

MAGGIE AND I HAD been on the road for a little under two hours after leaving Skowhegan when I pulled off the highway and took the exit into Freeport. I drove down Main Street, on the lookout for a pay phone without much luck until I drove past a school and turned down Bow Street. I spotted a place called the Bow Street Market with a pay phone on the sidewalk in front of the building, just before the entrance.

"You have any change?" I said, fishing around in my pockets. I picked through mostly pennies left in the ashtray, and produced a crumpled-up dollar bill and a couple of dimes from my pocket. But a toll call from Maine to Massachusetts was seventy-five cents.

Maggie reached into her pocket, handing me three quarters and a nickel. "It's all I've got."

I didn't have time to go in the store to get change, so I'd have to make it a quick call. I dialed the number for my client, Jennie Vance, and the operator came on the line. "Please deposit seventy-five cents."

I dropped the three quarters in the slot and the phone rang twice.

The receptionist answered, "Vance Insurance."

"Hi, it's Jake Horn for Jennie, please?"

"Hi, Jake. Please hold."

I looked at my watch. It was 12:37.

A couple of minutes had gone by before Jennie Vance finally came on the line. "Jake? I was wondering when you were going to call me back."

"Call you back?"

"I called your office a few times, but you haven't answered. I don't understand why you don't have an answering machine."

"Oh," I said. "I guess I should look into it."

I felt that paying over a hundred dollars so someone could leave me a message—most likely a bill collector—didn't seem like it was worth the investment. To me, these new machines were nothing more than a luxury I wasn't sure I needed. "Listen, Jennie, is there any chance I can get a little more time with the Nolan's Auto Body case?"

"More time? Are you serious, Jake? I was calling you because, honestly, I'm not sure why it's taken you this long. All I need is a little proof on this one. A picture, or—"

"I wish it were as easy as you make it sound," I said. "Nolan's got that place buttoned up tight. You can't even see in the windows to his shop. You think I can just walk in with my camera and start shooting pictures?"

"You've never had trouble with it before," Jennie said, letting out a sigh. "What's the story, Jake? I get the feeling something's not quite right with you lately, like I'm not a priority anymore."

"No, no," I said. "That's not it at all." I didn't want to blow it with the one client who'd been feeding me work for the past year. "It's just... I've been busy. And I've committed to another case that's going to have me on the road quite a bit. So I'm just trying to balance everything."

"Why is that *my* problem?" she said. "All I'm hearing you say right now is that you're putting other clients ahead of me. Is that what you're trying to tell me? Because, I'm not sure I like hearing that. You know what *my* clients would say to me if I told them I had something more important to do?"

I wanted to laugh. Jennie was a hard-nosed businesswoman who didn't take an answer from anyone unless it was the one she wanted to hear. But that's what made her successful. "Nobody's more important than you," I said.

"Don't patronize me," Jennie said.

"Listen, all I'm asking is to give me a little more time. A week, I'll get what you need."

"A week? Jake, are you serious?"

There was a click and the operator came on the line: "Please deposit sixty-five cents for an additional three minutes."

I didn't have sixty-five cents.

I said, "I'm sorry, Jennie. When have I ever asked for more time?"

The line was probably thirty seconds from disconnecting.

"That's what I don't understand," she said. "I don't like the feeling I'm getting, that you're brushing me off."

"Just give me until the end of the week. I'll have this thing wrapped up; you won't have to worry about anything."

She sighed into the phone. "Friday?" she said. "Are you telling me you'll have everything I need to prove Teddy Nolan's committing fraud? And taking money out of my pocket?"

Insurance was, in most cases, a necessity. But for someone from the industry to tell me about taking money from someone else's pocket... I wanted to laugh into the phone.

"You have my word," I said.

And before she could respond, the phone disconnected. I couldn't even call her back to tell her I hadn't purposely hung up on her.

I climbed back behind the wheel and started the engine, banged a U-ey in the street and headed back toward the highway.

I was already feeling the stress, not knowing how I was going to manage two clients in two different states, helping Mrs. Bartlett and her brother while also taking care of my biggest client.

"Everything all right?" Maggie said.

I rolled down my window, rubbing the back of my neck. "I hope I'm not making a mistake," I said. "That was Jennie Vance. She's already pissed off I haven't wrapped up my latest assignment."

"The Teddy Nolan case?"

"Yeah, I had kind of promised her it would've been done last week."

Maggie said, "Is there anything else I can do to help?"

I shook my head, turning onto the ramp for 95. "She gave me until Friday."

***

We drove past Goose Rocks Beach on King's Highway and turned into the dirt road toward Beth's family's house. I had told Raymond we'd be coming by, but when I got out of the car and walked up to the screened-in porch, I noticed a yellow piece of paper folded and stuck in the doorjamb. It read,

Beth forced me to go to the beach. Come get me. -Raymond

Raymond liked being at the beach, as most any normal person would. But he didn't actually like being *on* the beach. He wasn't the kind of guy to stick his toes in the sand and relax in the sun. He was just as happy on the shaded, screened-in porch listening to the Red Sox on the radio, smelling the saltwater air.

I handed Maggie the note and looked toward the street. You couldn't quite see the water from the house, but you could *feel* it in the air.

"Do we have time?" Maggie said, handing me back the note. She looked at her watch. "We should probably be back on the road in an hour."

I opened my door and stuck my keys up over the visor. Being up in Kennebunkport wasn't like being in Boston; If I left my windows down with my keys over the visor outside my office, the car would be stolen.

It was also the reason they only needed a couple of police officers in Kennebunkport. Crime was just about nonexistent.

Until it wasn't.

Maggie and I walked toward the street, then along the sidewalk on King's Highway where we cut across to the beach once the handful of cars had passed.

We took the worn path through the tall grass on the dunes and out to the beach where I could see Raymond's big head sticking up over his beach chair, the floral umbrella over him. Beth and Raymond were down close to the water, and there weren't many people on the beach.

Maggie and I both took off our shoes and left them near the path. The warm sun felt good, and wasn't nearly as hot as it was when I was there a few days earlier.

I looked to the right toward the area where Casey Jilson's body had been. There was a group of people sitting there, unaware of the scene over the weekend. Five small kids chased each other, running in circles around the adults lying on blankets.

Maggie and I both had to stop short when a group of older women, who were walking toward us, had to go around us. But one of the women stopped and looked at me.

She wore a yellow, wide-brimmed sun hat and we both stared at each other through our sunglasses.

It was Mary Potter, the woman who lived in the yellow Cape Cod house, farther down the beach. She lifted her glasses from her face. "I know you," she said, smiling. "You're the private detective?"

"Jake," I said, nodding.

She looked at Maggie, who had continued walking toward Raymond and Beth without realizing I had stopped. "Who's the pretty lady?"

I cleared my throat and smiled. "Just a friend."

I recognized a few of the other women walking toward us from that morning on the beach. I spotted the younger-looking one in the group. Her name was Alice. I could usually remember names by associating them with something, and in this case it was the show, *Alice*, that had been on TV for the last couple of years.

Alice smiled at me and I looked away, toward Raymond and Beth, who at that point both had their heads turned, watching me. Maggie stood in front of them, eyes behind dark sunglasses, but I knew she was watching.

Mary Potter said, "You must've heard? Ron Tompkins' sister, Marilyn Bartlett—the owner of Bartlett's Dockside—confessed to murdering that poor woman?"

"I might've heard a little something about it," I said.

Mrs. Potter leaned toward me and whispered. "Rumors are that she confessed to protect her brother. Everyone knows he did it."

"Who's everyone?" I said, admittedly coming off a bit defensive.

A group of women, dressed in similar summer outfits, stood behind Mary.

Mary pulled a pink silk cloth from her pocket and wiped her forehead. "I don't like the idea of a murderer running free around this town."

I stared back at her nodding. "I'm not sure who does," I said.

She held her gaze on me, almost as if she wasn't sure what I'd said. "I do hope Marilyn smartens up," she said. "She can't spend her whole life protecting her brother the way she does. Besides, she needs to get back and open that restaurant." She laughed, looking at her friends, who all laughed with her, as if on cue. "We miss our lobster rolls, don't we, ladies?" They all nodded, like it was all a big joke.

One of the women, shorter and maybe the chubbiest one of the bunch, said to Mrs. Potter, "Brock will need another job if she doesn't open up soon."

Mary eyeballed the woman.

"Who's Brock?" I said.

"My grandson."

"Does he work over there? At Bartlett's?"

"Yes, he does."

"How old is he?" I said, wondering if he happened to be the kid in the kitchen I ran into that night.

I was sure she'd heard me, but she acted as if she hadn't.

"Well, if you'll excuse us," Mary said. "Come on, ladies. Let's go get those steps in. We have martinis waiting for us once we finish our exercise!" She started walking with her arms moving in robotic fashion, as if she were holding ski poles. The other women followed, like ducklings.

The younger of the group, Alice, waited while the others walked ahead. She stepped closer toward me, almost brushing up against me as she pulled her sunglasses from her eyes, looking at me over the top of them. "I'm Alice," she said.

I didn't say I already knew her name.

"Jake." I said.

She smiled. "Pleased to meet you, Jake." She looked back at me one more time over her bare shoulder, then went into a light jog and caught up with the others.

I walked over to Raymond, Beth, and Maggie. They'd already stopped paying attention to me and were facing the water. Maggie was sitting on a towel.

"What was that all about?" Raymond said, looking up at me.

"Be careful what you say to Mrs. Potter," Beth said, flipping through a magazine. "She's the town crier."

I faced the water and looked to my right down the beach, toward the women walking away from the shore in the direction of Mary Potter's yellow house. They continued through the gate of the white picket fence.

"Her grandson works at Bartlett's," I said, looking at Beth. "You don't know who he is, do you?"

She shook her head.

I said to Raymond. "I think he's the kid we saw outside the kitchen, the night Tompkins was arrested."

"The one who said he wasn't surprised they arrested him?" Raymond said. "Didn't that lady, Mrs. Potter, say the same thing?"

"She did," I said, and glanced at my watch. "We can't stick around much longer. I just wanted to swing by, tell you where things stand."

"Maggie filled us in," Raymond said, pushing himself up from the chair and ducking from under the rainbow-colored umbrella. "I'm happy to hear she'd like to hire you. But something about it sounds like Mrs. Bartlett's confusing you with a defense attorney."

"Why's that?"

"Well, you don't know yet if her brother's innocent or not. And it sounds to me she's expecting you to do whatever it takes to clear his name. So, you have to think if she was one-hundred-percent certain he was innocent, she wouldn't have sacrificed herself the way she did by confessing to a murder we all assume she didn't commit."

For the most part, I understood what Raymond was trying to say.

He said, "I just hope she's not being hopeful you can somehow help prove the brother's innocence, if it turns out there's evidence that proves he's not."

I had to think about what he was saying, but didn't want to get into it with him by asking him to clarify. I said, "I think Mrs. Bartlett understands what she and her brother are up against."

CHAPTER 8

WE MADE IT BACK into Boston in time for me to pick up Nancy from the pool in Canton and take her home before heading out to Foxboro once it was dark.

There was more traffic than I'd expected on Route 1 for that time of night, but I left it behind once I turned down the side street between the Dunkin' Donuts and Mike's Car Wash. A quarter of a mile down, I spotted the unlit sign for Nolan's Auto Body.

The body shop was a one-story brick building with three garage doors, the property enclosed with a chain-link fence and the double gate locked with a thick chain twisted around the middle posts. A yellow awning hung over the rust-colored steel door at the entrance.

A light rain had started to fall as I reached into the trunk for my bolt cutters, then snapped the lock on the gate without much trouble at all. I got back into the Nova and kept the lights off, driving into the parking lot and around the back of the building.

There were four cars parked along the fence: one a gold Trans Am that caught my eye, the other two vehicles, your everyday American sedans, each dented or smashed in one way or another. I parked next to a blue Dodge Aspen and stepped out onto the wet pavement.

The air smelled of summer rain, the way it mixed with the hot, dry sand on the asphalt.

The steel door on the back of the building had a single lock I knew I could pick without much trouble. But when I looked in through the window, with drops of rain sliding down it, I saw the white wires from an alarm running down the inside of the frame to the bottom of the window. I pulled the flashlight from my back pocket and shined it where the sash met the sill, seeing the switch for the alarm.

I went back to the Nova and opened the trunk, grabbing a roll of duct tape, a slotted screwdriver, and a putty knife, then gently closed the trunk lid.

With the flashlight off, my eyes adjusted to the darkness as I looked through the window into the body shop. A light from somewhere behind me reflected off the wet glass.

I slipped a long screwdriver's tip under the window. There was enough space to fit it because of the alarm switch, and it didn't take much effort to get the shaft all the way underneath.

With my free hand, I slid a flat metal putty knife between the sash and the sill, getting it over the switch to keep it down. That way I could open the window without the alarm going off. With a quick downward motion, I snapped the window open with the screwdriver, then lifted the window just enough to pop the lock, keeping pressure on the putty knife to keep the switch down.

Slipping my fingers under the window's sash, I lifted it open and used long pieces of duct tape to keep the putty knife in place on top of the alarm switch.

I put the tape and tools back in the trunk and grabbed my Konica camera. It was bulky and somewhat heavy, especially with the flash attached, but took good photos in low light. I hung the camera's strap around my neck and stopped in front of the window. I pulled myself up, making sure I didn't accidentally peel the tape off the switch and set off the alarm.

I poked my head through the open window and looked down at the workbench on the other side of the wall. It was covered with tools and cardboard boxes with gallon-sized cans I assumed were filled with paint. There was also a small metal tray filled with random pieces of hardware like screws, nuts, and bolts. I reached through the window and tried to clear some of the area to give myself a clean place to land, then took the camera off my neck and put it down inside, on the workbench.

I was already halfway through the window at that point, and pulled myself through the rest of the way, sliding my body over the sill and over the workbench. I made it onto my feet.

Inside was dark, other than the light coming in from the street and a slight glow from a small Cape style house behind the shop.

I reached into my back pocket for my flashlight, but it wasn't there. Looking out the window, I saw it had fallen from my pocket and onto the ground.

I couldn't turn the lights on, so waited for my eyes to adjust to the darkness. Within a few moments I was able to see some things in front of me, including the three garage doors on the far end from where I stood. Three cars were parked inside: one in front of each door. I grabbed my camera from the workbench and hung the strap around my neck.

The idea was for me to take photos of the cars and compare the damage to the accident reports my client, Jennie Vance, already had in her possession. It was, technically, an easy case. And it wasn't my first one either. The hardest part was getting close enough to the cars to get the photos needed for proof. Sometimes I'd go in as if I were a customer to see if I could get close enough to see the evidence right there, with lights on. But pulling out the camera to get a picture for evidence was never ideal.

Breaking into a place, on the other hand, was often my last resort. Being licensed as a private investigator didn't give me the go-ahead to break into a property illegally.

But I did what I had to do to get the job done.

Most of these auto-body guys all pulled the same stunts: they'd get the car in straight from the accident scene, and get right to work. Before the adjuster would show up, they'd take a sledgehammer to the car's exterior, smash in the door, or destroy the front end. Or they'd drive it around and sideswipe a tree or two... do whatever they'd have to so they could jack up the costs of repair. An average three-hundred-dollar claim could easily turn into a fifteen-hundred-dollar repair with a few extra dings and dents.

Often, the adjuster's hands had been greased too, so they'd turn their backs, even when it was obvious someone was playing the game.

For the most part, notes were never compared. And unless someone was paying attention, the auto-body owner would be home free once the repairs were complete.

So it was up to me to somehow catch them in the act.

A sliver of light came in from outside and reflected off the metal emblem on the side near the driver's-side door. It was a Chrysler New Yorker, although I couldn't tell if the car was black or dark blue. As long as I could focus the lens on my camera, which wasn't easy in the dark, the flash would take care of the details.

I held the camera up to my face, my eye in the viewfinder, and pressed the shutter-release button. The whole place lit up with the flash. I waited for the flash to be ready, walking around to the other side of the car to where the damage was obvious. But it was still hard to see the details. I raised the camera and, once again, the shop lit up from the flash.

I continued with the other cars until I'd gone through the whole roll of film and taken thirty-six pictures. I was tempted to disconnect the alarm—which took nothing more than disconnecting a single wire—and go right out the door. But that would mean I'd leave evidence behind.

I made my way to the workbench and climbed up on top of it, leaning out the window. I held my camera by the strap and eased it down to the damp ground, even though the rain had started to pick up. I couldn't afford to let the film get ruined, so I hurried through the window, head first.

But before I was all the way out, my foot caught on the sill. What resulted was I knocked the putty knife loose.

The alarm bell rang.

I fell to the ground, rain coming down hard now, and grabbed the camera. I ran toward the Nova, splashing through a puddle before I slid in behind the wheel.

A floodlight came on outside the house on the other side of the fence, a figure running out the front door. A man yelled, "Who the hell is that?" He ran toward me and slipped through an opening in the fence.

My hands were wet and I dropped my keys, reaching for the floor to find them. I picked them up and the man was outside my window, pounding with his fist on the glass.

He yanked open the door before I could lock it, grabbed me by the shirt and pulled me from the car.

I tried to grab the door to catch myself from falling but my hand slipped. We both crashed to the ground, splashing into the puddle outside my door.

"Becky!" the man yelled into the darkness. "Call the cops! Someone broke into the shop!" The man grabbed me by my shirt and lifted me from the ground. He tried to throw a punch, but I beat him to it.

I came up swinging and caught him with a shot to the chin. He stumbled away from me and I tried to get back in the car, but the man came charging right back for more, grabbing the back of my shirt.

He spun me around and threw me against the side of the car, throwing a punch that caught me upside the head. My head whipped back against the car's roof, then he threw me to the ground.

The man was not quite as tall as me, but he was strong, with arms thick and hard as steel.

I tried to pry him off me, both of his hands wrapped around my throat. "What the hell are you doing here!" he yelled, cocking his arm back ready to strike.

But I drove my knee into him before his fist came down, and he yelped like an injured dog when I connected, right between his legs. The man dropped to the wet ground, holding himself, crying.

The raindrops hit the Nova's steel roof like a machine gun as I jumped into it, got the key in the ignition and turned over the engine. Slapping the shifter into reverse, I did my best to avoid the man on the ground I believed was Teddy Nolan. I skidded, sliding and fishtailing on the wet pavement and into the road, slammed the pedal down and raced toward Route 1.

I grabbed the wet camera from the passenger seat, hoping the film had stayed dry.

At the light I turned right and drove north.

Blue lights flashed, coming over the hill as three police vehicles blew past me, heading south on Route 1 just before Schaefer Stadium.

CHAPTER 9

I SIPPED MY COFFEE with the *Boston Globe* open in front of me at the table, but kept my eyes down when Nancy came into the kitchen from upstairs.

"Dad?"

I looked up to her gaze, coming right at me.

"What happened to your face?" she said, pulling a chair from the table and sitting next to me.

I touched the bruise around my eye and leaned back from the table. "Well, I'm not sure we need to go into all the details. But I *did* manage to get the photos I needed for that insurance fraud job." I forced a grin and sipped my coffee, looking back at her over the rim.

She leaned in closer, studying my face. "Dad? Are you okay?"

"Yeah, it's nothing," I said. "The job's done, and now I can turn my full attention to helping Mrs. Bartlett and her brother." I moved the newspaper toward Nancy and pointed to the article I'd been reading. "Logan Reed's father has put up a reward for anyone who finds his son's killer."

Nancy pulled the paper closer and looked it over. "It says here the cops still don't know if he was killed or not."

"They don't," I said. "Not yet. But they'll know soon."

She got up from the table and grabbed a half gallon of milk and a box of Cheerios. She sat back down. "What does it mean for you that his dad's offering a reward?"

"What's it *mean*?" I said.

"Well, wouldn't you get the reward? If you solve the case?"

I thought about it, but shook my head. "Mrs. Bartlett—and her brother—they're my clients."

"I know," she said. "But what if it's the same person who killed Casey Jilson *and* her boyfriend?"

I leaned back in my chair, glancing out the window toward the street. "Well, if it turns out Logan Reed's case officially becomes a murder investigation, then the cops'll make the connection. And Ron Tompkins could end up being the main suspect in both cases."

Nancy said, "Even though he's out of jail?"

I stood up from the table. "He's out of jail, but the problem is nobody knows where he is."

I could tell by the look on Nancy's face her wheels were turning. They always were.

She said, "Doesn't that make him look guilty?"

"Of course it does. And as soon as Mrs. Bartlett's confession is retracted, assuming her attorney will be successful in front of the judge, there's likely going to be a new warrant for Mr. Tompkins' arrest."

I could tell something was bothering Nancy by the look on her face. "At first, I wanted you to help Mrs. Bartlett. But, now, something doesn't seem right. I guess I'm confused why..." She paused, looking down at her bowl of cereal. "Don't you worry that he's guilty?"

"Ron Tompkins?" I took a deep breath and exhaled. "Until I see something that tells me without a doubt he's guilty, I have to give my clients the benefit of doubt."

Nancy said, "Innocent until proven guilty?" She kept her eyes on me, stirring her spoon in the cereal. She hadn't even taken a bite, and I knew she had only begun with the questions. She said, "Why is Logan Reed's father offering the reward if they still don't know what happened?"

I walked to the sink, grabbing a towel and wiping my hands. "I'm sure he doesn't want to believe his son may have taken his own life."

Nancy always wanted to help me, even when she was just a little girl, although it was only as she got older I started to share more of the details of the cases I was working on.

But her idea of fun was trying to solve a crime right there at the kitchen table. The problem was, no case was ever that easy. Tossing around ideas was one thing, but guessing too early in the game and latching on to an idea was what usually sent a detective—including the ones in law enforcement—down the wrong path.

I had hoped Nancy would one day end up in law school, maybe take a different road than the one she'd always hinted at. I still remember the day when, at twelve years old—five years after her mother had been killed—Nancy told me she wanted to join the FBI.

She'd never once wavered from that idea, as much as I tried to persuade her otherwise.

The phone rang and Nancy jumped up, grabbing it off the wall. "Hello?" She nodded. "Yeah, he's right here." She handed me the phone. "It's cousin Raymond."

I took the phone and lifted the cord over Nancy as she ducked under it. "Hello?"

Raymond said, "You hear they found Ron Tompkins?"

"What? No, I haven't heard a thing. Where'd you... what have you heard?"

"He was in an accident, drove his car—actually, his sister's car—off the road. Drove it deep into the woods and claims he was unconscious since late afternoon yesterday. Police picked him up on Route 1, north of Biddeford."

"Was he hurt?"

"Well, he was unconscious for a full day. I don't know much else."

I glanced at Nancy watching me, like she wanted to listen in. I said to Raymond, "Where's the car?"

"I don't know. Why? Like I said, it was deep in the woods. Over fifty yards. Word is he fell asleep. Likely had been drinking. He claims he was on his way up to Skowhegan to see his sister. I guess that explains why he never called you back."

I thought about it. "Maybe. Where'd you hear all this? The news?"

"Actually, Beth ran into someone at the market, told her about it. So I made a call to a buddy of mine, an officer up in Biddeford. He said Tompkins was at Webber Hospital."

***

Although I tried to sneak in and out of the Vance Insurance office to drop off the photos and pick up my check without having to speak with Jennie Vance, it was just my luck she was standing out in the reception area, like she knew I was there.

I could see by the look on her face something wasn't good.

I handed her the envelope. "They're not perfect, considering it was pitch black inside the garage, but this should get you what you need. And there's some additional background information on Teddy Nolan you'll want to share with your attorney."

Jennie took the envelope and pointed over her shoulder to the glass door leading down the hall toward the offices. "Can we sit down and go over the next one? This one's urgent."

"I can't," I said. "Not right now. I'll have to get back to you."

Her eyebrows raised, and she pointed into her own chest. She said, "You'll... you'll get right back to me?"

The look she gave could burn holes.

"I'm sorry. I told you on the phone I have another client."

"And what did I say to you?" she said. "Do you remember? I said, 'if I told clients I had someone else more important, I'd be out of business.'"

"Jennie, you know I can handle more than one job at a time. But this one's out of town. It's a case up in Maine. In Kennebunkport. I'm sorry, but..."

Jennie folded her arms, the folder with the photos I'd given her dangling from her hand. "So, what you're telling me is you can't come back there and sit down with me to discuss another case? What am I supposed to say to that, Jake? For all I've done for you? I pay you pretty well for the work you do."

"I know that, but... I'm sorry." I took a step back, toward the door. "Just give me some time. I can meet later in the week, or early next week."

Jennie shook her head. "No," she said. "We're done. I'm moving on."

"Moving on?" I said.

"You're fired."

"You can't fire me," I said. "I'm not your employee."

She huffed, folding her arms. "I'll find someone else who actually appreciates the work I have available." She walked through the open door behind the reception area, disappearing as she slammed it closed behind her.

I wouldn't say I was shocked or surprised to hear her wanting to end what had turned out to be a decent business relationship. And I wouldn't say I was that upset about it. Just because Jennie Vance kept me busy with work didn't mean I was going to let her control me or try and stop me from having other clients. All along, for the time we'd worked together, she wanted me as her exclusive investigator. But I was never going to go for that, and she knew it.

I left the building, almost smiling.

I didn't like her that much anyway.

***

I pulled into a gas station on Main Street in Salisbury to call Maggie.

"Where's Nancy," she said, once I told her I was on my way up to see Ron Tompkins.

I said, "Well, that's part of why I'm calling. I'm staying with Beth and Raymond up there for the night, and probably won't be back until later tomorrow. I know you have to work tonight, but I was hoping you could at least check in with her at some point, if it's not too much trouble?"

73

"Of course not," she said.

I said, "She has a friend staying with her."

Maggie paused on the other end. "Then, are you sure she needs me checking up on her? If she's got her friend staying there... She's not a kid, you know."

"I know she's not. But it doesn't mean I don't worry about her. I guess... You don't have to actually go over there then. But if you could just give her a call? Don't tell her I asked you to or anything."

"Don't worry," Maggie said. "I'm on the clock for most of the night, but I'll check in with her."

Neither of us said a word for a handful of seconds.

Maggie said, "So what's your plan up there? You're going to talk to Tompkins? Then what?"

"Well, what I've heard is Mrs. Bartlett's lawyer ran into trouble with the judge, trying to get her confession overturned. Sounds to me the judge is playing hardball."

"Hardball? I don't know many judges who appreciate hearing someone plead for forgiveness after admitting to a false confession," Maggie said.

"I just hope they're not going to hold her longer up in Skowhegan," I said.

The operator came on the line and asked for another five cents to continue the call.

I said to Maggie, "I gotta run. I'll call you after I talk to Tompkins, assuming he's all right, or hasn't been dragged back to jail by the time I get up to the hospital."

CHAPTER 10

I WALKED INTO THE hospital room and barely recognized Ron Tompkins, lying in the bed with both eyes swollen, almost shut, and a bandage taped onto his forehead and cheek. The only other time I'd seen him was at the restaurant, the night he was arrested.

He turned his head on the pillow to his right, looking toward me as I got closer to him. "Who are *you*?" he said.

"Jake Horn. We spoke on the phone."

He pulled the blanket away with a free hand, showing me his other, handcuffed to the bed's rail.

I was somewhat surprised to see he was back in police custody, but not completely shocked. "When did they do this?"

"You just missed them. About twenty minutes ago."

"Biddeford Police?"

"Two of them were from Biddeford. Rick Hanley's the one who read me my rights. I don't know if you know him or not, the chief of police in Kennebunkport?"

"I know who he is," I said, looking at the sunlight coming in through the window. "Listen, Ron. Your sister is clearly concerned you're in some deep trouble here. If she had any faith you were going to get out of this situation on your own, I doubt she would've confessed to something I can only assume she had nothing to do with."

Ron looked at me through his swollen lids. "Didn't we already discuss this over the phone?"

I didn't appreciate the guy's attitude, but I let it slide, considering the condition he was in.

"If I'm going to help you, I'm going to ask you to be straight with me." I waited for his response, the man nodding after a moment. I said, "Have you spoken with your sister?"

"Marilyn?" He nodded, then placed his free hand on his neck, like the nod caused him pain. "I spoke to her on the phone, a little while before the cops showed up." He lifted his handcuffed hand. "Before they did this."

I looked toward the open door. "I'm surprised there's no cop outside. They just handcuffed you? And left?"

"I don't know. There was someone out there before. Maybe he went to get donuts." He grinned, as if he were in any position to be making a joke.

I walked to the window, moving the curtain aside to look out at the parking lot. I said, "Do you know Logan Reed?"

"Logan? Yeah, he's... Logan and Casey were engaged."

I turned from the window. "Do you know anything about what happened to him?"

Ron said, "No, I... Is he all right?"

I wondered if he was being honest with me. "Logan Reed is... He's dead."

Ron's puffy eyes opened as wide as they would go, his mouth hanging open like he wanted to talk, but didn't. "He's... Logan's dead? Are you..." He paused, taking a moment. "What happened?"

"They don't know yet," I said. "There was a gun in the car. There's a chance it could be suicide."

Ron held his free hand over his mouth, shaking his head. "Logan? I can't... I can't believe it." He looked up at me. "They're both dead?"

Either Ron was a good actor, or he was genuinely surprised.

Ron said, "Logan was my student at Westbrook College."

I watched him, the way his gaze shifted around the room.

He said, "He and Casey met in my class. We had a small group of students. All really talented, creative kids. The way it was set up, the students—all of us—we became close. We shared a lot. That's how I taught them to find stories: to pay attention to each other." He wiped the corner of his eye with his knuckle.

"I understand you ran into some trouble up there," I said.

Ron cleared his throat. "How much do you know?"

"Not enough," I said.

"Well, the simple truth is my whole life was taken from me. Working in the kitchen at my sister's restaurant wasn't exactly part of the plan."

"You never went back to teaching?"

"I was blacklisted," he said. "I couldn't get a job in a school as a janitor." His eyes met mine. "I smoked a little reefer with my students." He shrugged. "Big deal, right? But then, there was a drug bust on the campus. Someone was dealing, and they came after me."

"But you were cleared," I said.

"Legally, in a court of law? Yes. But, I still lost my job. They didn't care what the judge had to say."

"Who's 'they'? The school?"

"The school board. I was never even given a chance. A group of wealthy parents wanted me gone, and that was the end of it."

"The Reeds?" I said.

He swallowed, nodding. "Casey's parents were the only ones who didn't partake in the witch hunt," he said.

"I understand they were killed in an accident?" I said. "What do you know about that?"

He shrugged, shaking his head. "They were on their way back to their home in Maine, after visiting Casey at school. It was just a freak accident, as far as I know. I was out of the school at that point, but I went out of my way to help Casey. She didn't have much family around here at the time, so I did what I could to help."

"So you've always kept in touch with her?"

Ron nodded, and again grabbed his neck.

"Did you see her at all?" I said. "When she was in Kennebunkport? I mean, before she was killed?"

Ron didn't answer me right away. "I saw her the day before she... I saw her Friday afternoon. She came by the restaurant."

"Do the cops know that?" I said.

"Yes. I told them. I've been honest with them from the start. But honesty hasn't helped me much. I'm not sure it ever has." He looked up at me with a small grin on his swollen face.

I walked back to the window and sat on the ledge in front of it. "I find it interesting that Chief Hanley was involved in your case at the school."

Ron said, "He was just an officer in Portland, trying to make a name for himself. I think he had some kind of connection to Logan Reed's father, but I don't know how. He walked into the classroom, took me into custody in front of my students. That's why—that evening at the restaurant—it was like deja vu the way he showed up and arrested me like that, everyone staring at me."

The warmth of the sun came through the glass and onto my back. "Don't take this the wrong way," I said. "But if I were in Hanley's shoes..."

"I know how it looks," he said. "But you've got to believe me. I'm not a killer. And I certainly would never hurt Casey. Never. She was a wonderful person, for all that she'd been through."

I stood up, looking out the window toward the parking lot again. I could see the Nova, toward the back of the lot. "Is there a chance someone would set you up? I mean, that's clearly what's happened here, assuming—"

"Assuming I didn't do it?" He nodded. "I understand. My truck was there. I had a relationship with Casey." He took a deep breath, appearing to struggle with it, then exhaled with a sigh. "People talk about me around town, like I'm some crazy person who lost his mind. I know how it looks, a former college professor flipping burgers..." He brushed his long, gray hair back with his hand. "I look like a hippy. And, yeah, I smoke a little reefer. I swear, it's just to calm the anxiety a bit, you know?" Ron cleared his throat. "But I can't think of a single person who would want to kill Casey. And then go out of their way to make it look like it was me?" He leaned his head back on the pillow and looked up at the ceiling. "Do they even know if the truck is what actually killed her?"

I walked toward him. "I don't know."

"What if she was already dead?" he said. "What if she was dead before my truck was stolen, and someone brought it onto that beach?"

"Anything's possible," I said.

I didn't have a lot to go by, but I had to believe this guy was innocent. And since I'd already, for the most part, committed to helping prove it, it didn't make sense for me to think otherwise. At least in the early stages of my investigation.

I said, "Can we talk about this accident? The cops say your car was fifty yards in the woods. You mind telling me how it happened?"

He shrugged, shaking his head. "I... I honestly don't know. I hadn't eaten much of anything at all. I just blacked out, driving down Route 9. It was raining, and..."

"Were you drinking?" I said.

His Adam's apple jumped in his throat.

"I had a couple of beers," he said.

"A couple? You know you could've killed someone?"

As soon as the words left my mouth, I knew there must've been a better phrase I could've used.

There were a couple moments of silence.

"Listen, I know. It was stupid. But with all the stress of every-thing..."

I thought about it, looking him over. "Has that ever happened before? Where you blacked out and didn't remember anything?"

He glared back at me. "Are you asking me if there's a chance I blacked out, took my truck on the beach, and killed Casey?"

"I'm just asking questions," I said.

"Excuse me," a voice came from the doorway. "Can I help you?"

I saw it was the young officer from Kennebunkport I hadn't yet personally met, Thomas Silva.

"I'm just checking on my friend," I said.

"He's not allowed to have visitors," he said, like a nervous kid, the first say on the job. "I'm going to have to ask you to leave." He narrowed his eyes. "Do I know you?"

I shrugged, holding my gaze on his. "I don't know. Do you?"

He pulled at his chin, eyes squinted. "You were on the beach, at Goose Rocks." He glanced from me to Ron, then back to me. "You were there the morning we found Ms. Jilson's body on the beach."

"I don't know. I might've been." I wasn't going to get into it with the young officer, or tell him much of anything. I gave Ron a nod and told him I'd talk to him later, then walked out the door without another word to Officer Silva.

Chapter 11

IT WAS FAIRLY QUIET inside Bartlett's when I first walked in, three men at the counter with their backs to the door and barely half the tables in the dining area occupied.

The seafood smells coming from the kitchen made me hungrier than I already was.

Mrs. Bartlett approached me, knowing ahead of time I'd be there. "We can talk toward the back," she said, walking ahead of me and around the corner to a booth somewhat separate from the main dining area.

She placed a menu on the table. "Are you hungry?" She slid onto the seat across from me.

"I could eat," I said, but pushed the menu aside.

She looked at her watch. "I've got to get up there to see Ron at the hospital, before they move him. But I'm still in a little bit of hot water myself," she said. "I'm lucky I'm even here right now."

"Because of your confession?" I said.

She nodded. "I know it was a mistake. I hadn't really thought it through when I showed up at the station."

"How was the judge?"

"Well, I said I'd do anything for my brother." She shrugged. "He seemed at least somewhat sympathetic, which isn't always the case with most people. But, as of right now, I'll have another day in court. He actually said I could have been sent back to jail for what he referred to as a 'stunt' a handful of times." She let out a sigh. "This doesn't look good for Ron, you know."

I paused, nodding. "I'd have to agree."

"Did you know it was my car he drove into the woods?"

"He told me," I said. "So what are you driving?"

"My husband's truck. It hasn't been driven since he passed."

We both sat, saying nothing for a couple of moments.

I said, "They have him handcuffed to the bed."

She closed her eyes and kept them closed for a moment, slowly shaking her head. "I hope you haven't changed your mind about helping us, have you?"

"I gave you my word," I said. "I just hope your brother's going to—"

"Ron's all I've got," she said. "He's my only family around here. I... I have a son out on the West Coast, but, well, we had a falling out after my husband passed away. I can't tell you the last time I've even heard from him."

"I'm sorry," I said.

"His wife... She and I never got along. Not for a minute. We almost didn't get invited to their wedding."

I sat, listening.

"It got worse when my husband passed away, because they expected I was going to hand over this restaurant to them. Apparently, my husband had made them a promise it would be theirs."

"Didn't he have a will?"

She shook her head. "He thought he'd live to be a hundred." She nodded, forcing a small grin. "He never made it to sixty."

"How old is your son?"

"Thirty-four. His wife is younger by a few years. She must be thirty by now." She nodded toward the menu. "How about a bowl of the lobster bisque?" She got up from the booth without waiting for my answer and disappeared around the corner.

I had a feeling discussing what sounded like an estranged son wasn't something she'd be interested in going any deeper into.

I opened the menu and looked it over. There was something about Mrs. Bartlett I liked. She reminded me of my own mother, somewhat. Even her brother seemed like a decent enough guy who may not've been perfect, but—thinking with my gut—he didn't seem like a killer.

I eyeballed the lobster roll on the menu and pulled out my wallet to make sure I had enough cash. The gas on the Nova was low, and I needed to fill up. I counted twenty-seven dollars in bills. I had a check Jennie Vance handed me for the Teddy Nolan job before she tossed me out of her office. I wished I'd stopped at the bank to deposit it before I drove up to Maine. But I hadn't.

I realized maybe I wasn't as prepared as I thought I was to stay overnight in Kennebunkport.

Mrs. Bartlett rounded the corner and put a bowl on the table, then placed a check in front of me. "I hope this is enough to get you started?"

I picked it up and saw she'd paid me with a check from Bartlett Restaurant, Inc. It was for five hundred dollars and already made out to Horn Investigations.

I said, "I didn't ask for a deposit."

"I wanted to give you a little something to make sure you stick around."

I placed the check on the table.

"I'd sell this restaurant and use the money if that's what it'll take to make sure Ron stays out of jail." She stood next to the table, like she was waiting on me. "What else would you like?"

"Oh, I haven't even looked at the menu," I said, even though I had. I was caught off guard by the check.

"How about a lobster roll?" she said. "And a cola? We have RC."

I nodded. "That sounds good."

She turned the corner without another word.

I looked toward one of the front windows and saw the kid I recognized from the night Ron was arrested. He was walking around from the back of the restaurant and across the parking lot toward the street.

I jumped up from my seat and hurried for the front door before he disappeared.

"Hey," I said, following after him.

But he kept walking as if he didn't hear me.

I yelled, "Hey, kid! Wait up."

He looked at me, but kept walking as if he wasn't sure I was talking to him.

I picked up the pace, breaking into a light jog to catch up with him.

"Hey," I said, walking up behind him. "Don't you work back there? At Bartlett's?"

He had a smug look on his face. "None of your business, weirdo." He kept walking.

I wanted to smack the punk in the back of the head. "You're Mary Potter's grandson, aren't you?"

He stopped.

I said, "It's Brock, right?"

He stood just before the bridge between Kennebunk and downtown Kennebunkport. He wasn't very tall, maybe five and a half feet with a somewhat scrawny build and dark messy hair. He had a pack of cigarettes rolled up in the sleeve of his black T-shirt. "What do you want?"

"I saw you the other night, when you were out back throwing out trash. I was back there, in the parking lot."

He stared back at me, holding his gaze.

I said, "You said something to me about Ron Tompkins, along the lines that you weren't surprised he was arrested?" I wasn't sure how old the kid was, but maybe not even old enough to drive.

"What are you, a cop?" he said.

"Nope."

He took the cigarette pack from his sleeve, removed a cigarette and stuck it in his mouth. With a silver Zippo lighter, he gave it a light and took a drag, blowing the smoke straight at my face. "You want to know something about Ron Tompkins? Go ask the police."

I stared back at him, and thought about what kind of trouble I'd get into for tossing this kid off the bridge and into the water. "You have something against him?"

He dragged on his cigarette. "I'll tell you what," he said. "I don't really remember talking to you. I think you have the wrong guy." He started to walk away from me, but after two steps turned back. "How do you know my grandmother?"

"From the beach," I said, and left it at that.

Brock looked back at the restaurant. "You know that lady was hit with Ron's truck, don't you?"

"That may or may not be true," I said.

"Why's that? Because his truck was supposedly stolen?" He laughed. "Wouldn't you say your truck was stolen, too, if you were going to use it to run over your girlfriend?"

"His girlfriend?" I said.

He leaned against the railing on the bridge. "Well, she'd been here to see him before. And she was here the day before, and they left together."

I held my gaze without getting into it with the kid.

He said, "Listen, I don't know what you want from me. I don't know what happened." He continued again along the bridge, smoke from his cigarette rising up from in front of him.

I looked back at the restaurant and guessed Mrs. Bartlett must've been wondering where I'd gone. I let the kid walk away.

Mrs. Bartlett was already waiting for me when I walked back through the entrance. "What was that all about?" she said.

"Just asking the kid some questions," I said. "But he didn't seem to be up for talking."

Mrs. Bartlett looked through the plate-glass door. "Brock's a funny kid. He's been in a bit of trouble here and there himself." She started toward the back area where we had been sitting.

I followed her. "Do you know his grandmother?"

Mrs. Bartlett looked back at me, nodding. "*Everyone* knows Mary," she said. "The Queen of Goose Rocks." She sat down in the booth where a soda and a lobster roll were already waiting for me, along with the lobster bisque I hadn't touched.

She said, "This is all on the house, by the way."

"No, I pay for my own meals."

"You said two hundred a day plus expenses. I thought I'd rather feed you at my cost."

"Those expenses don't include my meals. I'd like to pay for whatever I eat." I stuck a fresh-cut french fry in my mouth. "So, why is Mary Potter called the 'Queen of Goose Rocks?'"

Mrs. Bartlett rolled her eyes. "She acts like she owns that beach. She acts like she owns the whole town, really. I guess some people seem to think, just because they have money..." She wiped her hand across the table and used her other hand to catch whatever it was off the edge. "You know, she and her husband—ever since they bought that house—have tried to make it so people couldn't walk on the beach in front of her house. It would be trespassing, anywhere from her white picket fence to some point along the shoreline."

"She can do that?" I said, doubting it would be the case.

"No, she can't. But she's been trying for as long as I can remember. Luckily, the town has yet to allow it."

I stuck another fry in my mouth. I was hungry to a point where I could finish the entire lobster roll in a couple of bites if Mrs. Bartlett wasn't sitting there, watching me eat. "You don't like her?" I said.

"I don't know if I'd say I don't like her. But I could certainly think of plenty of other people I'd prefer to be around."

"What about your brother?" I said. "He knows Mary?"

"Ron is one of those people who thinks money is the root of all evil. Or, I should say, he thinks the people who have lots of money are evil."

"In a lot of cases, I'd say he's not very far off base with his belief," I said, smiling. I thought about what Mary had said to me on the beach. "Mrs. Potter made a comment on the beach, when I was there with my daughter. She was pretty quick to place blame on Ron. Considering his truck was there, you could see why. But there seemed to be more to it."

"I didn't know you were on the beach that morning," she said.

I realized I hadn't told her that, but it didn't matter much either way. I said, "She was with a group of women."

"Her little club," she said. "They all bow to her, like she's the queen."

"There was another woman I met, who apparently was the one who had first discovered the body, when they were all out walking. She was younger than the others."

"That must be Alice." Mrs. Bartlett gave me a weary look. "I know that redhead you brought up to see me isn't your wife. And I don't see a ring. Should I assume you're not married?"

"I was."

"Divorced?"

I paused, shaking my head. "My wife was murdered. Twelve years ago."

Mrs. Bartlett stared back at me, her eyes wide. "Oh, I... I'm sorry, I—"

"Why do you ask?" I said.

She held her gaze, like she'd forgotten what she'd said.

I said, "You said you assumed I'm not married..."

"Oh, yes, I was... I was going to say, well, that Alice tends to be attracted to married men. Usually older ones. But I didn't mean to—"

"It's all right," I said.

She leaned with her hands folded on the table. "What was your wife's name?"

I didn't want to get into it. Some people tried to change the subject when what happened somehow came up. Others wanted to know more. I said, "Her name was Barbara."

"I assume they got the person who did it?"

"They have someone in prison. But he's not the one who killed her."

"You mean, they have the wrong man?"

I cleared my throat and nodded. "As far as I'm concerned, yes. And I'd be lying if I said it didn't keep me awake every night, thinking about the real killer, who's still out there."

Mrs. Bartlett straightened up, turning to look toward the rest of the dining area. "Is this why you're willing to help Ron? Because you know, firsthand, the police don't always get it right?"

I didn't answer, looking at the lobster roll in front of me. I thought it might be rude if I took it to go, but I didn't feel like eating with Mrs. Bartlett watching me. I might've lost my appetite and tried to get the conversation back on track.

"Does this woman, Alice... Does she know your brother?"

Mrs. Bartlett paused. "She does," she said, but didn't go into any details. She started to get up from the booth. "I'll leave you alone, so you can eat."

"No, that's all right," I said. "Sit down." I lifted the lobster roll from my plate and took a bite. It was so good, I thought I'd gone to heaven.

Mrs. Bartlett sat back down and smiled. "I was actually going to go in the kitchen to have a cigarette."

I actually did mind, especially while I was eating. But that's not what I said to her. I wiped my mouth with my napkin. "I don't mind if you have one right here. I'd rather keep talking."

She got up and walked around the corner again, then came back ten seconds later with a cigarette in her hand, already lit. "Since the other night, I haven't been able to stop. It's been a long time since I smoked. With all that's going on, I have an excuse to start up again."

I took another bite of my sandwich, trying to ignore the odor from the cigarette smoke hanging over the table. I swallowed and wiped my hands on the napkin. "Did you know the father of Logan Reed has offered a reward for any information about the person who killed his son?"

"Logan Reed?" she said. "That's the young man who was engaged to Casey Jilson?"

"It is."

"But I heard he took his own life?"

"Well, he may have," I said. "But they haven't come to any definite conclusions yet."

"But the father's already offering a reward?"

"Well, he's most likely trying to get out ahead of the police."

She drew from her cigarette and blew a stream of smoke toward the ceiling. "Have you spoken with him?" she said. "The man's father?"

"I'm thinking of heading back to Boston tonight, maybe go see them. Logan Reed's parents."

"You're not staying up here?" she said.

"I was planning on it, but like I said, I've got to head back."

"Is it because you need somewhere to stay?"

I shook my head, smiling. "No. I have a place. I just..."

"Okay, but if you need a place to stay..." She drew from her cigarette, then crushed it out in the ashtray.

"Thank you, Mrs. Bartlett, but I—"

"I wish you would stop calling me that," she said. "I thought I mentioned it already. I prefer you call me Marilyn."

CHAPTER 12

RAYMOND WAS OUT ON the screened-in porch, asleep in the chair, feet up with half of the newspaper in his hand, the other half on the floor where it had fallen.

"Must be nice," I said, loud enough to wake him.

He sat up, startled, eyes wide open, and looked through the screen at my car. It looked like it would take him half a minute to figure out where he was. He cleared his throat. "How long've you been here?"

I said, "I just pulled in."

"You bring your suitcase?"

"It's in the trunk. But I think I'm going to go home."

He gave me a look, like he disapproved. "I thought the whole thing about taking this case was you didn't want to have to drive back and forth?"

"I don't," I said. "But I need to hit the bank."

He picked the sections of the newspaper that had fallen to the floor, folding it all together, then stood up from the chair. Stretching his arms, he yawned, his fingers practically scraping the tongue-and-groove pine ceiling. "You need some cash?" he said.

"No. I just want to deposit a check."

"So you're going to drive all the way down there, to deposit a check?"

"Two checks, actually," I said.

The truth, at least part of it, was that I'd left in somewhat of a hurry in the first place early in the morning. Nancy certainly wasn't a kid, but I felt like I'd left her behind without really discussing my trip with her in detail. Of course, I knew I was overthinking it. And she was probably glad to get rid of me and have the house to herself. One of her friends was staying over.

If it had been earlier in the summer, it would have been different. But she'd be off to school in two weeks, and I just felt I should've waited before I left her.

I said, "Do you mind if I bring Nancy back with me?"

"I thought you said she had to work?"

"She does. Or, she did. But it's not like she needs the money. She's probably got more in her pocket than I do, from working all summer."

Raymond looked through the open door into the house. "Beth was actually wondering why you hadn't brought her with you. But I told her you were coming up here to work, not for a family vacation."

"Well, I probably should've thought things through a little more. The problem is it's her last week at the pool. I'm not even sure she can get her shifts covered."

"Oh," he said, nodding. "Is that why you didn't want to take the case? Because of Nancy?" He huffed out a laugh. "I know how depressed you get when she goes back to school."

I sat down in the white wicker chair in the opposite corner from where Raymond was standing.

He sat down and leaned forward in the chair, elbows on his knees. "Have you spoken to Mrs. Bartlett?"

I pulled the check out and showed it to him. "She gave me a few hundred, to make sure I wouldn't back out of the case. I'd like to get this in the bank, which is why I need to go home for the night."

"Where was she?"

"At the restaurant."

"I guess that means she's out of Skowhegan?"

"She is, and went right back to work. As soon as the judge agreed to let her go, they took Ron back into custody."

"He's still in the hospital, isn't he?"

"Yeah, cuffed to the bed," I said.

"No repercussions for filing a false confession?"

I shook my head. "There may be. Her attorney's dealing with it."

Raymond said, "She's lucky to be out of there already. I can't imagine the cops—or the judge—are too happy she confessed to a crime she didn't commit."

"But it would've been all right if the cops forced a confession," I said. "But it's not like that's ever happened."

Raymond rolled his eyes. "Here we go. Are you really going to turn it around, like the cops are at fault?"

"Not this time," I said.

As a retired cop, Raymond was always the first to defend the actions of law-enforcement officials, good or bad. I was the one on the other side of it.

It wasn't that I didn't like cops. But I was well aware there was often a fine line between the men in uniform and the crooks on the other side. Especially in Boston, where cops—some that Raymond knew personally over the years—had a reputation for crossing that line.

He said, "Have you talked to anyone over there, with Kennebunkport PD?"

"There are only a couple of them," I said. "But I'm going to go see if Chief Hanley'll be willing to talk. Any chance you'd want to come with me?"

Raymond pointed toward his chest. "You want *me* to go?" He looked like he was about to shake his head, but didn't.

"I thought maybe if you were there," I said, "the chief would be more open to talking. I can't imagine he'll be too excited to hear a PI from Boston's up here sniffing around his murder case."

Raymond leaned back in the chair. I could tell his wheels were turning. "I'm sorry," he said. "I can't do it. You know I'll do whatever I can to help you out, but I'd prefer to hang in the background. I don't need my name out there, Jake. You understand, don't you?"

***

The wooden sign with grass growing up around it, had Kennebunkport Police Department carved into it. The clapboard-sided building was a Cape Cod-style house, and if it weren't for the tall antennas on either side of the roof's peak, you'd think it was someone's personal home. The building had Kennebunkport Communications Department painted in black letters on the white fascia board under the roof.

I parked next to the only police vehicle in the lot, to the right of the entrance. Stepping out of my car, I noticed the white-haired man in uniform looking out the picture window at me.

It was Chief Hanley. He sipped from a coffee mug, watching me, but disappeared from view as I headed for the front door.

I tried to open the door but it was apparently swollen into the frame from the humid ocean air. I leaned into it with my shoulder and gave it a shove. The sound of the door opening was a *snap*, like I'd cracked something. It creaked when I opened it.

A woman sat behind a desk with the phone up to her ear, her eyes on me moving toward her.

There were five desks in total inside the wide-open area, but only one was occupied, toward the back of the room. A man in plain clothes was seated at the desk, his back to me, and didn't bother turning to look at who had just come through the door.

The woman behind the desk had red hair that reminded me of Maggie's, although by the look of her face I guessed she was quite a bit older. I couldn't tell for sure, but I guessed her hair was colored to look the way it did.

The man with his back to me was somewhat slouched over his desk, his head resting in one hand and writing diligently with the other. From where I stood, it looked like he had maps open in front of him.

I glanced at two closed doors across the room. One had a sign on it I couldn't read from where I was. The other door was slightly ajar with almost total darkness on the other side of it.

The woman at the desk in front of me nodded into the phone. "Yes, Mr. Carlson. I do understand. And when the chief returns, I'll make sure he calls you." She listened, giving me a look as she rolled her eyes, nodding. "I know you have, Mr. Carlson. I assure you, he will call you back this time." She grinned, still nodding. "All right. I'll see to it. Have a good day, Mr. Carlson." She hung up the phone and let out a heavy sigh. "May I help you?"

"Did I hear you say Chief Hanley's not here?"

"That's right," she said, looking down at the papers in front of her.

I glanced at the closed door on the other side. "But I just saw him in the window when I pulled up."

She straightened out the papers on her desk, looking up at me this time, holding her gaze. I could tell she didn't appreciate the pushback. "Chief Hanley is not available for visitors at this moment. I'm sorry. But if you'd like to leave your name..."

I looked at a wooden bench to the left of the door, under a long wooden coatrack attached to the wall. "How about I wait right there on that bench, would that be all right?"

She looked as if she was becoming annoyed. "He's very busy, sir. If you would just tell me what your matter is, I can relay the message to him and perhaps you can come back at a better time."

I looked at my watch. "I'm sure he'll be out at some point."

Chief Hanley must have been listening, because his office door opened and he came out. "Is there something I can help you with?" he said, walking toward me.

"Chief Hanley," I said, extending my hand. "Jake Horn."

He shook my hand, although seemed a bit hesitant in doing so. "Is there something I can help you with?"

"Yeah, there is," I said. "If there's somewhere we can speak in private?"

He glanced at the woman behind the desk watching us, then nodded. "If you'd tell me what this is all about, maybe we can—"

"Casey Jilson," I said.

Chief Hanley stared at me for a moment without a word. "Are you a reporter?"

I didn't answer. "I just need a few minutes," I said.

The chief stood, then started toward his office. "I don't have much time."

"I'll try not to take much of it," I said, following him.

A man seated at a desk looked at me over his shoulder, then went right back to whatever it was he was doing.

The chief's office was small, with his wooden desk facing the door and not much else in there, other than an umbrella in the corner and a small rack on the wall inside the door. He had a phone on his desk with a folder and a yellow pad with notes scribbled on it.

Chief Hanley walked past me and out of the office, coming back with a wooden chair he placed in front of his desk. "Have a seat," he said, then closed the door and sat behind his desk.

"So, you didn't answer me. Are you a reporter?" he said.

"No, I'm not." I sat in the chair.

"A lawyer?"

"Sorry, no. I'm a private investigator, investigating Casey Jilson's death."

He stared back at me. "Who're you working for?"

I paused before answering. "Marilyn Bartlett."

The chief leaned forward on his desk, pushing the pad and folder aside. "You from around here?"

"Boston."

He narrowed his eyes. "Marilyn Bartlett hired a PI from Boston?"

"She did. And she believes her brother's innocent."

The chief cracked a slight smile, looking like he was about to roll his eyes. But he didn't. "Nobody ever wants to believe a family member could do such a thing as what happened to that poor young woman. Most wouldn't take things as far as she did, confessing to the crime just to protect him."

"You knew it was a false confession," I said. "So then why'd you throw her in jail?"

Hanley cleared his throat. "Once the judge gets involved, it's out of my hands. That's just how these things work around here. We have evidence now. Enough that we were able to bring Ron Tompkins into custody, without question."

I said, "But it seems to me you arrested him the first time based on the fact his truck was on that beach. A truck he'd reported stolen the night before. You call that evidence?"

Hanley held his gaze on me, like he knew he didn't have to answer to me. "I didn't say what kind of evidence we have. Of course, the truck is just a piece of the story. But if you want to go on trying to prove a man like Ron Tompkins wouldn't do something like this..."

"What's that supposed to mean?" I said.

"It means I'm guessing, with you not being from around here, you don't know much about him."

I waited for more.

The chief said, "You don't think it says something about a man, gets behind the wheel like he did, takes his sister's vehicle a football-field deep into the woods... because he can't manage to keep himself clean?"

"Clean? He did admit he had a couple of drinks."

"He had marijuana in him too," Hanley said.

"Is that true?"

Hanley paused, and followed it up with a slight shrug. "Biddeford isn't my jurisdiction, of course. But police up there found it in his car."

"Just like up in Portland?" I said.

Chief Hanley stood up from the desk, his eyes narrowed. "Excuse me?"

"I know all about what happened between you and Ron up at that college."

Hanley said, "This case has nothing to do with Portland, or anything else you may have heard about from the past." He walked toward the door and opened it, his hand on the knob. "If you'll excuse me now, I don't have time for some two-bit private investigator questioning official police business. You want to help some drunk, stoned hippie, you can do it on your own time."

CHAPTER 13

IT WAS DARK OUT by the time I made it into Milton and turned onto Pagoda Street. I stopped in front of my grandmother's house, where I lived and had spent a good part of my life as a kid. She left the house for me and Nancy after she died, along with the '74 Nova.

But when I pulled up, I wasn't expecting all the cars parked in the driveway and along the street.

There were people everywhere—teenagers or maybe twenty somethings—standing on the lawn and in the driveway, leaning on cars and gathered around the steps at the front door. With the lights on in the house, I could see even more of them inside through the windows.

I shifted into park, killed the engine, and put the hazards on. I got out, leaving the Nova in the middle of the road.

The first group of kids I saw seemed to be the first to notice the six-foot-two grown man moving toward them from the street. Most of them quickly dispersed, other than one kid who had his back to me and didn't seem to notice when I walked up behind him.

"What's going on here?" I said, and the kid turned to look at me, holding a can of 'Gansette beer I had a feeling he took from my fridge.

I recognized the scrawny kid from Nancy's class in high school, although he looked to be no more than twelve.

He stood, frozen, and hid the beer behind his back. "Mr... Mr. Horn?"

I didn't know the kid's name.

The group hanging on the steps by the front door were watching, quietly, then moved away and headed toward the street when I looked toward them.

I heard one of them say, "Who's the old man?"

Old man? I remembered a time when I thought someone in their forties looked old too. But I still didn't appreciate it.

I grabbed the can from the kid's hand and dumped it, crushing it with one hand, then giving it back to him. "Get your friends, and tell them the party's over." I looked toward the house. "Where's Nancy?"

"I... uh... she... she's, uh..."

I didn't wait around for the stuttering fool to answer, and walked in through the front door to Van Halen's "Jamie's Cryin'" blasting on my stereo. Cigarette smoke hung in the air mixed with the smell of sweaty teenagers and cheap perfume.

I yelled for Nancy. The ten or so teenagers sitting on my couch in front of the TV all turned to me with stunned looks on their faces. I walked over and shut off the stereo in the cabinet under the TV and lifted the needle off the record. "In case you haven't figured it out," I said, "party's over."

A female voice from somewhere in the the kitchen said, "I think Nancy's dad is here."

The kids in the family room all scurried out the front door, although a few stragglers still hadn't moved. "Hey!" I said. "Are you deaf? You don't have to go home, but you can't stay here."

I walked into the kitchen where a group of kids who looked older than Nancy by quite a few years were smoking cigarettes and drinking beers. I said, "Where's Nancy?"

They all looked at each other but nobody answered. Not at first.

A man with long hair and a scraggly, uneven beard who had to've been somewhere in his mid-to-upper twenties, if I had to guess, stared back at me without moving. He said, "Who's Nancy?" and took a drag from his cigarette, his eyes lazy and half closed. He sipped from a can of beer, staring back at me.

"You don't know who Nancy is?" I said. "Then what the hell are you doing in this house?"

"Hey, man, why you buggin' out?" he said, followed by a goofy laugh.

I took a step toward the man. "Why am I buggin' out?" I looked him over, and glanced at the four others standing in the kitchen, all staring back at me with their bloodshot eyes. "I want you all out of my house, before I call the cops. And I'm not going to say it again."

The skinny, hippy-looking man gave me a nod. "Hey, dude. Take a chill pill. We're just hangin'. Why don't you grab a beer out of the fridge?" He laughed, looking at his friends as if to see if they were entertained. "The man could use a drink, am I right?"

I guessed by the way his friends moved to the doorway and from the kitchen they could see it in my face: the last thing I was going to do was take a "chill pill." Far from it.

"You've got five seconds to get out of here," I said.

The man smirked at me and sipped his beer. He didn't move, and had clearly chosen to see how far he could push me.

I sized him up, looking him over. He wasn't a kid, but a grown man who not only didn't know Nancy, but wasn't going to leave.

He put his cigarette in the ashtray next to him and reached for his back pocket, coming out with a switchblade he flipped open, holding it up in front of his face. "You wanna dance, old man?"

I grabbed the phone off the wall, held it by the chord and swung it hard at the man, catching him just above the eye with the handset.

He dropped the knife and his beer, grabbing his face. He screamed. Blood dripped over his eye.

I kicked the knife out of the way, grabbed him by the back of the shirt and dragged him past his friends and out the front door. I tossed him down the steps and he collapsed onto the walkway. "I ever see you around here again..." I said, pointing at him.

"Dad?" I looked toward the driveway, where Nancy had just come around from the side of the house.

"I want everyone out of here, now!" I yelled, walking down the steps. I'd taken my eyes off the man on the ground for a split second, and gave him just enough time to charge toward me, wrapping his arms around my waist and tackling me into the shrubs under the picture window.

Nancy screamed, "Dad!" and started toward me, but I was already up on my feet.

I grabbed the hippie punk and dragged him by his feet across the lawn and into the street. He tried to swing on me as he attempted to get to his feet, but I caught his fist and bent his wrist back, dropping him to his knees.

I let go and he stumbled as he stood up, trying to get away from me, then disappeared into the darkness with his buddies running after him.

"Who the hell was that?" I said.

Nancy shook her head. "I... I don't know. They just showed up." She looked down. "I'm so sorry. I invited a few friends over, just to hang out. But word spread that I was having a party. Next thing I knew, these people showed up."

I yelled at whoever was still standing around watching the scene. "Move those cars out of my driveway, or they're getting towed!" I walked down to my car, backed it out of the way and waited for everyone who was left to clear out.

It took five minutes until I finally pulled the Nova into the driveway and parked.

Nancy came over to me. "Don't you believe me?"

I was mad, and not in a place to have a normal conversation with her, the way my adrenaline was still pumping through my veins. "Just get everyone out of here," I said, walking away and into the house.

The place wasn't as much of a mess as I thought it would be once everyone cleared out, but even having a small amount to clean up was more than I felt like dealing with at that point.

Nancy walked in from outside.

"I'm disappointed in you," I said, something I rarely, if ever, had said to her She was a good kid. She was *always* a good kid. And once the foolish words left my mouth, I wished I hadn't said it at all.

"I tried to get everyone to leave," she said. "I swear."

"How many people did you actually invite?"

She shrugged, and before she answered, her friend Renee walked in the front door.

"Hi, Mr. Horn," Renee said. "This wasn't Nancy's fault. It got out of control *really* fast. She was trying to get people out of here the whole time."

I picked up a handful of beer cans from the coffee table in front of the couch, most with beer in them —dead soldiers, as they were called when I was a kid—and carried them into the kitchen. I didn't want to get into it with Nancy *or* her friend. I yelled out to them, "I want this place cleaned up!"

Nancy's friend walked in the kitchen. "Mr. Horn, you know that guy you threw out? He was causing trouble the whole time. Nancy couldn't get him to leave."

I didn't bother asking where Nancy was when the kid was in the kitchen. "I'm sorry that happened," I said. "That man pulled a knife, and the right thing would've been to call the cops."

Nancy walked through the doorway with cans in her hand, and dumped them in the sink. "I'm sorry," she said.

I pulled the garbage can from under the sink. "I could get in trouble, you know, having kids drinking here."

"Most of them were old enough," Nancy said, looking out the window into the darkness outside. "I was out back, yelling at everyone to leave. You only saw half of them. The rest ran when they heard you were here. Everyone—my friends, at least—are still scared of you."

I liked hearing that, turning to Nancy with a half grin on my face.

I picked up an ashtray from the counter and ran it under water to make sure there weren't any hot ashes. I said to Nancy, "Was anyone upstairs?"

She shook her head. "I don't think so."

I didn't say much else while we picked up whatever else was left on the counter.

Nancy had a broom, sweeping the floor. "How come you came home?" she said. "I thought you were staying with Raymond and Beth?"

"I was planning on it," I said, pulling the plastic garbage bag from the can. "I need to run by the bank in the morning. And I think I'm going to go to Cambridge so I can talk to Logan Reed's parents." I tied up the bag and left it by the side door. I said, "I'd like you to come up to Maine with me tomorrow."

She seemed surprised, at least by the look on her face. "I have to work."

"Then get someone to cover your shifts."

"I could, I guess. But I wanted to make a little more money to take back to school."

"Don't worry about money."

"You say that," she said, "but then you're always worried about it."

I smiled. "Listen, I'm going to be spending a lot of time in Maine, and I hate the fact that you go back to school in a couple of weeks. Not to mention, I'd rather not have you down here trashing the house with your big blowout parties."

I think she knew I was kidding, but her shoulders dropped. "I swear, Dad, I didn't—"

"It's actually not the parties I worry about," I said. "It's the losers that tend to show up uninvited. They always do." I said. I ran some water over the other ashtray filled with cigarette butts and left it in the sink. There was a time I smoked, when I was younger and didn't know any better. But the odor coming from the ashtray, not to mention the smoke still hanging in the house, made my stomach turn.

I said, "Beth would love to have you up there. You know she loves having you around. So, maybe it's not a bad idea you take a break, enjoy what's left of the summer. And if I can come up with some things for you to help me with…"

She looked into the family room where her friend was cleaning up. Nancy kept her voice to a whisper and said, "Is it still okay if Renee stays tonight?"

"That's fine," I said, wishing I had the house to myself and Nancy. But I wasn't going to send the kid home at that point. I grabbed the phone off the wall and dialed.

A man answered on the other end, "Boston Police."

"Is Officer Donovan available?"

"I think so," the man said. "Can I tell her who's calling?"

"Jake Horn."

There was brief silence and what might've been a sigh. "Hold on."

A handful of minutes went by before Maggie finally picked up the phone. "Jake?"

"Are you busy?"

"Always," she said. "But I'm off in twenty minutes. Where are you?"

"Milton."

"Your home?"

"I needed to come back, take care of something." I looked at my watch. It was 9:40.

She said, "Did you hear about Logan Reed?"

"No, I haven't heard anything."

She paused on the other end. "The latest, according to the chief medical examiner in Maine, is that Logan Reed didn't take his own life. They're officially calling it a a homicide."

CHAPTER 14

I WENT OUTSIDE AFTER I finished a cup of coffee and read the *Globe*. Nancy and Renee were both sleeping, being that seven in the morning was a bit early for a couple of college kids.

The sun was up, shining over the neighbor's house across the street. It was cool out for a mid-August morning, and made it feel more like mid-September.

I picked up a can of beer in the bushes by the steps and placed it next to the garage door so I'd remember to take it in when I got back. With the sun reflecting off the windows of the Nova, I was puzzled by the way the car looked. I was still groggy after a sleepless night, and probably could've used one more cup of coffee to wake my brain.

But when I went over to the driver's-side door, I felt a bit taller than normal, the way the roof appeared to be lower than my chest. I looked the car over, then shifted my gaze to the front and back tires.

They were both flat.

I walked around to the other side and sure enough, all four were flat. I crouched down next to the passenger-side rear tire and felt the puncture wound in the rubber.

The tires had all been slashed and I was now without a car, on top of whatever cash I'd need for a tow and to replace four tires.

I looked out toward the street as a neighbor drove by and beeped his horn, most likely on his way to work.

But all I was thinking about was that hippie freak I got into it with the night before. Although he'd left his knife on the kitchen floor—and I'd left it on the counter—I knew it had to've been him. I didn't have time to deal with tracking him down. And calling the cops wasn't something I felt was necessary at the time. I'd deal with him later.

I went back inside, picked up the phone and called Maggie. She was going to meet me for breakfast before the bank opened at nine. But, clearly, I needed a ride.

Nancy's friend's car, her parents' Oldsmobile Vista station wagon, was parked out in the street. I walked down and checked her tires, which luckily were full of air. I thought about grabbing her keys, but I needed to wait to get my car towed. Which meant I'd need to get to the bank to cash the checks to pay for it, and whatever the tires would cost.

The morning was already off to a bad start.

***

Nancy and her friend were outside standing with me by the time Maggie pulled in the driveway. Neither knew the man's name from the party, which bothered me as much as everything else that had already happened.

I said to Nancy, "I know we already discussed this, but the fact that someone was in my house and you have no idea who he was or what his name was..." I shook my head. "I know you didn't mean for any of this to happen. But it did. It's a crazy world out there. You know that. Next time someone shows up uninvited and just walks in like that, you either call the cops or... shoot him if you have to." I took it back right away. "Maybe not the shooting part, but..."

All I wanted was for Nancy to be safe. It was hard enough, just the two of us.

We tried to live normal lives, and I think we did a pretty good job of it. But that touch of skeptical paranoia never went away. I didn't trust many people, and luckily Maggie—my wife Barbara's best friend—had come back into our lives a few months earlier. That was when I was wrapped up in a case involving a woman I'd dated and, almost at one time, mistakenly married.

Maggie was out of her car and looking over the Nova. "Do you have any idea who did it?"

"We don't know his name," I said. "But I think we can find out. Hopefully someone from Nancy's big bash'll know who he is."

Maggie kept walking toward Nancy and gave her a hug. "Next time, you'll have to invite me." She smiled, but Nancy looked embarrassed, even though Maggie was trying to make light of the situation.

"Dad said you would've had Milton Police over here with the paddy wagon."

Maggie let out a slight laugh, but I didn't know if she thought any of it was funny.

***

111

With my car in the shop, Maggie and I drove into Boston and stopped at the main library so I could pull up some newspapers from when Ron Tompkins was arrested at Westbrook College.

It didn't appear to be big news outside of Portland, but it was covered by the *Portland Press Herald*.

There were numerous accusations against Ron, although most apparently unproven. He was quoted in the paper as saying the parents were out to get him, because they didn't believe a teacher should socialize with students.

I wouldn't say they were wrong—and the statement seemed a bit off—but there seemed to be more to it.

And as I dug a little deeper, I discovered Chief Hanley—Officer Hanley, at the time—may have had the tables turned on him by the attorney representing Ron claiming the drugs found in the trunk of Ron's car were planted there by Hanley.

As with the case against Ron Tompkins, the claim against Officer Hanley being the one who planted the drugs went unproven. Although, as Hanley had claimed, the attorney ruined his reputation as an officer in Portland. Turns out, he didn't lose his job. And, as most things were, the case was short-lived in the press. Hanley went on to become chief of police in Kennebunkport, so in his case, it turned out just fine.

I couldn't help thinking he still held a grudge against Ron Tompkins.

Maggie called me over to where she was sitting, in front of another microfilm projector at the other end of the table. "Look at this," she said, standing from the chair.

I sat down and skimmed over the article in front of me. The headline read: "Westbrook Professor Ousted After Heated Battle."

Tom and Kathryn Jilson were mentioned as the parents of student Casey Jilson who didn't believe Ron Tompkins should lose his job.

I read a few more lines and looked back at Maggie. "Logan Reed's parents were leading the charge to see to it he was dismissed?"

She nodded. "Casey's parents tried to help him, clearly on the other side of the line from Logan."

"They were killed in a car accident soon after," I said. "I'd say it's a bit suspicious, wouldn't you?"

Maggie paused before answering. "I'm not sure you can say there's a connection, but..."

"And then Logan and Casey end up engaged?" I said. "It's all a bit strange."

"Engaged. And both dead, in two separate incidents," Maggie said, sitting back down in front of the microfilm projector. "Did you see the part about Ron Tompkins having parties and inviting the students?"

"I didn't read the whole thing," I said.

Maggie rolled the film and said, "Logan Reed took a semester off, his junior year." She looked back at me. "He was in rehab. For a drug problem. And the parents blamed Ron Tompkins."

We both sat, no words, thinking it all through.

I said, "Do you mind taking me over to see the Reeds?"

"Jake, are you serious?"

"Why not?"

Maggie took a moment, like she had to think about it. "I certainly can't go over there," she said. "Do you know what kind of trouble I'd be in? And Eddie knows you're working on the Casey Jilson case."

"Eddie?"

Maggie nodded. "Eddie Kelly. Officer Kelly, with Cambridge PD. You know, he's the one who called the house, when—"

"Yeah, I know who he is," I said. "But how'd he know I was working the case?"

Maggie shrugged, and her white Irish face turned a deep shade of red. "I'm sorry, Jake. I... we were just talking. I didn't know you wanted to keep it a secret."

I left it at that. I wasn't sure if I was as much bothered by the fact she'd told a cop—one who was potentially involved in a case I had no doubt was tied to the one I was involved with—or that I didn't know she was buddy-buddy with this guy, Eddie Kelly. Not that it was any of my business...

I said, "If you don't want to go over there with me, would it be all right if I used your car? I'll drop you off at your apartment, head over there, and be back in an hour. I need to go see them, before I head back to Maine."

"I guess so," she said, but seemed a bit hesitant about it.

We both headed for the exit and down the library steps onto Boylston Street. With the sun shining bright, I slipped my sunglasses over my eyes.

"Maybe you should talk to Eddie," she said. "Instead of the parents?"

I glanced at her through my shades, then started toward a pay phone at the next corner, on Exeter. "I have to make a quick call," I said, and reached into my pocketful of quarters. I'd made sure I stocked up before I left the house.

I picked up the handset and dropped three quarters in the slot for the toll call to Maine.

A woman answered the phone. "Bartlett's."

"Morning," I said. "Is Marilyn available?" I had to force myself to use her first name, although I wasn't sure why it was so uncomfortable calling her anything but Mrs. Bartlett. Maybe it was out of respect, or because she was older. Or the fact I'd always referred to her as Mrs. Bartlett, before I ever met her. *Everyone* called her Mrs. Bartlett, including Raymond and Beth, who had been going to her restaurant for plenty of summers before I showed up.

She picked up the phone. "Hello?"

"Good morning," I said. "It's Jake."

"I'm glad you called. I've been trying to reach you."

"Oh. I'm sorry. I haven't been in the office. Is everything all right?"

"Well, Ron is going to be released on bail, but they want to talk to both of us about what happened up in Bar Harbor."

"*Who* wants to talk to you?"

"The Maine state police."

I glanced at Maggie with her back to me, facing Boylston.

I said, "What else did they say?"

Marilyn waited before she spoke softly into the phone. "A witness who was at Acadia claims to have seen a brown Oldsmobile Cutlass leaving the parking lot around the time that young man was found in his car."

"A brown Cutlass?" I said, unsure at first of the significance.

"I own a brown Cutlass," she said. "That's the vehicle Ron drove into the woods, in Biddeford."

CHAPTER 15

I DROVE MAGGIE'S SCAMP out to the Avon Hill neighborhood in Cambridge and stopped in front of a Craftsman-style, gable-roof bungalow with a front porch that stretched from one end of the house to the other. It's not that I was some kind of expert in residential architecture by any means, but when Barbara and I first got married, we used to drive out to Cambridge on the weekends. She'd point out the houses she wanted to buy, if we ever somehow became rich. Although I had to remind her on every drive that if she wanted to be rich, she shouldn't have married a private investigator. She always liked Cambridge, with the Charles River in its backyard and the biggest brains from the wealthiest families in the country hanging around town.

The Reeds' house was on a tree-lined residential street not far from Porter and Harvard Squares. I thought about how much Barbara would have loved a house like the Reeds' as I walked up the steps and onto the porch. I knocked on the door, and felt the thickness of it on my knuckles. There was a gold-colored door knocker, but it never felt quite right using one.

The door opened and a woman who I knew was older than me by twelve years actually appeared a lot younger. But that was only at first glance. It took a moment to notice the way her skin was pulled back and stretched tight from her lips, tucked somewhere behind her jaw, her blonde hair as natural-looking as the skin on her surgically modified face.

But I wasn't there to judge the woman who had just lost her son. The rich were different from the rest of us, and if plastic surgery was what they wanted to spend their money on, then more power to them.

"Mrs. Reed?" I said.

She paused before she answered, looking me over. She had a glass of red wine in her hand. "Who are you?"

"My name's Jake Horn."

She stared back at me, waiting for more.

"I'm a private investigator. I was hoping you and your husband might be able to answer some questions for me?"

"Private investigator? Who... Did Carl hire you?"

"Your husband?" I shook my head. "No."

I thought she was going to say something else, the way her lips had moved, but she didn't.

"I know this is a very difficult time for you, but if you and your husband have a few minutes..."

"Carl isn't here," she said. "Can you please tell me who hired you?"

"Well, I'm not exactly involved in what happened to your son."

She held her gaze on me for a moment, like she wasn't sure what to say next. "What did you say your name was?"

"Jake. Jake Horn. I have an office not far from here, in Southie."

I knew at some point I'd have to tell her who I was working for, but at the time I thought I could ask questions without getting into it. Especially considering the man I was hired to help was a suspect in both Casey *and* Logan's deaths.

"I'm somewhat involved in the Casey Jilson investigation."

She closed her eyes. "I... I can't believe what's happened," she said. "Casey... and now... my poor Logan." She started to cry.

"I'm sorry," I said.

Darlene Reed pulled a tissue from her pocket and dabbed the corners of her eyes.

"Do you mind if I ask you a few questions about what happened in Portland? At Westbrook?"

She raised her eyebrows. "Excuse me?"

"I know all about it. Everything that happened up there with Ron Tompkins and you and your husband. And, of course, Chief Hanley."

There was a brief moment of silence, while Mrs. Reed sipped her wine, her gaze toward the decking on the porch.

She said, "I... I don't know what you want. But I'm not going to get into what happened up there. It was a long time ago."

"Eight years," I said. "And, as I'm sure you know, the police arrested Ron Tompkins for Casey Jilson's murder. And, now he's also a suspect in your son's case."

Darlene Reed looked back into her house, then came out onto the porch, pulling the door shut behind her.

I got the feeling someone was inside the house, but I didn't ask.

She said, "I don't know how much you know about Ron Tompkins, or what you know about Casey, but it doesn't make any sense at all that he would kill her. After her parents were killed, he was there for her. It made me regret the way things happened up there, the way we went after him."

"From what I understand, you and your husband were the ones leading the charge to have him removed from his position. Isn't that right?"

"All we were doing was trying to protect our son," she said. "Isn't that what a parent is supposed to do?"

I watched her finish off her glass of wine.

I said, "So, what you're telling me is you regret going after Ron Tompkins? And you don't believe he could have killed Casey *or* your son? Have you shared any of this with the police? Or your friend Rick Hanley?"

"He's not a friend," she said. "Far from it."

"Would your husband say the same thing?"

She looked into her empty glass and let out a deep sigh. "Rick Hanley pressured Carl and some of the other parents to go to the board and have Ron Tompkins removed from the school."

I said, "Even after he was found innocent, in a court of law?"

She nodded. "Rick Hanley believed the judge made a mistake. And he wouldn't let it go. But he couldn't be directly involved, so pressured all of us to push for Ron's ouster."

"He was mad the defense attorney flipped the narrative on him," I said. "Isn't that right?"

A tear dropped down her cheek. "I'm sorry, but my son is dead. And nothing you or anybody else can do will bring him back."

"But don't you want the *right* person to pay for what happened? Because, right now, Ron Tompkins could end up going down for both murders, whether he's guilty or not."

She stared back at me without a response.

119

I wasn't sure if she knew about Ron's sister's car—or the identical make, model, and color—being spotted at the scene where Logan was found dead. She didn't mention it. And I didn't think I needed to.

"Is that who hired you?" she said. "Ron Tompkins?"

I paused, pondering if I could keep it up without revealing my client. "His sister hired me," I said. "Or, at least she's the one footing the bill."

"His sister? You mean, the sister who confessed to killing poor Casey, but then changed her mind?" She rolled her eyes.

"Do you know her?" I said.

"We met for the first time, up at the college," she said, looking into her empty glass. "Would you like a drink?"

I shook my head.

"Well, I need a refill. I'm doing all I can to keep it together."

"I don't think anyone would expect someone in your position to keep anything together," I said.

"Carl does," she said, then excused herself and walked back into the house. She came back out with her wine glass filled almost to the top.

I wanted to ask her what she meant, about Carl expecting her to keep it together.

But she said, "Logan was a good kid, you know. He had his problems, but..." She placed the glass on the railing.

"What kind of problems?" I said.

"I'm not sure I want to get into any of that with you, Mr. Horn."

"But, I think it's—"

"I'm sorry," she said. "I'm just not going to get into it. Not today."

I understood. I was pushing it already, just by showing up at her door.

She picked up her glass and took a drink from it. When she put the glass down, it was already half empty.

I looked at my watch. "Do you know when your husband will be home?"

"I wish I did," she said.

"I saw in the paper he's offered a reward to anyone who finds the person who did this to your son?"

"Is that why you're here?"

"No. I already told you why I'm here. And who I'm working for. But I'm wondering if he believes the cops have their man, or..."

"I honestly don't know what he thinks right now," she said, leaning on the railing with her glass in her hand, looking out across their small yard and into the street.

"Would it be all right if I gave you my card? And can you ask your husband to give me a call when he gets home?" I held the card out.

Darlene took it from my hand and looked it over. "Jake, huh?" She cracked a slight smile and looked me over. "Is it okay if I call you that, *Jake*?"

CHAPTER 16

I PICKED UP MAGGIE from her apartment building on Beacon Street, but she got in the passenger side and told me to drive.

She slid onto the seat and slammed the door closed. "Any luck?"

"I'm not sure," I said. "The father, Carl Reed, wasn't there. And I'm not sure Mrs. Reed was in the mood for a deep discussion about what happened. She'd already cracked a bottle of wine."

Maggie looked at the analog clock on the dash. "I guess I can understand. I'd start drinking early, too, if I lost my only son."

I had the window down, with mild, fresh air that was a lot more comfortable now that the summer heat wave had finally moved out of the area. "I think I'd like to dig in a little more into what happened at that college," I said.

"You mean... with Chief Hanley?" Maggie said.

I told her what Mrs. Reed had said, and how it was Rick Hanley who pushed the parents to get Ron fired. "It's like he had—or has—a vendetta."

"Because the drug charges fell through? He got his way in the end, didn't he?"

"You would think so," I said. "But if the defense lawyer made him look like a fool..."

I went down Pond Street in Jamaica Plain. "The guy, Hanley, goes out of his way, after his case falls through, to get this man fired. And then he ends up chief of police in the same town Tompkins grew up in?"

Maggie said, "Are you saying Hanley took the job as chief just to get closer to Ron Tompkins? For what? To kill a woman and set him up for murder?" She stared back at me, waiting for a response.

I said, "That's not what I'm saying. But, I'll go back to that morning on the beach... You should have seen Hanley, and the young officer, Thomas Silva. The scene was a mess: not wearing gloves, walking all over the sand and whatever footprints may have been there..."

Maggie said, "There are plenty of incompetent people in law enforcement, I won't deny that. But if you're trying to say they purposefully botched an investigation and destroyed a crime scene..." She had a look on her face, like she was questioning my sanity.

I said, "I'm just throwing it out there that something's way off with this case."

We drove past the south side of Franklin Park Zoo, then down Blue Hill Avenue through Mattapan.

Maggie reached for the radio and turned on the Red Sox game. It was the first inning of a day game out in Oakland.

"Tiant's on the mound," I said. "They need to pick up a game in the standings."

We continued south on 138 until I saw the sign in the distance for Buddy's Tire and Auto. I took a quick right onto Canton Avenue, drove a quarter mile and into the lot.

The Nova was parked out front. I parked in the space next to it, admiring the shiny black tires. They made the car look new.

Before I got out, I said, "I did tell you they saw Marilyn Bartlett's car up there at Acadia National Park, right?"

She stared at me, looking somewhat surprised. "Doesn't that concern you?"

We both got out of the car and Maggie walked around the front end of the Scamp. I left the keys in the ignition. "Of course it concerns me. It doesn't look good. Not at all."

"But you're not having doubts? About taking the case?"

I started toward the entrance to Buddy's. "I already took the case, Maggie. But I haven't even had a chance to talk to him about it. And as far as I know, the witness never got a plate, and wasn't even sure about the color."

***

I pulled the Nova into the driveway at the house and Maggie, in the Scamp, came in right behind me. I was already behind schedule, but also wished I could go back to Cambridge to see if Carl Reed ever made it home.

Nancy already had her bag packed and by the door. She sat at the table in the kitchen eating a sandwich, when Maggie and I walked in.

"Are you all squared away at the pool?" I said.

She nodded, finishing what was already in her mouth. "All of my shifts are covered."

I said, "Your boss was okay with you taking off for a few days?"

"They're cool with it, as long as I had someone work for me."

Maggie leaned inside the kitchen doorway behind me. "I wish I could go with you," she said. "But hopefully there's some way I can help out while I'm down here."

I opened the door to the fridge, then turned to Maggie. "Do you want anything to eat?"

She looked at her watch. "I need to get home and feed Max before my shift starts. He'll eat the couch if he doesn't get his food."

Maggie's cat was the size of a dog, especially with the way he ate. It's why we all called him "Fat Max."

I closed the refrigerator, pulled a ten-dollar bill from my wallet and handed it to Maggie. "I should have stopped to fill the tank, but I wasn't thinking. Thanks for letting me use the car."

Maggie waved it off. "Don't worry about it. I'm sure you'll return the favor, if my tires ever get slashed and I need a ride."

"Oh," Nancy said, grabbing a pad from next to her plate. "I got that man's name."

"The one who slashed his tires?" Maggie said, reaching for the pad. She looked at the name. "Brian Jones? Do you want me to do anything with this?"

I said to Nancy, "How'd you get his name?"

She shrugged. "I made some calls. None of my friends even knew him, but I asked around."

"Good detective work," I said, smiling, then said to Maggie. "Don't do anything yet. I'll take care of it."

She said, "I don't think it's a good idea, taking the law into your own hands. If that's what you're thinking."

"I didn't say I was going to do anything. Not right now."

Maggie said, "You sure you don't want me to talk to anyone at the Milford PD?"

I shook my head. "I'll handle it."

Maggie walked to the door. "All right. Call me if you need anything."

Nancy got up from the table. "Bye, Maggie. Maybe you can come up to Maine on your day off?"

Maggie opened the door and looked back, nodding with a slight shrug. "Maybe."

She walked out and Nancy watched her drive away through the kitchen window.

Nancy said, "Is everything all right with you two?"

"I guess so. Why?"

"I don't know. You were both acting weird. Like something was wrong."

"We were discussing the case a bit. It's nothing."

Nancy gave me a look, like she didn't like my answer. "Stop treating me like that," she said. "You can't just say it's 'nothing,' when you know it's not *nothing*."

I took a loaf of bread out of the bread box. "There's a lot of baggage between Chief Hanley and Ron Tompkins, and it makes me a bit suspicious."

"Of Chief Hanley?"

I shrugged. I was hungry, and couldn't even think straight enough to answer all of Nancy's questions.

She said, "Do you think the chief of police had something to do with Casey Jilson's death?"

I gave up, and went ahead filling her in on much of the history surrounding Ron Tompkins, the Reeds, and Chief Hanley, although there were still too many missing pieces.

And, sure enough, Nancy asked the same questions as Maggie did. That included why someone would kill an innocent woman like Casey Jilson just to get back at someone.

"It doesn't make sense," Nancy said.

"No, it doesn't." I opened the fridge again and pulled out the Polish ham and some American cheese to make a sandwich. "Nothing makes sense in the early stages of an investigation. But it doesn't mean you should cross anything—or anyone—off your list."

"But what if it sends you in the wrong direction?" she said.

I had my back to her, making my sandwich at the counter. "Even the wrong direction will lead you somewhere," I said.

My uncle, who taught me the business and, as one of the most well-known private investigators in Boston, used to tell me the same thing all the time. He'd say, "Don't be afraid to make mistakes."

He also warned me once or twice to stop making mistakes, so...

I sat down at the table with my plate and took a bite of the sandwich, eating it like it was my first meal in weeks.

Nancy watched me scarf it down, but I could tell by the look on her face, her wheels were turning.

Although I always shared the details of my cases with her, I had started to be more specific with them more recently, as she got older and absorbed a lot of what she'd been learning as a criminal-justice major at college.

I got up from the table and grabbed the phone off the wall when I noticed the time. I pulled a piece of paper from my pocket and dialed the Reeds' phone number, trying to finish the sandwich I was still chewing.

"Who are you calling?" Nancy said.

"Logan Reed's parents."

The phone rang twice and, before the third ring, a woman answered: "Hello?"

I said, "Mrs. Reed?"

"Yes?"

"This is Jake Horn, I was out at your house earlier..."

"You say that like I wouldn't remember you," she said, not sounding quite as somber as she had earlier. I guessed she'd finished the bottle of wine, considering her words seemed to be somewhat slurred. "Can I help you with something?"

"Actually, I was hoping your husband was available."

She paused on the other end. "I wasn't completely honest with you earlier," she said. "Carl hasn't been staying here."

"Oh," I said. "Do you mean—"

"We've been having trouble for a while now," she said.

"He moved out?"

"Well, not officially. He still has a lot of his things here. But, I can't imagine he'll be coming back."

"I'm sorry," I said.

"You don't have to be," she said. "When the love is gone, you know it."

I wasn't sure what to say. I knew how difficult it was for her to lose her son, and now learning that her marriage had fallen apart made me question the whole situation.

"Do you know where he is?" I said.

The line went quiet, until she said, "He's in Maine."

"Oh, but you made it sound earlier like you didn't know where he was."

More silence.

"I don't. I mean, I don't know where he's staying. Most likely at a friend's house."

"Does his friend have a name?"

"Carl grew up on Cape Elizabeth, outside Portland. He knows a lot of people up there."

"I didn't know that," I said, thinking for a moment. "Did he, by any chance, know Rick Hanley? I mean, prior to the incident at the college?"

There was a pause on the other end. "I can't answer that."

"You can't? Or you don't want to."

"As I already said. Carl knows a lot of people in Maine. I'll just leave it at that."

CHAPTER 17

IT WAS LATE BY the time Nancy and I got up to Maine, and I had to take off as soon as we got to Raymond and Beth's so I could get over to Bartlett's Dockside before they closed.

I drove around the side of the building and parked near the screen door leading to the kitchen. I stepped out of the Nova and glanced through the screen into the kitchen, seeing Mary Potter's grandson washing dishes at the stainless-steel sink. I looked over toward the other side of the kitchen, to where Ron Tompkins was standing by the grill with his back to me. He appeared to be cleaning up.

I was surprised to see him there.

Neither of the two noticed me standing in the dark, outside the screen door.

I went around to the front entrance and went inside.

A young waitress I recognized approached me right away. "I'm sorry," she said. "The kitchen's closed."

Most of the tables were empty, and the other waitresses looked to be cleaning up, one sweeping the floor and another wiping down tables with a small plastic bucket in her hand.

"I'm here to talk to Mrs. Bartlett," I said. "Can you tell her Jake Horn's here to see her?"

The waitress looked me over with what seemed like a bit of suspicion, then nodded. "I'll let her know." She walked away, around the empty counter and through the door to the kitchen.

Ron walked out the same door, passing the waitress. He had an empty glass in his hand and poured himself a soda from the fountain with RC Cola printed on the front of it.

"Ron?" I said.

He looked surprised and maybe somewhat startled when he turned. His face looked a little better than it did in the hospital, although his eyes were still swollen and black underneath. He had a bandage on his forehead and looked at me, appearing somewhat confused. He said, "Did you just say my name?"

For some reason, it appeared he didn't recognize me.

"It's me," I said. "Jake Horn."

He rolled his eyes and huffed out a slight laugh. "I'm so sorry, I didn't even recognize you. My eyes were so swelled up in that hospital I could hardly see." He came around the counter and I could see he had a limp. His arm was bandaged too.

"I'm surprised to see you here," I said, keeping my voice low considering there were still a few people left in the restaurant.

He said, "I made bail. Of course, Marilyn took care of it for me. So, the least I could do was get back here to work and help her out."

The kitchen door swung again and this time Marilyn walked out. "Hi, Jake. I was worried you weren't coming back."

"I gave you my word," I said.

Ron looked confused, looking at his sister, then at me.

She asked me if I was hungry.

And I was. "Thank you, but I just want to talk to you." I nodded with my chin at Ron. "I was surprised to see him here. But it's good that he is. Can we sit down somewhere? To talk?"

Ron sipped from his glass and started back into the kitchen. "Let me finish getting things cleaned up," he said, and disappeared through the swinging door.

Marilyn waved for me to follow her. "Let's go back to my office."

I walked around the counter and followed her through the kitchen, past the ovens and stoves and a long steel sink with three bays: one filled with dirty pots and pans and one in the middle filled with water and soap foam on top.

Her office door was just to the left of the sink, but before we walked in I turned when I heard the screen door open.

Mary Potter's grandson, Brock, walked into the kitchen carrying a gray plastic garbage barrel. He looked at me, taking a moment, then went ahead with his work and acted like I wasn't there.

I didn't say a word to him, and instead continued behind Marilyn into her office.

She closed the door behind me.

The space was tight, with two desks taking up a lot of room, one piled high with papers and cardboard boxes. A filing cabinet in the corner had a Devil's ivy plant on top of it, although hers didn't seem to be doing so well.

I said, "I have the same plant in my office, I've had it since... I've had it for over twelve years." I didn't tell her my wife, Barbara, had given it to me, and that I did everything possible to keep it alive beyond its normal lifespan.

"I don't have a green thumb," she said. "I'm sure the fact there are no windows in here doesn't help the poor thing."

The other desk faced the wall where a cork board hung in front of it with photos and papers attached with multicolored plastic push pins. A calendar with a photo of the ocean hung on a nail to the right of the cork board, although it was still open to the month of June. I looked closer and saw the date was 1977.

Marilyn grabbed a folding chair that was closed and leaning against the wall. She opened it and placed it down in front of me.

She pulled another chair from one of the desks and sat down, turning to face me.

I sat in the folding chair with the door closed behind me.

"I was surprised to see Ron here," I said.

"He wanted to help out. I had to come up with ten thousand dollars bail," she said. "Although, if they find any other evidence he might've been up there in Bar Harbor with my car... I don't know what's going to happen."

"What did he say about that?"

She sat down and grabbed a pack of Newports from her desk, slipped a cigarette in her mouth and gave it a light, acting like she didn't want to answer. She took a drag, squinting from the smoke rising from the cigarette and into her face. "I had to pick him up at York County. He just wanted to get back here and work, act like everything's normal. Ron's like that, tends to go out of his way to pretend things are all right when they're not." She shrugged. "Maybe that's what the marijuana does for him. Who knows. I've never touched the stuff."

Mrs. Bartlett drew from her cigarette and filled the small office with smoke when she exhaled. "The police still aren't sure the Cutlass someone spotted up there is mine or not."

"I heard," I said. "Are you driving your husband's truck?"

She shook her head. "I already got the Cutlass back. The damage wasn't that bad, considering he drove it deep into those woods up there. It'll still need to be repaired, but I can drive it."

I looked at the photos she had on her cork board. From what I could see, most were of her with people inside the restaurant.

There was a knock at the door.

"Come in," Marilyn said.

I stood and dragged the folding chair out of the way.

Ron poked his head inside. He said, "Brock just left."

"He *left*?" Marilyn looked at the clock up over her desk. "Already?" She stood, and moved past her brother, out into the kitchen, then turned back to Ron. "Are you sure? Why would he leave?"

Ron stood in the doorway with his back to me. "I don't know. He took off his apron and just walked out. He said he was done."

Marilyn said, "And you're sure he's not outside, having a cigarette?"

Ron nodded. "I looked."

Marilyn walked back into the office, shaking her head. She took another drag from her cigarette and sat in the chair. "Kids these days..."

"Is it possible he left because I'm here?" I said.

She gave me a somewhat odd look, like she didn't understand. "Why would he leave if you're here? He's got a job to do."

"Remember I spoke to him the other day? Maybe he was afraid I was going to ask him more questions."

"I don't think Brock has anything to hide," she said, crushing her cigarette out in the translucent brown-glass ashtray. There were already a dozen or so crushed cigarette butts inside it, with flecks of white ash scattered around the top of her desk.

"How do you know he has nothing to hide?" I said.

Ron had walked away but came back and leaned in the doorway.

I said to Ron, "The other night, when you were first arrested, he said he wasn't surprised you were in trouble."

"Brock?" He seemed to force a smile. "He's like my kid brother. Why would he..." He swallowed, looking from me to Marilyn. "Why would he say something like that?"

Mrs. Bartlett pulled another cigarette from her pack, taking her time. "The rumors around this town have never stopped. Some people just don't know how to forgive someone for their past."

I watched her light her smoke, and could feel Ron staring at her, his eyes wide.

"Are you talking about Portland?" I said. "Or, is there something else that might've happened you haven't told me about?"

Neither responded to me.

Ron said to Marilyn, "That has nothing to do with—"

"If you want him to help you," she said, gazing back at Ron in the doorway, "Then we have to tell him everything."

Ron looked toward the floor for a moment, then raised his gaze to mine. "There's just something you should know."

I said, "Please tell me it doesn't have something to do with you and Casey Jilson."

Ron shook his head, his eyes open wide. "What? No!" He looked over his shoulder, toward the kitchen, and kept his voice low. "When I was younger... I was just getting started in teaching, and I—" He stopped and went inside the small office, standing only inches from where I had sat back down in the folding chair.

I stood and moved over to the desk with the boxes and papers, to give us both a little more breathing room.

Ron leaned against the door. "I was a substitute teacher at Biddeford High School, teaching English while the regular teacher was on maternity leave. And there was a student, Elizabeth Green, who approached me because she needed help with the class. She told me she wanted to be a writer but, frankly, she wasn't very good. She just..."

"That's not important," Marilyn said, holding her cigarette up in front of her mouth between her two fingers. "Get to the point, Ron."

He said, "Well, she asked if I could help her, and I told her I would, after school. So we met in the library, and I got the feeling there was something else going on. I don't know why. She didn't flirt with me or anything, but clearly her writing didn't seem to be the reason she was there. She just wanted to talk about stuff... asking me personal questions, like if I had a girlfriend."

I said, "Do I have to guess where this is going?"

I was starting to get impatient with the story, and knew it wasn't going to end well. I was afraid, at that point, I'd made a mistake getting involved.

"Nothing happened," he said. "If that's what you're thinking. But she did start calling me at my apartment. Then one night she showed up at my door."

"Did you let her in?" I said.

Ron shook his head. "No. In fact, I was dating someone at the time. She answered the door and told her I wasn't there."

Marilyn said to Ron, "Tell him who it was. The girl you were dating."

Ron said, "Alice Jennings."

That one caught me off guard. "Alice? The woman from the beach?"

Marilyn crushed out her cigarette in the ashtray. "I was going to tell you, but..."

Ron said, "Turns out, someone saw Elizabeth leaving my apartment. Not exactly my apartment, but in the building, going down the stairs. Some of the students found out she was there, and rumors spread like wildfire. Next thing you know, I'm being questioned about being involved with a student."

I closed my eyes, shaking my head. "This isn't good," I said. "I don't even know if I want to hear anything else."

"Elizabeth denied anything had happened," Ron said. "There was no lying. All we did was tell the truth. But nobody believed us."

I said, "Were you arrested?"

Ron shook his head. "No, it never even went that far. I was only a substitute, so it wasn't like I was fired. But they replaced me right away."

"Does this have anything to do with what happened at Westbrook?" I said.

"Well," Ron said, "the whole reason that escalated the way it did, that I was fired from my college teaching job, was because somehow the story of what happened got around Westbrook. And when the drug situation went down, even after the charges were dropped, the department chair, the dean, the parents, and everyone above me wanted me out."

I had my arms folded, staring at the photos on the cork board. I saw one of Ron and Marilyn, clearly from when they were younger. "Okay, so, you have some baggage that's followed you around all these years. And now we have a young woman, who also happened to be your student, who was killed with your truck."

Ron nodded, watching me like he was waiting to hear where I was going.

I didn't speak.

Nobody did.

On one hand, all I could think was that Ron Tompkins was guilty. Possibly of everything he told me he *hadn't* been guilty of, starting with the affair with the high school student, and then dealing drugs on campus. Did it mean he had something to do with Casey Jilson's death?

I didn't know.

If I'd learned anything in all my years as a private investigator, it was to believe a person was, without a doubt, innocent until proven guilty. My Uncle Pat had always said the cops didn't believe it should be the case. The ones he knew—including those he worked alongside before he started Horn Investigations—tended to lean toward guilty. Uncle Pat said it was just easier for them that way, and why he felt a third of prisoners behind bars were probably innocent.

"Can I be honest?" I said, looking from Ron to his sister. "I'm having a hard time here. As I hope I mentioned, it's rare I take a case like this, where my client—or my client's *brother*—is the one being charged with a crime. Normally, I end up on the victim's side, or the family. Just being honest here; I'm worried about how this all looks."

"So, you don't believe me?" Ron said.

My mind was shifting back and forth. There was, no doubt, something about him—the look on his face—that came across as honest and sincere. But that same look was what had me thinking there was a chance he was guilty.

I glanced at Marilyn and shifted my stance, straightening up. I said to Ron, "Can you be straight with me?"

He nodded.

"Did you take Marilyn's car to Acadia National Park, before you drove it into the woods?"

He paused, appearing hesitant, staring at Marilyn for a moment until he finally answered. "I did go up there. But I didn't have anything to do with what happened. I went there to talk to Logan."

CHAPTER 18

RON TOMPKINS' ATTORNEY WILLIE Hamme had been hired by Mrs. Bartlett, who'd hired him the first time when a woman from Rhode Island allegedly slipped on a french fry in the restaurant and tried to sue Mrs. Bartlett and her husband. Willie Hamme had the case thrown out after proving the woman had faked her fall, and had never been injured in the first place.

Whether or not Mr. Hamme was the right man to defend Ron was the question. Slip and fall wasn't murder, but Mrs. Bartlett seemed to trust him.

Willie stood at the top of the stone steps leading down to the driveway at his house. He was dressed in suit pants with a white, buttoned shirt, sleeves rolled up, with red suspenders stretched around the big belly that hung over his belt. He had a cigar hanging from his mouth, although it didn't appear to be lit; his graying hair was greased back on his balding head. He walked with a limp, careful with each step as he walked down the stone steps to greet me.

A dark-stained wooden sign by the bottom step had WILLIE HAMME, ESQUIRE carved into the base of the sign surrounded by flowers. A carved arrow on top of the sign pointed up the steps.

I met him halfway and he reached out his sweaty hand. "Willie Hamme," he said. "Jack, is it?"

"Jake," I said. "Jake Horn."

Willie headed back up, slow with each step, his breathing heavy.

I followed him along a stone walkway around the house and toward a large barn-like structure out back. A smaller version of the carved sign, without the arrow, hung on the grayed cedar shingles to the left of the building's door.

"Thanks for coming out," he said. "I used to have an office downtown, but purchased this property a couple of years back. I prefer the privacy. Doesn't hurt that I wake up, take ten steps and I'm at the office."

I glanced back at his Cape Cod-style house with the matching gray cedar shingles on the exterior.

He pushed open the red door and stood, holding it open. "Come on inside," he said. "Can I offer you a drink?"

"Not right now," I said.

I stepped into the wide-open space with rafters exposed above with a fan hanging down, humming as it turned. The place was well lit from the sunlight coming through the tall windows, with a hint of mildew odor in the air, although the cologne Willie wore was stronger.

The desk was made of what looked like cherrywood with a full-sized green leather chair behind it. A wall of shelves were filled with leather-bound law books.

A long table that matched his desk had four chairs on either side of it with a file box on top of it.

Willie walked over to a wet bar with a handful of liquor bottles on the shelf. He held up a bottle of Crown Royal. "You sure you don't want something?"

I waved him off. "Too early for me. But thank you."

He looked at his watch and laughed. "I guess maybe you're right. I tend to like to wait at least until eleven." He laughed again, loud, and sat at the table. "Have a seat," he said, gesturing toward the chairs on the other side from him.

"So, Jack, are you—"

"Jake," I said, wondering if the guy was doing it on purpose.

Willie let out a rolling laugh. "I'm sorry. I had a friend named Jack."

"Not a problem," I said, rolling the chair back from the table. I sat down across from him and he pulled out a stack of folders from a box.

"So, just so we're both on the same page here, uh, *Jake*." He grinned, like getting my name right was a big accomplishment. "Normally I hire my own private investigators. In fact, I have a man I work with... a former police detective from down New Hampshire. Someone I've learned to trust. However, I do understand Mrs. Bartlett went ahead and hired you on her own." He opened one of the folders, looked at whatever was inside, and closed it. "Is your background similar?"

"Similar?" I said.

"Were you an officer of the law at any point in your life?"

I didn't exactly answer. "I'm a private detective. Been doing it for most of my adult life. If there's something specific you'd like to ask..."

Willie shook his head. "Oh, no. I'm sorry if I offended you in any way. I was simply curious, if..." He cleared his throat and grabbed another folder from the file box and opened it, glancing over whatever was inside. "I just like to be sure we're all in capable hands."

"Mrs. Bartlett is my client," I said. "Maybe I should be the one to ask about your background?" I looked around the office. "As you know, Ron Tompkins is not in a good situation. I don't know how much work you've done that's involved defending a man suspected of murder, but this isn't someone slipping on a french fry. So if you want to try and pick apart someone's experience..."

Willie said, "Maybe we should just get past the questioning about who is or isn't capable, and move on to discussing what it is we'll need to do to help prove Ronald Tompkins' innocence?"

"That works for me," I said.

Willie got up from the table. "I think I'm going to pour that drink now." He had his back to me and reached into a cabinet for a glass. "You sure you wouldn't like a drink?"

I looked at my watch. I needed caffeine more than I needed a buzz. "Any chance you have coffee?"

He nodded. "I've got some made in the house, if you'd like?" He went and opened the door. "How do you like it?"

"Black," I said.

He gave a quick nod and left the building, closing the door behind him.

I watched him through the window as he walked into his house, then pulled the folders toward me to see what he had in his notes.

The first one I opened had a copy of a medical examiner's report, with Casey Jilson's name typed in the box where it said Decedent.

I hadn't yet gotten my hands on the report, and assumed Willie had planned to share it with me.

I looked over my shoulder toward the door and made sure he wasn't coming, quickly glancing over the report. I first looked at the space under Pathological Diagnosis: hip fracture... cracked kneecap, deep contusion on right thigh, shattered occipital bone...

The knob on the door turned and I closed the folder, pushing it toward Willie's side of the table. I leaned back in the chair just as Willie walked into the office and placed a mug down next to me, with Willie Hamme, Esquire printed in gold on the side of it.

Steam rose from the top of the coffee.

"That was fast," I said.

"Had actually just made a pot before you arrived."

He sat across the table again. "I'm sure you already know most of the story, how Ron had reported that truck missing when he got off work?"

I nodded. "But I'm not clear why the cops don't believe it was stolen."

"They're saying Miss Jilson's death was premeditated, and that Ron reported the truck stolen as part of his cover-up."

"Premeditated?" I said. "You're planning to murder someone, I can come up with at least twenty different ways you could do it without having to run someone down on the beach in the middle of the night."

Willie just stared back at me, maybe wondering what the twenty ways might've been.

He said, "Part of the issue for Ron right now is the relationship between himself and Miss Jilson."

"But he doesn't seem to be a fool," I said. "I'd say he's far from a perfect human, but not foolish enough to run her over and leave his truck there."

Willie leaned back in his chair. "Anything's plausible, if the police want it to be."

I lifted my coffee and took a sip. "Something doesn't smell right."

"It's supposed to be good coffee," Willie said.

"I don't mean the coffee." I wasn't sure if Willie was kidding or not, but he kept a straight face. I said, "Did you know I was at the scene the morning Casey Jilson's body was found?"

He appeared surprised. "At Goose Rocks?"

"Uh-huh. And the scene was a mess. The two cops... all I could think about was what amateurs they were. I've been involved with or witnessed enough homicide investigations to, well... if you ask me, Chief Hanley and Officer Silva either had no idea what they were doing, or were causing a mess on purpose. They weren't the least bit careful the way they trounced around on that sand."

Willie Hamme removed a photo from one of the folders and slid it across the table.

"Did you know they have a print from the sand that matches one of Ron's shoes?"

I shook my head and reached for the photo. "No, I didn't know that." This wasn't good news. "What did he say about it?"

"Ron? Just that he wasn't wearing those shoes, that he'd left them in the back of the truck. He told the police he couldn't remember the last time he wore them."

I was having a hard time trying to tell if Willie believed Ron was innocent, or if he was just doing the job he'd been paid for.

"Do you believe him?" I said. "I watched Chief Hanley and Officer Silva going through Ron's truck, tossing things everywhere like two kids digging through a toy box... walking all over the place with Casey Jilson's covered body on the ground at the front of it. The scene wasn't taped off, with various footprints all around the truck, like the whole area had been trampled. Even the women who were there watching had apparently walked all over the crime scene." I thought of that morning and leaned forward, my arms folded on the table. "In fact I saw someone's footprints going down toward the water." I handed him back the photo. "The simple fact, aside from everything else that doesn't add up, is why would he leave the truck there with her body?"

"Well, the truck ran out of gas," he said. "You didn't know that?"

I shook my head, admittedly somewhat embarrassed for not knowing a basic fact about the investigation.

Willie said, "So, it's assumed the person driving it had no intention of leaving it there. I'm not sure how much you've seen or heard, but there was a witness, lives right there on the beach, said she'd heard an engine running outside for most of the night but didn't think much of it."

"Didn't think much of a truck's engine running on the beach?" I rolled my eyes.

Willie said, "The woman's name is Mary Potter. She just happened to be with a group of ladies who'd first spotted the body."

"I know exactly who she is," I said. "I met her that morning on the beach." I looked into the coffee, raising it to take a sip but stopped, placing the mug back on the table. "Was the key in the ignition?"

"Yes. In the on position."

I said, "So they're saying the truck was left running, and it ran out of gas?"

Willie nodded. "That's correct."

"Did Mrs. Potter say how long she heard the engine?"

"She said she fell back asleep without even thinking about it."

Willie took the photo with the footprint in the sand and slid it back in the folder. "I appreciate your feedback on all this. But, if we can be honest with each other, things have only gotten more challenging with Ron admitting he drove up to Acadia National Park." He looked over toward his desk, which was mostly clear other than the black rotary phone on top of it. "I'm expecting a phone call any moment now, to see where things stand."

"I'm not sure why he waited to say anything," I said. "It certainly has me questioning what else he hasn't told me."

Willie nodded, like he agreed. "We don't need more surprises. I'm afraid it's come to a point I'll have no choice but to recommend Ron enter a different plea."

"Yeah?"

"Well, we're looking at *not guilty*, as things stand. But when he admitted to taking his sister's car up to Bar Harbor, as you know... it takes our defense in a completely different direction." He looked down at the folder in front of him. "Do you know the father?"

I said, "Whose father?"

"Carl Reed. Logan Reed's father."

"What about him?"

"Well," Willie said, "he's going to go out of his way to make sure someone pays for what happened to his son."

"Do you blame him?" I said.

Willie shook his head. "Of course not. But, I mean... I assume you know the whole history with him and Ron?"

"Of course," I said, making sure he knew I'd done my fair share of digging.

Willie said, "He grew up here, built his company..."

"He's in some kind of chemical business," I said.

"Yes, that's correct. But, as I was saying, he built his company in Portland but moved to Brighten, Mass ten years ago, in the fall of '68. Sent his son to his alma mater in '72, where he—Logan—met Casey Jilson."

I said, "It sounds like Carl knew Rick Hanley, even before what happened with Ron, up at the school?"

"Where'd you hear that?" Willie said.

"Mrs. Reed."

"I didn't know you spoke to her," he said. "What for?"

"Well, when I saw in the paper Carl Reed had offered a reward for finding the person responsible..."

"You went there for the reward?"

I shook my head. "Not at all. I went there because I found it suspicious, considering it hadn't yet been determined whether it was a suicide or not."

"Why would that make you suspicious?"

I thought about it. "Just like I said; it was just a little early in the investigation, to be able to get it in the papers, and—"

"So you going over there had nothing to do with you putting a few extra bills in your pocket?" He stared back at me. "Between that, and whatever Mrs. Bartlett's paying you, you'd be doing all right."

"I'm not interested in the reward," I said.

Willie grinned. "Is that the truth? Or are you afraid someone'll say you're double-dipping?"

"I couldn't care less what anyone thinks. I've been hired to do a job. And I gave Mrs. Bartlett my word I'd see it through."

"Your *word*?" He said, a slight smirk on his face. "You say that as if she's not paying you?"

"Of course she's paying me," I said.

I wondered why Willie had suddenly become less friendly, actually somewhat hostile, once I brought up that reward.

He said, "Well, the way you said it, it's like you're doing it out of the goodness of your heart." He was being a bit smug.

I wasn't exactly clear where he was going. "All I told you was I gave her my word. I'd like to think that's worth something."

Willie picked up his glass and held it in front of his mouth, looking at me over the top. "I'm just thinking out loud here, but what if, maybe, the two of us put our heads together, maybe you talk to Carl Reed about that reward, and as a team we—"

"I already said I'm not interested," I said.

"You didn't let me finish."

I pushed back the chair and stood up from the table, heading for the door. "I didn't have to."

CHAPTER 19

I TURNED OFF KING's Highway and into the circular driveway, parking behind the white Lincoln Continental with the black vinyl roof. The front door of the yellow Cape Cod-style house was open behind the white-aluminum exterior door. I could see inside through the screen.

The smell of something sweet came from inside the house, maybe cookies or something else baking in the oven. I pressed the doorbell and watched through the screen as Mary Potter took the corner and walked toward me from the back of the house.

"Oh," she said, wiping her hands on the red apron she wore, with a lobster printed in white on the front. "I thought you would be someone else." She looked toward the driveway and my car. "She's always late."

Mary pushed open the door and I didn't ask who she'd been expecting.

She held it open, inviting me inside.

I followed her down the hall and into the kitchen.

"So, to what do I owe this visit?" she said. "I've already answered all the questions I can about that poor girl on the beach. And, then..." She shook her head, in a what-a-shame kind of way. "Did you hear about her fiancé?"

"Yes, of course," I said.

Mary slipped floral-design oven mitts on her hands and opened the oven door, pulling out a pan of what looked like muffins rising up over the top of it. She placed them on the stove. "Hard to beat muffins with fresh Maine blueberries." She opened a cabinet door and took a toothpick out of a small box, stuck it in one of the muffins, then opened the oven door and slid the pan back inside. "They're not quite ready."

She removed the mitts from her hand and placed them on the counter. "Would you like a drink?"

I waved her off. "Not right now, thank you."

She laughed. "Not right now? How long do you plan to hang around, if not now?"

I stared back at her, and was starting to get the feeling she felt she had something over me, if nothing more than the money was in her bank account.

I looked through the sliding glass door at the beach, a view most people could only dream of. "I understand you heard a truck running in the middle of the night?" I turned to her, waiting for a response.

"A truck?" She appeared to act, at least for a brief moment, like she had no idea what I was asking about. Do you mean, the night before that woman's body was found?"

What else would I mean? "Yes, that night. Do you mind sharing the details with me?"

She paused, clearing her throat. "I heard something I guess we know now was an engine. However, at the time I first heard it, I didn't even know it was coming from the beach. I got up out of bed and looked out front, toward the road, but didn't see anything. Or anyone. It didn't even cross my mind to look out back for something on the beach."

"So, you didn't see anything?" I said.

"Oh, I'm sure it was Ron's truck."

"But you didn't see it?"

"Well, let's remember, whatever happened out there occurred Saturday morning." She laughed. "And I'd had quite a few Manhattans out back on the deck that evening. I wasn't worried about what I'd heard."

"Nobody else was here?" I said.

"What kind of question is that?" She appeared offended.

"I'm just asking if you were the only one here, if anyone else happened to be here with you," I said. "You *are* married, aren't you? I thought perhaps your husband might've been here with you."

She shook her head. "He's in Germany."

"Germany? What's he doing there?"

"He's a scientist," she said.

"No kidding? Was he there for President Carter's visit?"

She laughed, shaking her head. "No, I don't believe my husband is interested in being associated with President Carter." She went to the oven and pulled out the muffin tin. "It's about the only thing we don't agree on: our politics." She touched one of the muffins with her finger, then licked it. "My husband is holding out hope Ronald Reagan will run again."

Politics wasn't my thing, and was the last thing I wanted to discuss with anyone. It was something my grandmother had told me to avoid, back when I was young, even though she had her own strong opinions. She said you'll never be able to persuade anyone to believe anything other than what was already set in their own minds, and that politics only divided the country. Over the years, I came to realize she was right.

There was a knock at the door. Mrs. Potter removed her apron, hung it on a wooden coatrack on the wall, and left the kitchen. I heard her say, "I thought you'd be here sooner."

I looked out the sliding glass door into her yard, beyond the narrow deck just off the house, with steps leading to a brick patio. There was a long table on it with a blue umbrella and eight wood chairs surrounding it. There were also six lounge chairs facing the ocean, the yard enclosed by a white picket fence with bushy, flowering rhododendrons within.

"Jake?"

Mary Potter stood behind me with her younger friend, Alice.

"You remember Alice?" she said.

"Of course," I said. I gave Alice a nod.

She smiled back at me, biting a chunk of her lower lip. "Hi, Jake."

Mary said to Alice, "He's been hired by Marilyn Bartlett to get her brother off the hook."

Alice's eyes opened wide, and she appeared to try to hide her swallow.

"I'm not sure I'd put it that way," I said.

The two just stared back at me, like they were confused.

I said, "It's my job to look for—and find—the truth."

Mary said, "But don't you have to believe he's innocent? Otherwise I'd imagine you'd end up in quite the precarious position, no? And now, from what I hear, Ron may be facing charges for *two* murders?"

I said, "I get the feeling you're already convinced he's guilty?"

Mary shrugged. "Well, the evidence seems to be clear to me. But Alice would certainly be on the other side of the argument."

"Is that so?" I said.

Alice shrugged. "Ron's not a perfect man. He never was. But he's not a killer."

"You know him fairly well?" I said. "From what I understand?"

Alice nodded. "We dated. But it was nothing serious."

I said, "But I understand you were with him, at the time there were some rumors swirling around?"

"Rumors?" Mary said. "You mean, with that young girl? Apparently, he's always had something for his students."

I acted as if I didn't hear Mary Potter. Her opinions about Ron were obvious.

Alice said, "I didn't believe him at first, when he told me he had nothing to do with her. I was there that night, when she showed up at his door. I was upset with him, but it turned out none of it was true. Part of me regrets not sticking up for him more than I did, but I was young myself at the time. We both were. And, of course, my parents demanded I stay away from him."

"And what about now?" I said. "When was the last time you talked to him?"

"To Ron?" Alice shrugged. "Other than seeing him at the restaurant a couple of times, I wouldn't say I've really spoken to him lately."

"Lately?" I said. "Can you be more specific?"

Mary said. "Why are you trying to put her on the spot? It's not like she's done anything wrong."

I looked from Mary to Alice, shaking my head. "I'm just trying to get some answers. And, they're not easy to come by in this town."

Alice gave Mary a look, like she didn't mind the questions. At least not as much as Mary appeared to. She said, "Well, I think I saw him out, oh, I don't know... it must have been a few months ago. He was at the bar, over at Fran's Place."

I had no idea what Fran's Place was. "And you talked to him?"

"A little. But he's not the same person he was when we were younger. He used to be so happy all the time. And he was a good-looking man, with his long wavy hair, his blue eyes..." She cracked a crooked smile. "You could understand why his students were attracted to him."

"Students? Plural? Do you mean there were others? Besides the girl from Biddeford High, who showed up at his apartment?"

"There were others. I couldn't take it anymore. Not that I ever thought he'd do anything, but..."

"Others? You mean, other students?" I said.

She nodded. "Elizabeth Green was the last straw for me," she said. "I trusted Ron, but I guess it bothered me how close he'd get with the students."

"Close?"

"I don't know. He was friendly with everyone. He'd drop whatever he was doing if one of his students needed him."

"What about Casey Jilson?" I said. "Did you know anything about her?"

"I thought I told you," Mary said, "Alice was the first one to find her on the beach. Of *course* she didn't know who she was."

I hoped Alice would have a different answer.

She said, "We all knew what was happening in Portland. But I never knew any of the details at the time. I'd never heard of Casey Jilson before." She walked over to the stove, helped herself to a muffin and took a bite. She caught the crumbs with her hand held under her chin. "Mmmmm. These are delicious, Mary."

Mary took a small dish down from the upper cabinet and slipped it into Alice's hand under the muffin.

"Fresh Maine blueberries," Mary said. "That's the secret."

I felt like Alice was trying to divert my attention. Maybe she just wanted a muffin.

"So, Alice, didn't you know it was Ron's truck?" I said. "When you saw it on the beach?"

Alice and Mary both looked at each other, nodding.

Mary said, "I had already called the police about the truck before we even walked down there, when I first saw it. The last thing any of us expected was to see that poor girl." She had her back to me now and lifted the blueberry muffins from the tin, placing each one in a small wicker basket she pulled from under the cabinet.

Alice said, "I hope you're not trying to imply I knew something about it, or had anything to do with it?"

Mary turned from the stove, holding the basket of muffins, staring at me like she was waiting for the answer.

I thought about it for a moment. "I think it's just that in a small town like this, you all know each other. Everyone has secrets." I looked at Mary. "When you called the cops, did both Chief Hanley and Officer Silva show up right away?"

Mary waited, like she was afraid to answer. "Thomas showed up alone, at first. He came right after I called about the truck. By the time he got there we'd already walked down and saw the body. Chief Hanley showed up a few minutes later."

"How long?" I said. "Do you remember?"

"I wasn't paying attention," Mary said. "But it must've been ten, maybe twenty minutes?"

I said, "And what did Thomas do the whole time?"

"To be honest," Mary said, "the poor boy looked scared. You could tell he was nervous, at least at first. I'm sure he'd never even seen a dead body before."

"And what about Chief Hanley?"

"What about him?"

"What was his reaction once he arrived?"

Alice laughed. "Now you sound like you think the cops had something to do with it."

I gave her a look, just to let her know I wasn't screwing around.

Mary answered me: "The chief was calm. He didn't say much at all, seemingly more concerned with Thomas keeping us from getting too close."

I said, "And when did you tell him about hearing the engine in the middle of the night?"

Mary replied, "I don't know. I told Thomas I heard it when he first showed up, but he didn't seem to think much of it. Like I said, he seemed nervous." She grabbed the basket of muffins and held it out toward me. "Would you like one?"

"Maybe for the road," I said.

Mary looked at the clock on the wall. "I'll wrap it up for you. Because, I hate to say it, but Alice and I have to meet the others soon, so..."

"Can I just ask one more question? What's the story with your grandson? He made a similar comment to the one you did, that morning on the beach."

"What comment was that?" Mary said.

"How you seemed to have little doubt Ron was responsible."

"His truck was on the beach. I don't know what else you need to see."

I didn't need to go into it with her.

"Your grandson seemed to have similar feelings."

"Brock?" Mary waved her hand at me, as if brushing me off. "I can't answer for him. He's got a mind of his own and isn't afraid to speak his mind. But I wouldn't think too much about it. He's a good boy."

Chapter 20

RAYMOND WAS OUT ON the porch with the radio on, reading the *Globe*. "You alone?" I said, opening the screen door.

He nodded, eyes still on the newspaper. "I thought I'd wait here, see if you'd show up. Beth took Nancy to the library."

"The library?"

"I guess Nance had some work to do, but the way she was talking, I have a feeling something more to do with your investigation."

"Are you kidding me?"

Raymond shook his head. "Well, she was asking questions, most of which I couldn't answer. Beth wanted to take her to the beach, but it sounds like she'd rather help out her old man."

I cracked a smile, looking into the driveway toward my car. "Maybe I should take a ride over there."

"To the library?" Raymond folded the paper over and dropped it on the floor next to his chair. "Any progress?"

I sat in the rocker on the other side of the porch from him, in the corner. "I'm not sure I'd call any of it progress at this point. I can't help but think everyone's in on some kind of secret around here."

"It's a small town," he said. "Probably don't want to be bothered by some hotshot PI from Boston. And, you know, the summers are short up here. I can't imagine many people want the weight of a murder on their shoulders."

I thought about it. But there was more to it. It was like nobody wanted to talk. "You know that woman, Alice? The one who found the body?"

"Is she that pretty one you were talking to on the beach, with Mrs. Potter?"

I nodded. "It turns out she dated Tompkins, back when they were younger."

Raymond said, "Those two? I can't see that. She's got that look, like she's from money. Then there's this guy, Ron, some hippie Deadhead."

"It was a long time ago," I said. "But the thing is, it happened when he first got in hot water, when a young high school student showed up at his apartment."

Raymond waited, listening.

"But, besides that, there's something about her and Mary Potter. I'm not even sure how they're friends. There must be twenty years between them."

Raymond stared back at me, eyes squinted, like he was thinking something through. "And then there's the grandson," he said.

I leaned back in the chair and rubbed the side of my face. I could've used a shave, but on the other hand didn't feel the need to deal with it. "It's like they all have something against him," I said. "Not to mention she seems to be bothered by the fact the guy smokes pot."

Raymond said, "You say it like doing drugs is legal."

I rolled my eyes. "Take it easy, Officer Horn," I laughed. "He's hardly the only hippy in Maine who smokes grass." I stood up from the chair. "I'm going to go see if I can find Nancy. Was Beth staying with her, or did she just drop her off?"

Raymond picked up the newspaper and opened it, his face hidden behind it. "Beth was supposed to call me. But I haven't heard from her."

***

I stopped to use the pay phone outside the library and saw Nancy walking out of the building. I'd just dropped the coins in the slot, calling Maggie, and didn't want to hang up. I waved and yelled, "Nancy! Over here!"

She saw me and smiled, walked down the steps and along the sidewalk toward me. "When did you get here?" she said.

"Just now." I held up my finger for Nancy to wait when Maggie answered on the other end.

"Where are you?" Maggie said.

"Kennebunk Library. I just thought I'd check to see if you spoke with your friend."

"My *friend*? You mean Eddie? Do you have to keep calling him that?"

"Calling him what?"

"My 'friend.' The way you say it... You know his name now, don't you?"

I huffed out a laugh. "I don't know. Sorry, I was just—"

"I left a message with Raymond," Maggie said. "About five minutes ago."

"I just left there. Did your officer friend have something?"

Maggie paused on the other end. She probably knew there was something up with the way I addressed Eddie Kelly. Some might say I was being a fool, acting the way I did. But I couldn't help but think there was something going on between them. Even if there was, it wasn't like it bothered me.

Or maybe it did.

Maggie said, "Eddie said Carl Reed is staying at a friend's house, up in Old Orchard Beach. He seems to think Carl's there by himself, but he wasn't sure."

I wrote the address she gave me on the back of my business card.

"What's his name?" I said. "The friend he's staying with…"

"Chuck Johnson," she said. "He's an attorney in Boston."

"Johnson? Name sounds familiar. What kind of attorney?"

"Patent, I believe."

I looked at my watch and glanced at Nancy watching me, and gave her a quick nod with my chin. I said to Maggie, "I appreciate the help."

"There's something else," she said. "Eddie talked to one of the troopers, with Maine state police. He wasn't on the scene, but talk is there was some internal rift about the cause of death."

"Logan Reed's cause of death?"

"Yes, more about the way the chief medical examiner seemed to step in and get involved right away. Reversing the cause of death has apparently ruffled some feathers."

"Ruffled feathers?" I said. "Because an autopsy didn't go their way?"

"Eddie said the cops on the scene felt the initial evidence showed Logan Reed had taken his own life."

"You sure it's not just a handful of cops who are upset they might've gotten it wrong?" I said. "It wouldn't be the first time."

Maggie said nothing on the other end. She was similar to Raymond in a way, being a bit defensive or maybe even oversensitive whenever I'd question the police or said something negative about law enforcement officials. It wasn't that I didn't respect the men and women in blue. Quite the opposite. But cops were human. They made mistakes just like the rest of us. Of course, most were good and well-meaning. But I'd known a few, personally, who were pure narcissists: power-hungry and corrupt without an ounce of empathy... more interested in getting their names in the paper.

I told Maggie about my meeting with Ron's attorney, Willie Hamme, and how he had a copy of the medical report but didn't share it with me.

"Did you see anything that stood out?" she said.

"The injuries she sustained has me thinking," I said. "I'm not sure they match up with someone who'd been hit by a truck."

"In what way?" she said.

I had to think about it. "I'm not sure, to be honest. But... if I remember, there was also something about the way she was there on the sand. The position of her body... the proximity to the truck's bumper... It just doesn't add up. And I can't stop thinking about the mess those cops made of the crime scene. I've never seen anything like it."

Maggie said, "But you spoke with Chief Hanley, didn't you?"

"He didn't have much to say."

"What about the other officer? Did you talk to him?"

"Not yet." I noticed Nancy walking away. I said, "Listen, I gotta run. Did Beth call you? She said she was going to see if you wanted to come up."

"She did call. But I told her I had to check on a few things. I have to call her back."

"You should just come up," I said.

"I'd have to check with my neighbor," she said. "Make sure she can feed Max while I'm gone."

The operator came on the line and asked me to deposit thirty-five cents to continue the call.

Maggie said, "I'll let you go. If you need to reach me, call the station and let the desk know it's you. I'll be on the streets tonight, so I'll call you back when I have a chance."

I said goodbye, hung up, and turned to Nancy, now seated on a park bench under a big maple tree not far from where I stood. "Sorry about that," I said, walking toward her.

She stood and shrugged. "No biggie. What'd Maggie say? Is she coming up here?"

I looked toward Fletcher Street and straightened my sunglasses. "Maybe."

Nancy said, "I found something in the library, you know."

"Like what? A book? I hear they have lots of them."

Nancy rolled her eyes. She didn't laugh. When she was little, my so-called humor went over much better. "I'm serious," she said. "I thought I'd try to help you, show you that I'm not incompetent."

"Who said you were incompetent?" I shook my head. "I've never thought that for a second."

"Well, you don't want me helping you, so..."

"You know that's not true," I said. "But I don't want you to get in any trouble either." We both sat on the bench, the sun shining through the branches over us.

Nancy pulled a folded piece of paper from her back pocket and handed it to me. "Here."

I took it and looked over her handwritten notes. Logan Reed's name was written in blue ink on top of the paper:

August 3rd 1965

Brian Justice, 15 years old

Fell from boat, drowned in Great Pond, Cape Elizabeth, fishing with friend, Logan Reed

I looked up from the paper. "Where'd you find this?"

She shrugged. "I just looked through microfilm of old newspapers from up here. Remember, I had that Library Research class last year..."

"Which newspaper?"

"The *Cape Elizabeth Observer*."

"Was there anything else about it?"

"Not really. It was a short article, only a few paragraphs. I tried to find more about it, but I didn't have any luck."

I stared at the piece of paper with Nancy's notes. "I'm not sure what it means, if anything at all, but you never know." I gave her a smile. "This is good work, Nance."

CHAPTER 21

My job was to investigate the death of Casey Jilson for the sole purpose of proving Ron Tompkins was not the killer, as most people believed he was. Of course, I had my own doubts he was innocent, but I was committed to getting my facts straight.

The problem was, my involvement had gone far beyond my initial plan, especially considering Logan Reed's death had complicated the investigation not only for me, but for the various law enforcement departments involved.

From Cambridge to Maine, there were at least four police departments involved, including, but not limited to: Kennebunkport, the Maine state police, Biddeford Police because of Ron's accident, and now, to a lesser extent, the Cambridge Police in Massachusetts.

My initial thought was to focus on Casey Jilson's death, and, of course, her life leading up to it. But it wasn't as easy as I'd hoped. There was no record of her staying anywhere in the area. No witnesses saw her on the beach the night before her death, or at any other time. Not until it was too late. The deeper I dug into what could have happened, the more questions I had. One thing I was almost certain of—and any decent detective could've figured it out—was that whoever was behind Casey's murder had also killed Logan Reed.

At that point, I almost felt as if it didn't matter which death I investigated. Either would lead me to the killer.

With the two cases being covered by the local news, the citizens of Kennebunkport believed without a doubt the cops had it right from the moment a truck belonging to Ron Tompkins seemed to provide all the evidence that was needed. It was only a matter of time before Ron ended up behind bars.

I waited in the Nova, parked off the side of the road in a wooded area fifty yards from the entrance to the Kennebunkport police station. I was parked far enough away to avoid being noticed, but close enough where I could see who was coming in or out of the station.

I had learned Officer Thomas Silva left every single day at twelve forty-five to pick up lunch. And, like clockwork, he got in his blue Ford Fairmont station wagon and left the station. He turned out of the parking lot and drove right past me without even noticing I was there.

I waited before I pulled out and got behind him, staying far enough back he hopefully wouldn't notice I was following.

Officer Silva pulled into a parking space in front of the Dock Square Market. I drove ahead and grabbed the first spot I saw, a few spaces from the entrance to the store. I jumped out and hurried to catch up with him.

But he'd already gone inside.

He was at the counter when I walked in after him, removing his hat as he sat on the last red-padded stool toward the end.

The woman behind the counter told him his sandwiches would be ready soon.

Thomas Silva watched me sit on the stool next to him. "Afternoon," he said with a nod.

A woman with two young boys in tow walked by, on their way toward the door. "Hi Thomas," she said, smiling.

He said hi to the woman and her two kids, but didn't get into any kind of conversation with them. He turned back to me with a look like he wondered why I sat so close to him when all the other stools were empty. "Do I know you?"

"I don't think so." I reached out to shake his hand. "Jake Horn."

"Horn?" He stared back at me, his eyes squinted, like he was thinking. "You're the private investigator been sniffing around here, aren't you?"

The woman behind the counter walked over and asked me if I wanted to order something.

I glanced at the menu written on a chalkboard behind her. "Can I just get a coffee for now?"

She nodded, turned and walked away without another word.

Thomas Silva said, "You've been going around asking people questions about the Casey Jilson murder, isn't that right? Chief Hanley said you showed up at the station, stirring up trouble."

"I wouldn't say I was stirring up anything. I'm just looking for some answers. Same as I assume you and the chief are."

The woman came over with a coffee. She placed it in front of me with a stainless-steel creamer and a glass sugar pourer. "Let me know if you'd like to order anything else." She gave Thomas a nod. "Your food'll be ready in a few minutes, hon. We got a little busy, for lunch."

"Chief's hungry," he said. "You know how he gets when he hasn't eaten." He laughed, and the woman walked away, toward the register at the front of the store.

"I was there that morning," I said.

Officer Silva turned to me. "You were where?"

"At the beach. When you were there, with Casey Jilson."

He stared back at me with his chin raised, like he was thinking. "I knew I'd seen you somewhere," he said. "You were with a girl, about my age?"

"My daughter," I said. "How old are you?"

"Twenty-two."

"Nancy turns twenty in November." I sipped my coffee. "You like being a cop?"

He had a confused look on his face, maybe wondering why I was asking him a random, personal question. "Uh, yeah. Of course. Something I wanted to do my entire life."

"Probably never expected you'd be dealing with a murder up here in Kennebunkport though, right?"

Thomas didn't reply.

I sipped the coffee, looking up at the chalkboard. I hadn't eaten a thing all day, not since the muffin Mrs. Potter had given me.

"Is the food any good here?" I said.

Thomas nodded toward the swinging door to what looked like a kitchen. "Mr. Barns makes a good sandwich."

"Any suggestions that don't have to do with lobster?"

Thomas pulled at his chin, looking up at the menu. "Well, I suppose if you don't want the lobster roll... Can't go wrong with the Reuben."

I waved for the woman, now standing behind the cash register by the door at the front of the store. "Can I order a Reuben? To go?"

She looked at me and gave a nod, then walked past us and back through the swinging door.

"So, that morning on the beach," I said. "When Mary Potter mentioned Ron Tompkins' name, you at first seemed to want to defend him. It didn't sound to me you believed he had anything to do with that girl's death, even though it was his truck."

"It *was* his truck," he said. "But it'd been reported stolen. It hadn't crossed my mind at the time someone would've submitted a false report, attempting to hide a crime before it had even occurred. If he hadn't run out of gas, maybe he would've gotten away with it."

"Do you really believe that?" I said. "I don't see how it makes sense he'd report it stolen, then use his own truck to kill a woman right there on the beach in the middle of the night."

Thomas's face turned a shade of red. The more I looked at him, the more I could see he was just a kid. Even his uniform didn't seem to quite fit him right. He shook his head. "Sir, I don't know what you're implying."

"Have you ever investigated a murder before?" I said. "I'm guessing this was your first. And, to be honest, by the way things were being handled that morning, it wouldn't surprise me to hear it was Chief Hanley's first too."

"What's that supposed to mean?" he said.

"Do you really think it makes sense that Ron killed Miss Jilson? I just don't see how someone gets hit like that on a beach, unless she was waiting there for it."

"Mr. Horn..." Thomas showed his frustration, but kept his voice low, although there was nobody inside the place other than the two of us and whoever was back in the kitchen. "I don't know what your goal is or what you're doing here, but I'm not going to sit here and discuss this case with you. We have already thoroughly investigated the crime, and Ron Tompkins will be found guilty of this crime. I'm sorry to say that, but whatever you're trying to do... it's not going to change anyone's mind."

"Don't you have even the slightest touch of doubt he did it? Do you really want that weight on your shoulders, knowing you sent an innocent man to prison?"

Thomas swallowed, shaking his head. "Just because you said he didn't do it, doesn't mean—"

"I'm just asking you to think about it. Think about how it all went down. And ask yourself if you believe Ron Tompkins is guilty because the evidence really tells you so... or because Chief Hanley said he was."

Young Officer Silva stared back at me without a word. His lips moved, like he wanted to say something, but he didn't. He stood when the woman came out of the kitchen with a brown paper bag, holding it sideways with her hand on the bottom of it.

She placed the bag on the counter in front of Thomas. "Eat 'em while they're hot," she said. "You know the chief doesn't like his sandwich cold!"

CHAPTER 22

I PULLED ONTO SACO Avenue and continued to Union, in Old Orchard Beach. The house where Carl Reed was supposed to be staying was on Fourth Avenue: a road that ended right where the beach began, the sand covering over the asphalt.

The ocean was less than a football field's length away from where I'd stopped. The Nova idled.

There were NO PARKING signs on both sides of the road. The only available space was in the short driveway where a green Mercedes occupied one of two spots. The car was registered to Carl Reed.

I turned into the driveway and parked to the left of the Mercedes, looking up at the two-story home with gray, weathered cedar shingles and a porch that wrapped around the house on three sides.

Chuck Johnson, the owner of the house and friend of Carl Reed, had bought the vacation home years earlier, as I'd learned, with his primary residence back in Boston, where he practiced law. My first thought was it must be nice to have enough money to own two homes. My second was I'd rather be flat broke than be a lawyer. My

Uncle Pat, whenever we'd run up against an attorney, would tell the same joke: "How can you tell if a lawyer's lying? His lips are moving."

I actually had a couple of lawyer friends, but Uncle Pat never had a good thing to say about any of them. Over the years, his distaste for them rubbed off on me. Just a little.

I walked around the house to the backside facing the ocean. Behind a screened-in area of the porch was a woman in a bikini on a lounge chair, reading a book. I went up the steps and knocked on the wooden edge of the screen door. "Hello?"

The woman appeared startled at first, then straightened up on the chair. She turned her legs and placed her bare feet on the wooden floor. She covered herself with a towel as she stood from the chair.

I said, "I'm looking for Carl. Is he here?"

She walked to the door and unlatched the latch that held it closed. "Are you a friend of his?"

"An acquaintance," I said.

She looked me over, and backed away from the door and allowed me onto the porch. "I'll go see if he's available. I believe he's taking a nap."

"I'll wait here," I said, and watched her walk through the door into the house and close it behind her. I heard the lock click.

I looked out at the crowd on the beach and colorful umbrellas over chairs with adults resting. Dozens of children ran in and out of the water as the calm waves rolled up onto the sand.

I thought about the morning Casey Jilson's body was found, the way the water rushed up, getting closer to her body as high tide rolled in. I remembered the footprints that disappeared under the carelessness of Officer Silva and Chief Hanley, and the way footprints

173

from the truck—what were left, went straight toward the water and vanished in the sand.

But, somehow, they managed to get a footprint that matched one of Ron's shoes. I didn't buy it.

The door opened and a white-haired man with a thick mustache stepped outside onto the porch. His short-sleeved shirt was unbuttoned over a striped bathing suit. "May I help you?"

"Mr Reed?"

He looked me over. "Who are *you*?"

"My name's Jake Horn. I'm involved in the investigation of Casey Jilson's murder."

The woman, pretty and much younger than Carl Reed by at least twenty years, picked up her book from the lounge chair. "I'm going down to the water," she said, giving me a thin smile as she left through the screen door.

"Are you with the police?" he said.

"Not exactly," I said. "I'm a private detective."

"A PI?"

"That's right."

Carl Reed said, "Working for whom?"

"Well, it's confidential," I said, something I'd drop on occasion that was rarely questioned.

Carl didn't question it.

He pulled the door to the house closed behind him and walked across the porch, looking out through the screen toward the beach. With his back to me, he said, "Does this have something to do with Logan?"

"Considering Ron Tompkins is the prime suspect in both Casey and your son's case, I'd say it does."

Carl glanced back at me. "What do you want?"

174

"Well, first thing I'd like to know is if you're still offering a reward?"

He turned around to face me. "Is that what this is about?"

I shook my head. "No."

He said, "I had offered that before the police knew anything at all. But, at this stage, I'm confident they have the right man."

"Are you?" I said. "Because, although Ron has admitted to being up at Acadia National Park around the time your son was found in his car, and his truck was left on the beach where Casey was killed, there's no real motive. The evidence, to be honest, is weak."

"Weak?" he said. "As far as I understand, there's plenty of evidence. Not to mention, the motive, if you ask enough people, surrounds Ron's feelings for Casey." He folded his arms. "You're not much of a detective if that's news to you."

I'd considered the possibility. And there was clearly a relationship between Ron and Casey, but I understood it to be more of a student-teacher relationship than anything. At least that's the way I perceived it to be.

"Ron was friends with your son too," I said. "He was only up there at the park because Logan had called him, upset about what had happened to Casey."

"Is that what he told you?" Carl huffed. "I made sure that man never stepped foot near Logan. At least as much as I possibly could."

"I'm not sure he listened," I said.

Carl said, "Logan was a good kid. He knew right from wrong. He knew Tompkins was bad news."

"Is that what he told you?"

Carl paused, staring back at me for a moment. "I hope the man rots in jail. It's about time he paid a price."

"So, you've already made up your mind?" I said. "You have to remember, Ron Tompkins has never been convicted of anything. But you and Rick Hanley seem to've been hung up on bringing him down."

"He brought it all on himself," Carl said.

"You ruined the man's life."

Carl threw his hands in the air. "Is this what you came here for? To defend Ron Tompkins from something that happened eight or nine years ago? What's in the past has no bearing on what he's done this time. He needs to pay the price for what he's done."

"Would it surprise you if I told you I believe Ron's been set up?"

Carl held his gaze for a moment, then faced the screen door, looking toward the beach without a response.

I said, "Why did you offer that reward before you knew what happened to your son?"

He looked back at me. "What kind of question is that? I'm his father. I wasn't going to wait around for answers."

"Forgive me for asking this," I said, "but you never believed your son could have possibly taken his own life?"

"He's not some coward who..." He lowered his head, his eyes toward the floor. He turned again with his back to me, wiping the side of his face with his hand. "I'd like you to leave." With a furious look on his face, he pointed toward the door. "Get out of here, before I call the police. And don't you dare come back here!" He threw open the screen door.

I walked outside without arguing, but turned once I was on the steps. "I know about what happened with Logan and his friend, in Cape Elizabeth."

Carl stared back at me, his mouth slightly open like he was going to talk.

"It must have caused a lot of pain," I said. "For everyone. Including Logan."

His enraged reaction from a moment ago was replaced with calm. He looked down at me from the doorway. "We've all tried to put it behind us."

"Did Logan?"

Carl Reed closed his eyes. "Do you know what it's like to lose a child?"

"I know what it's like to lose someone you love," I said. "And I know you'd do anything to make up for it... To find an answer; even if it could be the wrong one."

He stared out at me, closed the screen door, and disappeared into the house.

Chapter 23

I took a left off of Beach Street into Saco and looked in the rearview at a powder-blue Chrysler that had been behind me since I'd left Old Orchard Beach. I tried not to think much of it, and wasn't ready to believe I was being followed.

With the Nova low on gas, I pulled into Don's Texaco.

The day had already started to slip away, with the sun starting to set. I didn't like that the days were already getting shorter. That was August, though—the month that always gave me a feeling of another summer gone by. As much as I enjoyed fall, I was never ready for those dark evenings with winter creeping around the corner.

Being born and raised in New England, it was always in the back of everyone's mind that the long winter would show up sooner than we'd hoped. We'd complain about the cold and snow and how much we wish it would be warm again. But then the heat of summer would have us wishing for cooler weather.

I cut the wheel into the lot, toward the pump. The bell rang when I drove over the black hose, and the serviceman in a green one-piece uniform immediately emerged from the building. I had my window down, and could smell the fumes from the gas pump.

"How much?" he said, standing outside my door next to the pump.

I handed him a fin. "Fill it up."

I watched him through the side view, sticking the nozzle into the tank. Looking around the outside of the car, I wasn't sure where the car had gone that I thought had followed me. I didn't see it. At least not until I glanced over my shoulder out the rear window.

The front end of the vehicle stuck out from the side of the brick building.

The man finished pumping and asked me to pop my hood. "I'll check your oil and fluids."

"No need today," I said, and thanked him before driving away from the pump. I drove so I could get a better look at the vehicle, but it was no longer there. The Chrysler was gone. I assumed I was mistaken, and started to head for the exit.

But at the last second I spun the Nova around and drove past the serviceman and around the back of the building.

The Chrysler was there, parked. I stopped behind it and was about to step out when a van pulled in close behind me and parked close enough to my rear end I couldn't go anywhere if I wanted to. All I could see was the van's grill.

A man got out of the driver's side of the Chrysler parked in front of me, and I reached under the seat for my .38. With the gun by my side, I got out and looked the man in the eye. "Something I can do for you?"

He stood still, watching me without a word. He was about my size, maybe an inch or two taller, but thin and dressed in a suit like he was on his way to an important meeting. He looked more like a businessman than some kind of goon. The man's gaze shifted to the gun in my hand, and he pulled his suit coat back enough so I could see that I wasn't the only one carrying a gun.

His gun was in a holster.

"We don't want any trouble," he said. "We just want to talk."

I glanced over my shoulder, but whoever was in the van still hadn't gotten out.

I didn't raise the gun. But I didn't put it away either. "Go ahead," I said. "Start talking."

The man said, "Can you please put away your gun?" He appeared calm and acted somewhat polite. There was no tough-guy act. At least not at first.

I wondered if he was a cop.

"How about you tell me what you want, and then I'll think about putting this away."

The man looked past me, toward the van, and gave a nod.

I looked back and the van's driver's-side door swung open, a man stepping down with his feet dangling, like he was too far from the ground. He was short, and looked like he could've used a step stool to get out of the van. The little guy wasn't dressed the way his friend was, instead showing off his thick arms and broad shoulders in a red sleeveless T-shirt.

His feet hit the ground and he walked toward me, barrel-chested with a snarl on his face and a bald head, and with tattoos running up and down his muscle-packed arms. Whatever he was missing in height he seemed to try to make up for in the gym.

"Is this your heavy?" I said, turning back to the well-dressed man in front of me.

He didn't answer. "I'm going to make this real simple," he said. "Walk away from your so-called investigation and go back to where you came from."

I laughed, although not because it was funny. I looked him over. "Who sent you? Carl Reed? Chief Hanley?"

"I'm giving you the courtesy of a simple warning," the man said. "And I'd advise you to take it for what it is, and not see how far you can push it. You're already in over your head, and if you don't do as I'm asking, you'll learn the hard way you've made a mistake coming to Maine."

I glanced behind me and didn't like the way the short gorilla-like man had gotten closer. I could smell whatever kind of gas-station cologne he was wearing, likely to cover up his body odor from too much time in the gym.

"I'm sorry," I said. "I don't scare that easily."

The tall one nodded at his friend behind me, and with another quick glance over my shoulder I saw him charge toward me. As he reached for me, I threw my elbow back, caught him in the chin and knocked him back a couple of steps. I spun around and followed it with a one-two punch and an uppercut that sent him stumbling into the front fender of his van.

But he caught his footing and lunged toward me, wrapping his arms around my midsection, pulling us both to the ground. His small size was hard to deal with as I fell on top of his sweaty body. He grabbed my wrist with both hands and tried to shake my gun free.

I kept my finger on the trigger and a shot fired in the direction of the thin man standing in front of us.

He ducked, pulled his gun, and came toward me with his hand out, holding the muzzle inches from my face. "I was warned you were going to make this more difficult than it had to be."

The goon on the ground underneath me had his arm wrapped around my neck from behind. He was strong, like a pit bull, holding my arm so I couldn't raise the .38.

The tall one reached down and peeled the gun from my hand, then made a swirling motion in the air with his finger. "Turn him around."

The goon flipped me over, like a pro wrestling move, and had my face down on the hot asphalt. The tall one slapped handcuffs on my wrists and lifted me to my feet.

There were spectators at that point peeking around the corner from the front of the building. Sirens could be heard in the distance, growing louder as he dragged me to his car and threw me into the back seat of the Chrysler. He ignored the onlookers, and still hadn't identified himself as a cop but I could only assume he was. "You should probably read me my rights, if you're..."

The door slammed in my face and the man got in the front behind the wheel, shifting the running car into drive. I fell back against the seat as he took off full speed, tires squealing. We headed toward Main Street.

I straightened up and looked out the rear window at my Nova, the driver's-side door left open.

The van followed.

"Where are we going?" I said. "If you're a cop, you should—"

"I'd like you to just be quiet for now," he said. He kept his eyes on the road. "I already told you, it was an easy request."

"Where do you work? Are you a statie? You can't be with Kennebunkport Police," I said. "Is Chief Hanley a bud of yours?"

The man said nothing, continuing toward Beach Street. He lifted a wired mic from a CB mounted under the dash, turning onto Route 1. "He didn't listen. I've got him in the car with me. I'll check back with you once we arrive." He turned the car into an empty parking lot of a youth baseball field, got out and opened the trunk, then came over and opened the passenger door to my right.

He reached in with what looked like a black pillow case and pulled it down over my head. Everything went dark, and I heard the sound of tape tearing from a roll. He wrapped the tape around my neck so I couldn't remove the pillow case or hood. The door slammed, followed by the door in front, and we were back in motion. The car skidded and I used my legs to keep myself from falling over.

"What the hell is going on here?" I said.

And just like before, I didn't get an answer.

Chapter 24

I sat in what felt like an uncomfortable lawn chair, the way the bar in front ran under my legs. I was in total darkness, and it was hard to breathe. All I could smell was my own sweat and breath inside the hood pulled over my head. Other than my hands being cuffed behind my back, I wasn't tied to the chair. And I could hear voices I believed belonged to the man in the suit and his goon friend somewhere outside the room or building they had me in.

The sound of a creaking door was followed by a light I could barely see through whatever the hood was they'd pulled over my head. "What the hell's going on here?" I said, my voice muffled with the way the hood stuck to my dry, sticky lips. The tape around my neck, to keep the hood in place, wasn't choking me. But I didn't like the feeling of it.

Luckily, whoever came in through the door yanked off the tape and ripped the hood from my head.

I squinted, giving my eyes a moment to adjust, and looked up at the tall, thin man. He'd removed his suit coat, although still in a tie, loosened, with his white dress shirt's sleeves rolled up to his elbows. His holster was gone.

"Mr. Horn," he said. "This is more than we wanted to have to do with you, but you gave me little choice. I'm sorry to be in this situation."

"You're sorry?" I said, lifting myself from the chair as if there was much I could do with my hands cuffed behind my back.

But he put his hands on my shoulders and eased me back down. "Just relax, all right?"

"Relax?" I said. "Tell me what the hell you want with me, and I'll think about it." I looked around what turned out to be the inside of a garage of some sort, with concrete, cinder-block walls and a bright fluorescent light on the ceiling that buzzed with a slight flicker. Stacks of heavy-looking bags—perhaps cement or fertilizer—were piled against one wall. Yard tools leaned against a ride-on lawnmower parked in the corner. "Where the hell are we?"

"Don't worry about that," he said. "But I need you to listen to me."

I looked the man in the eye. "If you're going to tell me what you already told me..." I shook my head. "You've only motivated me more. I'm just being honest with you."

"Motivated you? To continue your investigation?" He laughed.

I nodded. "That's right. I don't know who you are, but..." I looked him up and down with a forced expression of disgust. "A cop, I assume. But since I'm not down at the station with some kind of charge you know wouldn't stick... and you've got me holed up in some kind of garage... I'd guess you're a dirty one. So, at this point, maybe killing me will be your only option."

The man, now with a serious expression on his face, cleared his throat. "I'd hate to have to do that."

185

I said, "Why don't you tell me what this is all about? Clearly, I'm onto something, whether it's Carl or Chief Hanley, or..."

"I'm giving you a choice," the man said. "You can back away and go home, or pay the price for sticking around."

"You don't look as dumb as I'm thinking you are," I said. "You cover my head, but I'm looking right at you. You're not afraid I'll find out who you are?"

The man leaned down with his hands resting on his knees, staring into my eyes with his face so close I could smell the stink on his breath. "You can get as good a look as you'd like. All you'd need to do is know how much we already know about you. And that includes anyone else you care about."

"I'll take that as a threat," I said, staring into his dark eyes. "I don't take kindly to threats."

The man straightened up then walked, slowly, toward the door. He said, "What makes you think Ron Tompkins is innocent?"

"Because the whole thing is a joke. The truck on the beach, the woman's body... setting him up to somehow convince him to drive up to that park where Logan was killed. None of it makes sense. And I'm starting to wonder if this whole state is corrupt, from Chief Hanley to whoever else you're involved with."

"You are in over your head," the man said, turning back to me, his hands behind his back. He walked to a workbench built into the wall and grabbed a pair of pliers from a toolbox and walked toward me.

I used my feet to slide the chair back, the aluminum scraping across the floor until I was up against the wall behind me. "What are you doing?" I said, staring at the pliers in the man's hands.

"Ready!" he yelled, and the door swung open.

The short pit-bull-looking man from the van came in from the darkness outside. This time he was the one with a gun in his hand, and he walked toward me. Without a second of hesitation he swung the gun, striking me in the face.

My head snapped around and I felt the warmth of my own blood dripping down my face.

The taller one put his arm straight out, holding his buddy back from taking another shot at me. "Take it easy," he said, eyeballing his friend. "We don't want him dead. Not yet."

"What are you doing?" I said, looking at the pliers in the man's hand.

"You don't seem to want to believe we mean business," he said. "And I need your assurance you're going to leave this state, and never come back again."

The short goon tucked the gun in his pants and pulled me from the chair, holding me from behind with his arm tight around my neck. He squeezed my head, holding me by the chin and trying to stop me from moving around. He put pressure on my jaw, trying to get it open.

I shook my head, trying to get it free. But the goon was too strong, and with my hands cuffed behind my back there was little I could do to break free from his grasp.

I clenched my jaw, wondering what kind of psychos I was dealing with.

I tried to wiggle free, but it was no use.

The man with the pliers came toward my face, using his free hand to assist his friend trying to pry open my mouth with his fingers.

But as the pit bull pressed his body against me from behind, I felt the metal of the gun he'd stuck in the front of his pants rub against my cuffed hands. I grabbed it and, without a second thought, slipped my finger behind the trigger, firing a shot before I even got it out of his pants.

The scream was womanlike—a high-pitched cry. He fell to the ground.

I spun around with the gun in my hand behind my back and fired another two shots in the direction of the thin man with the pliers. I wasn't sure if I'd shot him once or twice, but I wasn't going to wait around to find out. As he stumbled back, I drove my shoulder into his chest and propelled him into the wall by the door.

He collapsed onto the concrete floor and I ran outside past the van and the Chrysler, toward the woods. I took a second to look back at the small concrete structure, and beyond it, in the distance, at a house I could barely make out. Dim lighting glowed from inside the windows.

I wasn't going to wait around to see if either of the two men would come after me, assuming either was alive. I continued toward the woods and ran as fast as I could to get away until I finally stopped to catch my breath. I was surrounded by nothing but trees and darkness, with the slight glow of the moon's light slicing through the tree canopy over my head.

I looked around, and seemed to have lost my sense of direction. I didn't know which way to go.

I didn't know where I was.

***

I walked for hours into the night. It was eerily quiet, and I could only hope I'd at least hear a vehicle or a plane or something to indicate I wasn't lost and in the middle of nowhere.

But it turned out that was nothing more than wishful thinking.

The fact my hands were still cuffed behind my back made being in the woods alone all the more uncomfortable. I still had the gun, tucked into the back of my pants, but wasn't much of a woods person. I'd spent a good part of my life in the city, and to say I knew how to survive in nature would be a stretch.

But I kept walking, assuming as long as I headed east toward the rising sun I'd eventually make it out of the woods. Whether or not it would be civilization was another question.

My eyes had somewhat adjusted to the darkness. I stopped to look around. There was nothing but trees. I wish I'd paid better attention when I ran away. I didn't even know which direction I'd started from, because I was more interested in getting out of there.

Thirsty and hungry, I had little choice but to keep going until, for one reason or another, I couldn't.

The cuffs were tight on my wrists. I wiggled them all I could as I continued walking, but I didn't think there was any way I'd be able to get out of them. But the thing about handcuffs was that they weren't foolproof. You could pick the lock, quite easily, but that would require something more than a stick from the woods.

The fact about handcuffs was that someone without thumbs couldn't be held in them. Of course, I wasn't, at that point, any- where close to being desperate enough to chew off my own thumb. But I did have a fairly high tolerance for pain, and realized if I had to somehow survive in the woods for a full day or two or even more... getting the handcuffs off my wrists was a priority.

I kept walking—wandering, really—thinking through my limited options. I was sure Raymond and Nancy, and most likely Maggie, had to be worried and out looking for me at that point. Whether or not they got anyone else involved, including the Kennebunkport

Police, was another question. If Chief Hanley was behind any of what had happened, then turning to him would be a dangerous mistake.

Having my hands cuffed behind my back was driving me crazy. I was defenseless. And sure enough, I took a step over a damp, downed tree and tripped on it, falling to the ground and holding my head up so I didn't crack it open. But I landed on my shoulder hard enough it felt like it'd popped out of the socket. I screamed in pain, although it was just as much frustration from being lost in the woods. My voice echoed through the forest when I cried out. But I was certain nobody heard me.

Chapter 25

I DON'T KNOW HOW many hours had gone by, but I'd finally noticed tiny lights, far off in the distance and moving through the trees. If I didn't know better, I'd've said they were fireflies. But I started to run in the direction of the lights, as fast as I could with my hands cuffed behind my back, until I was at a point where I could also hear sounds I knew—or at least hoped—came from vehicles out on the road.

But I slowed as I got closer, worried about being seen. I didn't know if I'd killed both men, or who they were. The one in charge, I was almost certain, was a cop. Or at least had some kind of law enforcement background. Maybe I was wrong, but my gut told me I was right if nothing more than because of the way he acted. If he was a cop—dirty or not—there was a good chance there'd be others out there looking for me.

And I wasn't going to take any chances.

I continued through the woods, but stopped when I heard a snap, a crunching of leaves and debris on the ground coming from somewhere behind me. Up to that point, I'd managed to avoid any kind of confrontation with a wild creature. Of course, Maine was known for large Moose and black bears. All I could think about was being attacked, after all the time so far being mostly drama-free, when I was just a few hundred feet from making it out alive.

A bear, of course, concerned me the most, although Raymond had recently dropped the fact that a moose can run thirty-five miles per hour.

I'd be lucky to hit twenty.

I looked back as I continued walking toward the road, but with the darkness around me, it was almost impossible to see whatever it was.

I heard the snaps and crunching again, and questioned if the fact I hadn't eaten or had anything to drink since morning was causing my mind to play games.

The sound of the vehicles grew louder, and I decided to run.

I ran for a few hundred yards and stopped, looking back as I heard whatever it was moving at the same pace as I was. I knew, without a doubt, I was being followed.

The .38 was in my hand, but I wouldn't be able to hit anything with my hands still cuffed. I was tempted to fire a shot, just to scare off whatever it was. I stopped to catch my breath and looked back. "Get out of here!" I yelled, as if it would listen. But at that point, I again started to run until I saw headlights close enough that I could make out the vehicles.

I moved as fast as I could until I stood on the edge of the road, with red lights from the back of a car that had gone by far down the road. It was the only vehicle at the time.

I looked into the woods, wondering if whatever had followed me was still there. The moon was brighter out in the open, glowing into the edge of the woods. What I saw, at least what I *think* I saw, were dark, glowing eyes staring back at me. So I crossed the road to the other side and started running again.

The paved road was narrow, barely enough room for two cars. I slowed to a walk, looking for a road sign or something to help me figure out exactly where I was.

Over a hill came lights from an oncoming vehicle. My first thought was to run back into the woods to hide. But I stood in place, watching as the vehicle slowed.

It was an old pickup truck, and the driver—an older man with a ratty white beard—looked out at me as he went by. He stopped a few feet past me, his brakes squeaking. The truck's reverse lights came on and brightened up the road.

He backed up and stopped next to me, rolling his window down. He looked me over. "Need a lift?"

My hands behind my back, I wasn't sure what he'd say once he noticed they were cuffed. It was dark enough outside, but I was afraid I wouldn't be able to hide them from the man.

I said, "My car broke down, and I ended up getting lost in the woods."

"You walked through *these* woods? At *night*?" His eyebrows were raised.

I nodded, but didn't look back or turn my body in any way, even though I wondered what had followed me. "I'm not even sure exactly where I am."

"Where's your car?" he said.

"Uh, well, through those woods, somewhere."

"The other side?" The man gave me a suspicious look, like he wasn't buying it. "Other side of these woods? Simpson Road?"

I nodded, even though I had no idea. "Yeah, Simpson Road."

"You didn't think to stay on the road? Couple of farms over there, I'm sure someone woulda helped you." The man nodded. "Get on in, I'll drive you to your vehicle."

"You know what?" I said. "I appreciate it, but I think I can walk from here. If you can just tell me where there's a pay phone?"

He looked at me like I had two heads. "I don't mind giving you a ride, if you'd like one."

"Thank you. I appreciate it. If you can just point me in the direction of a pay phone..."

He shifted the stick on the column and pointed toward the road ahead with his long, bony finger. "There's a phone out front of Henry's General, a mile that way." He huffed out a laugh, shook his head in wonder and slowly drove away.

I looked toward the woods, then started to run.

I was out of breath and dizzy by the time I made it to the general store, which was closed up for the night. The parking lot was empty and dark.

I had the .38 tucked into the back of my pants. It was a struggle trying to get my hand into my front pocket to fish out a dime. I wasn't even sure I had one.

Luckily, I did. Getting it out was no easy task, but I managed.

The hard part, I knew, was getting my hands raised enough to drop the dime in the slot. I stared at the phone, then looked around for something I could stand on. Walking around to the back of the building, I found a tall stack of plastic milk crates—piled higher than the top of my head—by the back door.

I grabbed the one closest to my hands and the whole stack fell to the ground. But I had what I think I needed.

I used the crate to step on top, raise my handcuffed hands and drop the dime in the slot.

I used my shoulder and squeezed the handset between it and my ear. As disgusting as it was, I had no choice but to use my tongue to press the zero.

I dialed the operator.

"Operator," the woman said.

"Can you please dial a number for me?"

"What's the number?"

My brain wasn't working, and it took me a moment to remember what it was.

But then it hit me. I gave it to the operator.

Beth answered on the first ring.

"Hello?"

The operator got off the line.

I said, "Beth, it's me."

"Jake? Oh my... Where are you? Thank *God* you're okay. Raymond's been out looking for you. He's out right now. Maggie and Nancy are too. You've been gone for so long."

"I know. I ran into a little trouble." I didn't need to go into details with Beth. "Do you know where they're looking?"

"Everywhere," she said. "They keep calling me, to see if you've called."

"I'm in Saco," I said. I looked up at the dark sign on the edge of the lot a few feet from the booth. "Henry's General Store."

"In Buxton?" she said.

"You know where it is?"

"I do. But I don't have a way to get out there. I stayed at the house, hoping you'd call. One of them should be checking in with me any minute and I'll send whoever calls right over."

***

I waited around the side of the store, hiding to stay out of sight as much as I could whenever I saw headlights going either way on the road. I ducked behind a steel barrel when a vehicle turned into the parking lot.

But I saw it was Maggie in her green Plymouth Scamp, and stepped out into the parking lot where they could see me.

She pulled up next to me and rolled down the window.

But before Maggie had fully stopped, Nancy jumped from the passenger side and ran up to me, wrapping her arms around me.

She had tears in her eyes.

"You're in handcuffs?" she said, turning me around to look. "Maggie!"

Maggie got out of the car with her keys in her hand, took the .38 from my waistband, and uncuffed me with a key.

I rubbed my sore, bloodied wrists.

Maggie reached back into the Scamp and came out with a paper back and a tall Thermos, opening the top and handing it to me. "Here. It's water and some snacks. I'm sure you're starving."

There were a couple of apples in the bag and what looked like a sandwich.

I took the Thermos and guzzled it until it was just about gone. It was the best water I'd ever had. "You're always prepared," I said, catching my breath after taking a long drink before taking a bite of the apple.

A moment later, headlights came toward us from the road. I felt panicked, taking the .38 from Maggie's hand and pushing Nancy behind me.

"Relax," Maggie said. "It's Raymond."

I recognized the square headlights on his brown Chrysler LeBaron.

He skidded into the parking lot and had his window down, hanging his head out. "You're all right?" he said, parking next to Maggie's car. He looked me over. "What the hell happened?"

"Can we get out of here first?" I said.

Raymond said, "You want to ride with me?"

I nodded, glancing over at Nancy with the worried look on her face. "Are you all right?"

She looked like she was holding back her tears, although appeared to be relieved her old man was alive and, at least somewhat, well.

I gave Nancy a hug and said to Maggie, "Get her out of here." I ducked into the passenger side of Raymond's car and turned to him as he slid in behind the wheel. "I need to get my car."

Maggie and Nancy got into Maggie's car and drove away, in the opposite direction from a car coming toward us.

Raymond didn't move, watching the vehicle with the headlights coming toward us.

"Let's go!" I said, with a bit more force.

Raymond glanced at me and got in the driver's side just as the car slowed on the road, going past us before it sped up and disappeared.

"You see what kind of car that was?" I said.

Raymond said, "A Ford. LTD. Should I follow it?"

But the car was already gone, the red lights disappearing over the hill.

"I was held up in a small building a few miles from here. Not exactly sure where. But we need to find it."

CHAPTER 26

I HAD MY EYES out the passenger side as Raymond drove slowly along Simpson Road. We were surrounded by woods, which made sense considering I'd spent quite a few hours lost in them. And it was mostly dark, at least until we came to a narrow, uphill driveway with what looked like lights from a house set far back from the road.

"Stop here," I said, and rolled down my window to get a good look up the driveway and around the heavily wooded area.

Raymond stopped in front of a mailbox and shifted into park. "You think this is it?"

"I have no idea," I said. "But I haven't seen anything but trees until now."

We both looked up the driveway.

"You said your hands were cuffed, but I'm still not sure I understand how you shot two men."

I looked at the mailbox, with the number six painted on the side of it. "Of course, he wasn't expecting me to grab the gun. I pulled the trigger without much thought."

"You shot him in the balls?"

"Like I said, I didn't think about it. The man in front of me had pliers in his hand, like he was going for my teeth. I'm not even sure why, other than a threat. But as soon as I pulled the trigger and ripped the gun from the guy's pants, I spun around and fired again. I don't know if I hit the other guy—the one with the pliers—but it seemed like it, the way he went down."

"That's impressive," Raymond said. He looked past me and out the passenger window toward the driveway. "I'm not sure it'd be smart to drive the car up there."

The house wasn't in clear view with all the trees surrounding it, especially in the dark, although there were lights in the distance.

Raymond said again, "You think this is the place?"

"I don't know."

"And you think the cop lives here?"

"No idea who lives here. And I don't know for sure if the guy was even a cop. He acted like one, that's all I'm saying."

We both stayed silent, looking around the area.

Raymond killed the engine. "I say we find out who lives here first, before we do anything else. Don't you think?"

I didn't want to leave until I had some answers. "I'm thinking you leave your car somewhere nobody will see it, and we'll walk up to the house. Maybe in the woods."

"You want me to park my brand-new car in the woods? It's going to get scratched."

"Then I'll go myself. You can wait here for me."

Raymond paused, like he was thinking it through. "No, I can't let you go up alone. You never know what—"

"It'd actually be better if you had your car ready to go," I said. "That way, I get in any trouble..."

"What if you find the building, and the two guys you shot? What if they're dead? And whoever lives there sees you. Then what?"

I pushed open the car door, closing it behind me, the window still down. "I'm not back in ten, you can make your own assumption." I started up the tree-lined driveway. The glow from the moon was the only light, other than what came through the trees from the house, or whatever it was, at the top of the driveway.

It felt like a good five-minute walk until I was close enough to see what was around me. There appeared to be a lot of open land. To my left was an open field, but it was too dark to see what was out there under the crescent moon. I had no idea if it was an active farm with crops or animals, or just open land.

I stood fifty yards from what turned out to be a two-story farmhouse, with a wraparound porch with a single light above the door. To the right of the house was a detached, three-car garage that matched the home's exterior.

With some lights on inside the house, I could see through the windows: some with closed curtains, others wide open. It was hard to tell if anyone was home or even awake as I stood looking in.

I glanced around the property surrounded by woods, but didn't see a building like the one I was held up inside of. I didn't see a van or the blue Chrysler, either, and started to wonder if this *was* the same place. I was tempted to knock on the door, pretend I was lost... maybe say my car had broken down out on the street. At least I could see who lived there. But the last thing I needed was to raise any alarms, even end up with a shotgun pointed out at me for showing up on the owner's doorstep in the middle of the night.

Even after eating the food Maggie had brought for me, I was still hungry. My stomach growled, and I started to wonder if I was even in the right frame of mind to be sneaking around the property.

I looked to my right, well past the garage and through the trees, and saw a tiny, dim glow of light far off in the distance. I stared, and realized it was moving, slowly, and coming toward me. It didn't take more than another moment or two to realize it was the beam of a flashlight, the light bouncing around in someone's hand.

I hurried toward the garage and around the side of it, crouching low in tall, uncut grass around the exterior. I poked my head out to look.

The light grew brighter, the person holding it coming closer.

But then it turned off. That's when I heard voices.

"I still think you oughta get that looked at."

"It's a superficial wound," another voice said.

I knew right away the second voice came from the man who grabbed me from the gas station—the one I thought might've been a cop. I assumed the "superficial wound" he referred to was the one that came from the bullet I fired with the .38.

The man continued, "Listen, let's not tell anyone about this until morning. We gotta find him."

A man with an older, somewhat raspy voice said, "It should've never gone this far."

"I didn't expect it to," the cop voice said.

"Well, now we've got a real problem," the older man said. "You're going to have to do what you have to do at this point. I knew we should've never gotten involved."

As the men got closer to the garage, where I was hiding, I moved farther away, toward the back of it.

Their voices were loud enough it felt like they were right next to me.

I heard the sound of a garage door open, a slight screeching noise, like metal against metal.

The man whose voice I didn't recognize, the older-sounding one, said, "Your friend didn't look too good. I wouldn't have let him drive off like that."

"He'll be fine."

"And what about you?" the other man said. "You said yourself, Jake Horn can ID you now."

The man I guessed was a cop said, "I'll have to find him. And when I do, he's going to regret it."

"Nobody wants him dead," the older man said. "All you were supposed to do was persuade him he'd be better off walking away, convince him Ron Tompkins was guilty. I'm not sure how you screwed it up the way you did."

"Horn's a little more stubborn than I'd expected. But just stop worrying. I'll take care of it."

The older man said, "Let's just hope he doesn't figure out you brought him here, to my property. That's all I need, this guy shows up at my door."

I couldn't see either man, at least not until the older one walked from the garage and toward the house. He continued up onto the porch and went inside without another word.

The light on the porch went out.

I walked along the side of the garage, toward the front, and stopped when I heard a car's engine start inside. The glow of red and white lights filled the driveway as the vehicle started to back out.

I poked my head out to catch a glance. Sure enough, it was the powder-blue Chrysler.

The vehicle was backed all the way out, the driver turning it around in the driveway where I was able to catch a glimpse of my cop friend behind the wheel.

He took off, full speed down the long driveway and toward the road.

I watched the rear lights through the trees until I couldn't see them anymore, and wondered if Raymond was still parked down there.

But Raymond was plenty smart enough to take off, even if he was waiting at the bottom of the driveway.

I looked over at the house. All but a couple of lights inside it had been turned off. I had to find out who the man was.

Clearly, he knew *exactly* who I was.

I came out from the side of the garage. The door had been left up. Glancing back at the house to make sure nobody was coming out, I snuck in through the opening and into the garage. Behind the other closed garage door in the middle was what looked like a hearse. I couldn't quite see what was on the other side of it, but it looked to be another vehicle, covered with some kind of tarp.

There was lettering on the door of the hearse, but I couldn't quite make out what it was until I crouched down and got a closer look. In what looked like gold handwriting, it said O'Reilly Funeral Home.

I tried to open the driver's-side door, but it was locked. I walked around it to try the passenger side, but that side was also locked.

I heard a door open with a squeak, then slam closed from somewhere outside. I assumed from the house.

I looked around for a place to hide, and ducked behind the front end of the hearse.

Footsteps outside grew louder, and whoever it was whistled a tune I'd never heard.

My breathing was heavy and loud, and the more I tried to control it, the louder I felt it had gotten. I stayed low and went around to the passenger side of the hearse and looked through the vehicle's window toward the open garage door.

The older man from earlier, dressed in a robe and slippers, reached up and pulled the door down. It slammed closed, followed by a clicking sound I could only guess was a lock.

I sat still in total darkness, crouched behind the hearse. There were no windows or any on the garage doors.

I felt my way around the vehicle with my arms out in front of me, being careful with each step. It took me a few moments and a couple of wrong turns, but I finally felt the door.

I stood still, trying to listen to make sure the man outside had gone back into his house.

I heard nothing.

But I waited another couple of moments, feeling around on the inside of the door for the handle, and finally grabbed on to it. I tried to turn it, but the damn thing wouldn't budge. It felt like it was locked, but there *had* to be a way to unlock it from the inside. I felt around the handle with both hands. No luck.

I carefully walked toward the backside of the garage, holding my hands out in front of me to make sure I didn't walk into anything. I hoped to find a regular door somewhere. I couldn't imagine there wasn't one.

Right then, I heard my name from somewhere outside, in a muffled, almost hushed voice I knew belonged to Raymond.

He called for me: "Jake? Jake? Where are you?"

I felt around and tripped over something that fell to the floor and smashed like glass, hurrying to the front of the garage. "Raymond?" I said, knocking on the garage door loud enough so he could hear it, but not loud enough to cause any alarm.

"Jake? Is that you?" he said, his voice on the other side of the door.

I had my face practically up against the wood panel inside. "Yes, it's me. Can you open the door? I think it's locked."

I heard the handle jiggle, but the door didn't open. "It's locked," he said.

"I just said that. Why do you think I'm still in here?"

He jiggled the handle again. "Hang on." Then it went quiet.

"Raymond?" I said. I heard nothing. "Where'd you go?"

I heard a bang toward the back of the garage. The door I was looking for opened, letting in just enough light from outside I could see Raymond's big silhouetted figure in the doorway.

"How'd you know I was in here?" I said.

"I didn't. I was just walking by looking for you. Someone left when I was walking up the driveway; I had to dive into the woods."

"Where's your car?"

Raymond let out a sigh. "I hid it in the woods. Any scratches, you're using your own money to buff them out."

I grinned, but then we both turned when we heard someone yell from the area of the house, "Who's out there?"

Raymond and I both took off, going all the way around the back of the garage and through the woods until we came out halfway down the driveway.

We continued running, and between breaths, I tried to tell him what I'd heard. A bright light came on outside, from somewhere behind us. I glanced over my shoulder and saw floodlights lighting up the entire area around the house like a football field.

Raymond and I kept running as fast as we could until we got to the road. I followed him another fifty yards and into the woods where he'd parked his car.

CHAPTER 27

RAYMOND DROVE AROUND THE side of Don's Texaco, where—through no choice of my own—I'd left the Nova.

It hit me like a brick when I saw that it was gone.

"You sure this is where you left it?" Raymond said, shifting his car into park.

I nodded, glancing around the parking lot, as if someone had simply moved it to a better parking space. "I guess there's a chance it got towed," I said.

"Or stolen," Raymond said.

"Yeah, of course. But I'm just being hopeful. I'd rather the cops have it. At least I'd have a chance of getting it back. When we were first leaving, after the guy put me in the back of his car, I heard the sirens. Don't forget, a shot was fired. Someone would've called the cops."

The gas station was dark inside, well past closing time.

"Where are your keys?" Raymond said.

I paused, hesitant to tell him about my mistake. "You're not going to believe it," I said. "But they were hanging from the ignition."

"Are you serious? Why wouldn't you take them with you?"

I laughed. "Why didn't I take them? Oh, I don't know. Maybe I was preoccupied with the gun I had pointed at my face?"

"But, I mean, why'd you leave them in the ignition in the first place?"

I rolled my eyes with a sigh. "I don't know why. I just did. But being a Monday-morning quarterback isn't going to help me right now."

Raymond drove around the building into the darkness, without a response, then around back and out the other side. He went past the gas pumps and out into the street. "I'll drive you here in the morning when they open; we can ask the clerk if anyone saw what happened to it. Unless you want to go to the police?"

I said, "The only problem with that is I'll have to explain to them what happened. And I'm not sure I trust any cops around here right now. Not if the guy who grabbed me turns out to be one of 'em."

"But they obviously know it's your car."

"I know," I said. "But I'd like to know who owns that house, before I get wrapped up in some mess at the Saco police station I can't get out of."

"But you already said the hearse you saw had O'Reilly Funeral Home on the side of it. Don't you think the guy's name is O'Reilly?"

"I guess, " I said. "But I don't know."

Raymond laughed, turning the wheel. "You think the guy just happens to drive a hearse?"

I rolled down the window to let in some cool air. It had gotten stuffy inside the car, and Raymond felt gas was too expensive to run the AC.

I said, "I'm just saying, just because it's in his garage doesn't mean his name is O'Reilly. Maybe he's a driver."

Raymond went left onto Log Cabin Road. "Why not go to the station, get the car, ask the officer on duty who lives in the house?"

I thought about it for a moment. "I'm just not sure I want to open that can of worms."

Raymond said, "Maybe you need to get over this lack of trust you have for law enforcement. You can't always think every cop is bad."

"I didn't say that. Maggie's not a bad cop. And you weren't too bad." I grinned at him.

"Come on, Jake," he said. "Everyone knows it's your MO."

I looked at the homes, one after the other along the road, most with small yards enclosed by a chain-link fence. "All right," I said. "Turn around."

Raymond looked at me, staring, like he wasn't sure I was serious. "Yeah?"

"I'll just tell them I had nothing to do with it. I'll need to come up with a reason why I left it there."

"Assuming the police actually have the car..."

***

The front door of the Saco police station was open a few inches with a brick placed on the concrete landing in front of it. I walked inside with Raymond behind me and stood at the tall service desk just inside the door.

An officer with his back to us turned, holding a white Styrofoam cup in his hand. "Can I help you?"

I glanced up at the clock and saw it was just a few minutes until midnight. "I'd like to report a stolen vehicle."

He nodded, reached under the counter and came up with a clipboard with a sheet of paper clipped to it. He dropped it in front of me. "Fill this out."

"Well, actually," I said, "I'm not one hundred percent certain it was stolen. It's a 1974 Chevy Nova I left parked on the side of the building at Don's Texaco."

The officer, looking disinterested at first, seemed to perk up a bit, placing his cup on the counter. He squinted, looking from me to Raymond, then walked away to a desk behind him. He grabbed a folder, opened it, and came back over to us, his eyes on whatever was inside it. "Your name Jake Horn?" he said. "Massachusetts registration IVJ-1015." He glanced up from the folder. "That you?"

I nodded. "Yes, sir."

"We had the car towed, impounded, because it was reported a gun was fired in the parking lot around the same area as your car."

I acted surprised. "A gunshot? I don't know anything about it." I glanced back at Raymond. "I left my car there, didn't think it'd be a problem." I faked a laugh. "I never imagined it would get stolen or, I guess what you're saying is it's been impounded? Is it here right now? Because, I'd love to be able to take it with me."

"It's locked up in back," the man said. "But I'm afraid you won't be able to take it with you. Not tonight. There's presently an investigation, considering, as I said, shots being fired at the gas station. And, on top of that, may I ask why you'd leave your keys in your car if you were parking it there?"

Raymond leaned with his hands on the counter, his voice hushed. "Jake's not the sharpest knife in the drawer, if you know what I'm saying." He reached out and offered to shake the officer's hand. "Raymond Horn. I'm a retired officer with the Boston Police Department. I'm afraid this is all just a simple misunderstanding."

"What makes it a misunderstanding?" the officer said, like he wasn't quite ready to let it slide.

"I mean," Raymond said, "I was the one who told Jake to leave his car after he filled up with gas. We drove around looking for a good fishing spot on the Saco River."

I glanced at Raymond, nodding. "Didn't make sense for both of us to have a car. When I decided to leave the Nova, I jumped in with Raymond without even thinking I'd left my keys in the ignition."

"It's not the first time he's done something like this," Raymond said, cracking a grin.

The officer stared back at us in a way I wasn't sure he was buying what we were telling him.

I said, "We drove out by Simpson Road heading toward a fishing spot we heard about on the Saco River, went out that way, past a yellow farmhouse, I think the owner's name is O'Reilly?"

"Ned O'Reilly?" he said. "What about it?"

I said, "Is that who owns that yellow farmhouse? Ned O'Reilly? From O'Reilly Funeral Home?"

The officer said, "Well, he doesn't own the funeral home any longer. His family sold out a couple of years back."

I said, "And now he's just a good ole farmer, huh?"

The officer looked at me with suspicion he didn't appear willing to let go.

"It looked like a nice piece of property," I said. "I noticed it when we drove by, on the way to the river. That's all. I always dreamed of moving to Maine, buying a farm." I glanced back at Raymond staring back at me, like we both knew it was time to be quiet.

The officer went over to the desk, reached inside a small white envelope and pulled out a set of keys. He came back over and placed them on the counter. "I'll need you to sign some papers."

I picked up the keys and looked at the silver, heart-shaped key chain on it—the one I'd given my wife Barbara when we'd first met.

***

I pulled into the driveway at the beach house and parked behind Raymond. Nancy came running off the screened-in porch, with Maggie following.

"Why didn't you call us?" Nancy said, giving me a look like an angry parent would. "I thought you'd be right back here. You had us worried!"

Beth poked her head out. "Jake, have you eaten? I made a sandwich, thinking you'd be here a couple of hours ago."

I pointed behind me at the Nova. "I had to get my car from the police station."

I was starving, and didn't see a single place open on the ride back or else I would have stopped. "I'm sorry," I said, putting my arm around Nancy. We walked together toward the porch. I said to Maggie, just ahead of us, "We have a lead."

We walked into the house, where Beth was pulling plastic wrap off a sandwich on a plate.

"Where's mine?" Raymond said, rubbing his stomach. "Don't I get to eat?"

Beth gave him a look, like she didn't want to hear it from him right then. She placed the plate down on the round wooden table in the dining area off the kitchen, by the window.

I gave them a brief rundown of the rest of the night, then sat down, with Maggie and Nancy on either side of me. Raymond went into the kitchen and came back out with two cans of Black Label beer. He pulled the tab off one and put it in front of me. "Anyone else want a beer?" He held up his can but all three women shook their heads. He pulled the tab off the top and took a couple of gulps, then sat down on a tall wooden stool in the corner by the window.

"Are you going to tell us what else you found?" Nancy said.

Maggie said, "We were afraid you were in trouble. Was it the car that drove by us at the general store you followed?"

"No," I said. "We drove around to where it looks like the area on the other side of the woods."

"But you never actually saw the building where they held you?" Maggie said.

I went ahead and told them all about the house, and about Ned O'Reilly and the funeral home his family used to own.

I turned to Beth leaning in the doorway to the kitchen. "You know anything about him?"

She said, "I've heard of O'Reilly Funeral Home, but..."

"The question is, what does this guy have to do with the case?" Raymond said.

"They want me to stop," I said. "But not bad enough to kill me, I guess."

"So how do you know the other guy's a cop?" Maggie said. "Is that what he told you?"

"Well, he didn't exactly admit to it," I said. "But, I know a cop when I see one."

Everyone was silent, staring back at me.

I said, "Either way, we know these people are all involved some-how."

"You didn't see the other man? The one driving the van?" Maggie said.

"He's the one I shot first. But I heard the other two talking—O'Reilly and the cop—and the way they talked was that he was still alive. But I don't know where he'd gone. Maybe the hospital."

Nancy said, "So you think this man, Ned O'Reilly, killed Casey? And Logan Reed?"

I had just taken a bite of my sandwich, and held my finger up for her to wait until I finished chewing. I washed it down with a sip of beer. "He's involved. But I don't know if he's the killer, or just part of trying to keep whatever happened covered up."

Maggie said, "But this guy—the alleged cop—would you be able to ID him? If you saw him?"

"He never bothered to hide his face or anything. Neither did the other guy he was with."

CHAPTER 28

THE MORNING CAME FAST. I didn't sleep much at all, and spent a good part of the night on the front porch, trying to run through all the possible scenarios in my head.

I was dressed and out the door without waking anyone else, on my way to Bartlett's Dockside. I had expected Marilyn to be there early, long before they opened, as she was on most days.

When I turned the Nova around alongside the restaurant, Marilyn's car was parked in the space by the door to the kitchen.

She still hadn't had it repaired after Ron's accident, and I wondered if it was because of all the money she'd been shelling out to help her brother. On top of paying me and the lawyer, Willie Hamme, there were other costs, including whatever she incurred making her unwise choice to confess to a murder to protect her brother.

I knocked on the wood frame on the back screen door, knowing the restaurant wasn't open for another hour. It took another couple of minutes and one more good knock before the door finally opened.

Marilyn stood behind the exterior screen door and appeared tired and exhausted. She managed a smile when she saw me, but her usual energy was missing. "Good morning, Jake." She held the door open. "Come on in."

I walked in and went into the kitchen. Ron was the only one in there, prepping food with his back to me at first, but then he turned to me, wiping his hands on his apron. He said, "We've been wondering where you've been."

I wasn't sure I liked the way he came across.

I said, "I don't normally check in with my clients as often as they'd sometimes like. I don't mean to leave you out of the loop, but, to be honest, sometimes it can slow things down. I know that sounds harsh, but if I were to come by or call every time I had a little something to report..."

"We'd just like to know where things stand," Marilyn said, stepping over to where her brother stood. "And right now, as you're fully aware, we're really up against the clock with Ron's trial."

"I understand," I said. "And I'm sorry. It's just... I've been a little tied up."

Marilyn said, "Have you come up with anything yet?" She walked through a doorway and was back within a moment, clutching a brown leather holder she pulled a cigarette out of. She stuck one in her mouth and dug into her pockets. "Where'd I put my damn lighter..."

Ron pulled a book of matches from his pocket and handed them to her. She looked at the matchbook cover. "Where'd you get these?" she said. "O'Reilly Funeral Home?"

Ron shrugged. "I don't know. I've just had them."

I was both surprised and perplexed that Ron had pulled a book of matches from O'Reilly Funeral Home. I knew there was no way it was just a coincidence. "You don't know where you got them?" I said. I opened the cover and ripped off a match, flicking it over the phosphorus strip on the back to give her a light. I looked over the cover with the logo printed in gold, like handwriting, the way it was on the door of the hearse in Ned O'Reilly's garage.

Ron pointed toward the front of the restaurant. "Probably got them from out front, under the counter. Business people leave them on the table all the time, hoping to get some free advertising."

I wondered if Ron was full of it. I handed him the matchbook. "When I said I was tied up, I wasn't kidding. You both should probably know, I was picked up by a couple of men up in Saco, handcuffed and dragged off to a building where they threatened me with a warning to back away from this case."

Marilyn exhaled a lung full of smoke and placed her hand over her mouth with a gasp. She looked at Ron, then me.

I said. "That's why I asked about those matches." I looked at the two. "Do either of you know Ned O'Reilly?"

They both nodded and Ron pulled the matches from his pocket. "*This* Ned O'Reilly?"

"Yes, *that* Ned O'Reilly. I was taken to his house. Which means he's somehow involved. I have no idea how or why."

Marilyn had a look of disbelief on her face. "Are you sure? There's no possible way Ned would..." She shook her head. "Do you mean... Are you saying he's involved in the murder?"

"I don't know," I said. "Maybe. But if he wasn't involved in the murder, he's got something to do with covering up whatever happened." I nodded at Ron. "For some reason, they've set you up to take the fall."

"But why?" Marilyn said. "Ned O'Reilly? I... I don't understand."

"I don't either," I said. "But when I broke out of the building and went back later in the night, the man who grabbed me was outside with an older man. I believe it was Ned O'Reilly." I said to Marilyn, "How well do you know him?"

"Ned?" Marilyn shrugged. "Not that well, other than as a customer. He comes in here quite often, usually once the tourists have all left for the season. I don't remember the last time he was here."

"I do," Ron said. "A couple of weeks ago." He shifted his gaze to Marilyn. "Don't you remember? You were talking to him."

She stared at Ned, like she was thinking. "I can't remember everyone I've spoken to in this place. Hundreds of people every week." She tapped the side of her head with her long, bony finger. "The mind doesn't remember the way it used to."

I was somewhat suspicious. But why would she lie about it? "So you don't remember the conversation?" I said.

"I'm sorry, I don't." Marilyn walked to the sink to run her cigarette under a stream of water from the faucet. "Would you like a coffee?" she said, her back to me.

"No, I'm fine, thank you." I was too busy running different ideas through my mind to think about coffee, although I probably could have used the caffeine. "Is there anything else you can tell me about Ned O'Reilly?"

Marilyn said, "Do you really think it was him? I still can't imagine he'd—"

"If he's the one who lives in the yellow farmhouse on Simpson Road in Saco," I said, then..."

Ron said, "I think that's where he lives, unless..." He pulled at his chin, turning his gaze to Marilyn. "The farm belonged to the Fuller family. I'm pretty sure they sold it a few years back, but kept it in the family."

"Who are the Fullers?" I said.

"Oh, just another family that's been around New England since their ancestors got off the boat in Plymouth. The Fullers came over on the Mayflower and became original settlers up here in Maine."

I said, "But you said they kept the property in the family. Is Ned O'Reilly related?"

Marilyn said, "Ned and Ralph Fuller are cousins."

"Ralph Fuller?" I had to think about why the name sounded so familiar.

"Well, there's Ralph Fuller the First, and Ralph the Second," Marilyn said.

Ron said, "Ralph Fuller the Second is the chief medical examiner here in Maine."

That's when I remembered Ralph Fuller's signature on Casey Jilson's autopsy report.

I was starting to see how the dots were possibly connected. The man who had performed, or at least signed off on the autopsies, was a blood relative of the man who had something to do with me being abducted and threatened.

"I imagine Ralph Fuller has his connections with most of the police departments around the state," I said.

Marilyn nodded. "He probably knows every cop in Maine. He's an appointed official, which makes him a somewhat powerful man in our state."

"So he knows Chief Hanley?" I said.

Marilyn and Ron both looked at each other but neither seemed to have an answer.

I waited. "Is that a no?"

"I don't know," Marilyn said. "My guess would be he does."

"What are you getting at?" Ron said. "Do you think Chief Hanley has something to do with Casey Jilson's death?"

Marilyn looked at her brother. "Does that really surprise you? The way he came after you, with very little evidence?"

"Well," Ron said. "They did find my truck on the beach."

"Of course," I said, "your past history with him makes the chief's actions seem a bit suspicious. I can't help but question his motives. On the other hand, it could be that he's not a very good investigator. You don't have to be a detective to become chief of police in a small town like this, you know." I looked around the kitchen. "When was the last time you spoke with Willie Hamme?"

Marilyn said, "Yesterday. But only for a couple of minutes. He didn't sound as confident as he had when I first hired him to help us."

"What makes you say that?" I said.

"Well, he said we're running out of time. I think he's waiting for you to bring him some answers."

I thought about Ralph Fuller, and how Logan Reed's autopsy was supposedly overturned by the chief medical examiner.

"Do you know if Willie saw Logan Reed's autopsy report?"

Marilyn and Ron both shook their heads.

I pulled out my wallet and checked to make sure I had Willie Hamme's number. I said to Marilyn, "Do you mind if I use your phone?"

She nodded toward her office door on the far side of the kitchen from where we stood. "Go ahead, whatever you need."

I started across the kitchen but stopped and looked at Ron and Marilyn, both standing still like they didn't know what to do with themselves. "Do you both trust Officer Silva?"

"Thomas?" Marilyn said. "He's a good kid."

"Thomas isn't a crooked cop, if that's what you're thinking," Ron said.

"No, I'm not. I want to talk to him, hopefully without Chief Hanley getting wind of it. I could use his help, although it won't be easy, considering it could get him in hot water."

Marilyn said. "He takes being a police officer very seriously. He's not going to cross any lines."

"I don't expect him to," I said. "But I hope he'd be willing to listen."

I went into the office and dialed the number on the card for Willie Hamme's office. By the third ring, he answered.

"Willie Hamme's office," he said.

"It's Jake Horn. You got a minute?" I looked into the kitchen where Ron had gone back to doing his work at the steel table. Marilyn had disappeared.

"What can I do for you?"

"A couple of things," I said. "When I was at your office, I happened to take a peek at Casey Jilson's file. I saw the copy of her autopsy and the injuries she sustained."

Willie said, "You went through my files? Without my knowledge? That report is not accurate. In fact, they don't even know I have it."

"They? Who's 'they'?"

"The staff at the medical examiner's office. Maybe the police too. I'm not sure what the story is. I just didn't expect someone to go through my files without my knowledge."

"I'm sorry about that," I said. "But can you just explain to me what the story is here? Why don't they know you have the report? You're the defendant's attorney."

"Well, it just so happens, Jake, that I called a contact up there in Augusta, at the ME's office. I drove up there and she brought me out a copy before it was officially released. But then she called me a few hours after I'd left, said the medical examiner who worked on it made some big mistakes, and that the chief medical examiner was pulling it back"

"Ralph Fuller?" I said. "He's the one who signed off on the one I looked at. I saw his signature."

"It was probably a stamp."

"You're telling me the one you have isn't accurate and has been replaced? Are you sure? Do you know the name of the medical examiner who performed the initial autopsy?"

"Let me see..." Willie Hamme paused on the other end. I could hear papers being riffled. "It looks like the man's name is Jason Strong."

"Jason Strong?" I said.

"It says it right here on the original report. But, by the sounds of it, I'm not even sure he's still working there. My contact seemed to believe he'd been let go."

CHAPTER 29

IT WAS 12:50 P.M. when Thomas Silva turned his Ford Fairmont into the parking space a few cars down from the front entrance to the Dock Square Market. He was right on schedule to pick up the sandwiches to bring back to the station.

"Officer Silva," I said, walking up to him on the sidewalk a few feet from the market's door.

"Good afternoon," he said, in such a way I had a feeling he didn't remember who I was.

"Thomas," I said. "Jake Horn."

He cleared his throat like a nervous kid on his first date. "I'm in a hurry," he said, trying to walk around me.

"I'm sure you are. But I'd like a word with you, if it's all right. It'll only take a minute."

He removed his hat to scratch his head as he looked down at the sidewalk. "Like I said, I'm in a hurry, Mr. Horn."

"The chief's lunch can wait a minute," I said, lowering my voice as an older couple walked out of the market, giving us both a smile and nod. "Chief Hanley is the subject I'd like to discuss with you."

"I know what you're up to," he said. "I'm sorry, but there's no... There's no way I'm going to be put in a position to—"

"I just want to ask you about that morning at the beach," I said. "When you first saw Casey's body. When I was there—I'm just being honest—from my professional viewpoint, the whole crime scene was a mess."

"Professional viewpoint?" Thomas cracked a slight grin. "Aren't you a *private* investigator?" He emphasized *private*, whatever that was supposed to imply.

"Just because I don't wear the badge, kid, doesn't mean I don't know what's supposed to go down at a murder scene."

I could see in the way he looked back at me, he didn't like my tone, or the idea I'd called him "kid." He took a deep breath, hanging his thumbs on his belt as his confidence appeared to grow.

I said, "I saw the two of you, and... I mean, just the way the footprints were all covered over and... well, I don't know what kind of fingerprints you could get from the truck, considering Ron's hands were obviously all over it already. And the way you were both just throwing things around in there, touching everything the way you were."

"What's your point, Mr. Horn? You don't like the way we do our jobs here? Well, I guess your opinion isn't worth two cents in this town." He glared into my eyes. "Maybe you should just go back to Boston."

I looked around to make sure nobody was close enough to listen to what I had to say. It was already worrisome enough hoping I could bring Thomas at least *somewhat* over to my side. But I could tell it wasn't going to be easy. I said, "The chief's been a cop for, what, fifteen years? And here he is, looking like a rookie on that murder scene. And he jumps right on the arrest of Ron Tompkins? A man everyone knows he has a history with?"

"The chief knows exactly what he's doing," Thomas said. "And I think you oughta be ashamed of yourself just for asking about it."

"You said it yourself that morning," I said, "Ron's truck had been stolen. Yet, there you were, not even twelve hours later, you and Chief Hanley show up at Bartlett's and take Ron into custody. But I was there that morning. You take the truck out of the equation, which I believe you should, and I don't see what proof there is Ron Tompkins killed that poor woman."

"He knew the victim," Thomas said. "The victim visited with him the night prior."

"There's no physical evidence besides that truck. You need to admit that."

"There's a shoe print," Thomas said.

"Yeah, and the shoes that made the print were in the back of Ron's truck with all the other junk he had back there. He's on record for saying he didn't remember the last time he'd worn them."

Thomas said, "That's assuming he's telling the truth. And that, as Chief Hanley has said, is part of the problem. Ron's never been known to be an honest person. His history tells us he's always had a problem with honesty, and that he's always had an interest in younger women. Even his own students."

"Let's not ignore Chief Hanley's past," I said. "This wouldn't be the first time he's tried to set someone up."

Thomas narrowed his eyes. "You'd better watch your step."

"Chief Hanley seemed to be doing his best to sabotage that crime," I said.

"You're out of line, Mr. Horn. If you don't—"

"Chief Hanley *also* knew the victim," I said. "You're well aware of that, I'm sure. Do you really think someone shouldn't be asking these questions?"

Thomas said, "If you are suggesting Chief Hanley in any way has attempted to cover up that crime..."

"Listen, Thomas. I'm just asking you to work with me here and listen to what I have to say. I need your help. You seem like a bright kid. You grew up in this town, right? I'm telling you, something's not right with this case. I know you respect the chief, but the way it's gone..."

"Ron Tompkins is guilty," Thomas said. "And I'm not going to discuss it with you any longer." He reached for the door and, without thinking, I put my hand on his arm and squeezed it, trying to stop him from walking away.

Thomas grabbed me, spun me around and pinned me up against the wall. I was surprised by his strength as he slapped the handcuffs on my wrists without giving me a chance to react. "You have the right to remain silent..."

"What the hell are you doing?"

"Anything you say can and will be used against you in a court of law. You have the right to..."

I waited as he finished reading me my rights and did my best to remain calm without trying to resist or put up a fight. I had the size and, I initially assumed, the strength over him. Doing anything I shouldn't at that point would only make the situation worse.

"You don't grab an officer of the law like that, Mr. Horn." He dragged me to his car and opened the door to the back seat, pushing my head down and guiding me into the vehicle.

He slammed the door in my face, but instead of getting in the front seat, he tapped on the window, pointing at me. "Don't you dare go anywhere."

I watched him walk toward the Dock Square Market and through the entrance.

A few moments later he came out with a paper bag filled with his grinders. He slid into the front seat behind the wheel. "I'm sorry, Mr. Horn. You can't come into my town and think you can push an officer around, like you're some hotshot from the big city who's above the law."

"Thomas... Officer Silva. Please, just listen to me."

He started the engine and cut the wheel, turning out of the parking spot and toward downtown. But he banged a U-turn and headed back toward the station without saying another word.

"Listen," I said. "I didn't mean to grab you like I did. I'm just asking you to... Chief Hanley—I don't know what you know about him—but he's got these friends, and..." I had to think through if I wanted to tell him exactly what had happened, fearing there was a chance Thomas couldn't be convinced his boss may have been crooked and possibly involved in at least one murder. Maybe two.

"I was kidnapped yesterday," I said, and waited to see his reaction. All he did was look at me in the rearview. "I was jumped. In Saco. These two men covered my head, handcuffed me, and took me to a location I escaped from."

"You expect me to believe you?" Thomas said.

"It's the truth," I said. "I was warned about continuing my investigation, and told I needed to leave it alone. This man, whoever he was, wasn't working alone. Whatever he was doing, it came down from someone in a position of authority in this very state."

Thomas kept his eyes ahead on the road. "What's that supposed to mean, someone of *authority*?"

"Well, I can't say for sure," I said. "But I can tell you where I was. I know who owns the property where I was taken. Not to mention the guy who grabbed me... I'm pretty sure he was a cop."

Thomas said, "A cop? He told you he was a cop?"

"No. But this man, the one who seemed to be in charge, dressed the part. I assure you, I know a cop when I see one. He took me to a farm in Saco, owned at one time by the Fuller family. But, now Ned O'Reilly lives there. You know who he is?"

Thomas didn't even turn or look in the rearview. After a couple of moments he finally nodded. "Are you trying to tell me Ned O'Reilly kidnapped you?" He laughed, shaking his head. "Now I *know* you're full of—"

"I was held captive in a building at his house," I said. "You know the house, right? That big yellow farmhouse off Simpson Road? He had a funeral car, a hearse, parked in his garage."

"That's where you were? In Mr. O'Reilly's *garage*?"

I could tell by his tone he still wasn't quite ready to believe me.

"Well, no. That's not where they put me. But I did go into his garage, at one point. But that was after I'd already escaped. I went back there, trying to figure out what was going on."

The handcuffs hurt my wrists, still somewhat sore from the previous day's cuffing.

Thomas cut the wheel toward Turbats Creek Road, pulling off to the side. He got out and came around to the rear door, opening it, and reaching in to pull me outside. "What did this so-called cop look like?" he said. "The one who allegedly abducted you?"

"He was tall, about my height. Thin, but strong. He had dark hair, a mustache... wore a suit, but without a tie. There was another guy with him. He was short and stocky, and drove a white van."

"And you're telling me you were on O'Reilly's property?"

I nodded. "I told you, the hearse was in the garage."

"Did you see him?"

"O'Reilly? No, not exactly. But, I mean, come on. If he lives there... I heard him talking to the other guy."

"The cop?"

"Yes. And I could tell by the way they were talking, there was someone else involved. Like they were either working for someone, or doing this person a favor by grabbing me."

Thomas turned me around and took the handcuffs off my wrists. "Chief Hanley might not be the best detective around, but he's not a crooked cop. I don't know who this other guy is, but I'd be willing to see what else I can find out, if that's what you're asking."

I rubbed my wrists. "Thank you. I appreciate it," I said. "But I think you should be careful. I wouldn't say a word to Hanley about what happened."

Thomas stood still for a moment, looking toward the other end of the road. "You'd better not be lying to me," he said, nodding toward the open door. "Get in."

"But I thought..."

"I'm driving you back to your car," Thomas said. "Unless you prefer to walk?"

CHAPTER 30

RAYMOND LOOKED OUT AT me through the screen door. "Where've you been?"

"At the restaurant, and then ran into Officer Silva."

Raymond said, "Ran into him? In what way? You didn't tell him what happened, did you?"

"I asked for his help," I said. "I'm just not sure yet he's willing to give it. At least when it comes to finding out what kind of connections Chief Hanley has to Ned O'Reilly and, as it turns out... his cousin."

"*Whose* cousin?"

"Ned O'Reilly's," I said. "He's related to Ralph Fuller, the chief medical examiner."

Raymond's eyes opened wide. "Are you kidding me?"

I shook my head, turning to look toward the road. With the trees and the way it curved, it was hard to see it. But I was worried, with good reason, that I might've been followed. "They're involved in this somehow. I just don't know why. It's some kind of cover-up."

Raymond said, "But, what'd you say to him?"

"I told him what I think's going on. And, like I said, asked him for his help."

"You really expect the kid will turn on the chief of police? Because some private investigator from Boston asked him to?"

"He was going to take me to jail," I said. "He had the cuffs on me."

"You were arrested?"

"He let me go, once I explained things. That's why I have a feeling he'll help me at least find who grabbed me."

"The one you think's a cop?"

I nodded. "Where is everyone?"

"The girls went for a walk on the beach," Raymond said. "Nancy was worried about you. Beth thought it would help her." He looked at his watch. "They'll be back soon, unless you want to walk over there?"

I thought for a moment, shaking my head. "I don't have time. I'd like to talk to Mrs. Potter again."

Raymond paused. "You think she knows something?"

"It's hard to say. She seems to keep herself involved in everyone's business around town. And her friend, Alice... I still think about that morning, how those women all just happened to be the first ones to find the body. Don't forget, Alice and Ron were together, as a couple."

Raymond said, "Yeah, but it doesn't make her a killer. And you said it was a long time ago."

"I can't rule anything out. It seems to me everyone in this town has something to hide. If I was any more foolish than I already am, I'd go knock on Ned O'Reilly's door myself, start asking questions. But if he has a dirty cop or two on his side..."

"You need to wait," Raymond said. "But I'm not sure you should be depending on some young officer who barely—"

"He may be a better cop than he's gotten credit for. I have a feeling part of the problem for him is everyone around here sees him as the little kid they all knew him as. I'm not sure he's taken very seriously." I rubbed my sore wrists. "And he's a lot tougher than he looks." I told Raymond how Thomas spun me around, had the cuffs on me before I even realized what was happening. "I gave him the number to the house here, in case he needs to reach me."

Raymond pointed with his thumb over his shoulder. "You wanna come in and eat before you go?"

I hesitated, knowing I was running out of time. But no sense trying to get through the days without food in my stomach. I started to follow Raymond inside, but stopped when I saw a police vehicle turn into the driveway toward us.

"Uh-oh," Raymond said.

The vehicle's lights on top were turned off, and it moved slowly, coming our way.

Once the car was close enough, I could see it was Chief Hanley behind the wheel, with Thomas Silva in the passenger seat. They stopped behind the Nova and both placed their hats on their heads as they stepped out of the car.

"Mr. Horn," the chief said, walking toward me.

"I guess I should have guessed you'd tell him," I said, my eyes on Thomas.

"Thomas is a loyal officer of the law," Hanley said. He stopped a few feet in front of me, looked at Raymond and gave him a nod, turning his gaze back my way. "You want to talk about what's going on?"

I hesitated a moment, unsure I wanted to go into any of it with the man, although clearly Thomas had already filled him in. But I wasn't about to ask him right out if he was involved. I knew what his answer would be. "I don't know what you want me to say."

Thomas stood a couple of feet behind the chief, his thumbs hooked in his belt. "Why don't you tell the chief what you told me in the car," he said.

I said, "Does it make sense repeating what I'm sure you already told him?"

"You think I'm a crooked cop?" Hanley said. "Are you basing it on the fact I have a history with Ron Tompkins?" He shook his head. "You're way off base. And, frankly, none of it even makes sense. You think I'd kill a young woman? Just so I could set a guy up?" He let out a laugh. "I could come up with a lot better ways to take care of him, if I really wanted to. But, the thing is, after all this time, the last thing I'm going to do is—"

"Maybe you didn't kill her," I said. "But somebody has gone out of their way to ensure whoever did, stays out of trouble. So if you're here to threaten me..."

"That's not why I'm here," Hanley said. "But I did make some calls. I have friends down in Boston." He looked at Raymond. "Friends of yours too." He turned back to me. "And from what I hear, you seem to have some kind of chip on your shoulder, and can't help but think every man in uniform is dirty, for whatever reason."

"Not *every* one." I nodded at Raymond. "He was a good, honest cop. My good friend, Maggie, is a good cop. I know a handful of others. But, for the most part... we all know there's a fine line between those who wear the uniform and those who are on the other side."

"Is that so?" Hanley said. "Tough way to go through life, being suspicious of everyone you come across, isn't it?"

I said, "Why's that any different from you being suspicious of Ron and going after him when all he was doing was teaching his students... connecting with them on their level?"

"By doing drugs with them?"

"He was found innocent in a court of law," I said. "But you kept going after him."

Hanley looked toward the ground. "I was asked by the parents to do what I could to keep their kids safe. Some didn't feel their children could be, with a grown man hanging around, throwing parties, getting their kids high."

I said, "You were never able to prove he did anything wrong. But you went ahead and destroyed his life anyway, taking away his career."

"All right, let's just be straight here for a moment," Hanley said. "Can we move on from the past? Is that all right with you?"

"I *am* being straight," I said. "But I feel like I may be the only one."

Hanley said, "Listen, Thomas told me about... I know some of these people you're accusing of being involved in whatever it is you believe happened. So if we can at least get on the same page, maybe you can tell me a little more about what you know. Or what you *think* you know."

"Are you referring to the men who grabbed me, handcuffed me and took me back to Ned O'Reilly's house?"

"I'm all ears," Hanley said, nodding.

"What do I need to tell you that you don't already know?" I said.

"Well, first, I can prove to you I had nothing to do with framing anyone or covering anything up. I understand you've been somewhat critical of my investigation so far, and maybe we did get a little sloppy. But I'm going to tell you straight out: I had nothing to do with that young woman's murder, and I am not about to cover up anyone's crime. I don't care *who* it is."

I said, "I believe the whole thing was a setup from the start, going back to the night Ron's truck disappeared from the restaurant."

Hanley stood still, like he was thinking. "What if I told you I believe you?"

"You're going to tell me you think Ron was set up? You expect me to believe that, after you've already arrested him and pressed charges?"

"I had no choice," he said. "I knew something wasn't right. Even the way that poor girl's body was on the beach. It didn't make sense. I have a feeling her body had been placed there, that the truck was brought onto the beach after the fact."

Raymond said, "And what about the kid up there in Bar Harbor? What do you know about that?"

Hanley shook his head. "Well, of course, there's little doubt the two are connected, but I don't have an answer. It's not easy, a small force like the one we have here, when you have people involved... on the inside. There's something more to this, but there's only so much I can do."

"Are you saying what I think you're saying?" I said.

Hanley looked up at Raymond, then at me. "I think we pull our resources together, maybe we can find an answer."

"But what if I can get O'Reilly to talk?"

"He's not going to talk," Hanley said. "He'll have you arrested as soon as you try and say he had something to do with any of this. Both O'Reilly and his mother's side of the family—the Fullers—have their hands in everything in this town. This whole state... It could be anyone... a friend of his, another cousin... He's just one layer of the corruption. I won't even be able to do anything through my office. It's not possible."

"So, you want to work with me?" I said. "Even though—"

"You may be closer to the truth than you realize," Hanley said.

CHAPTER 31

RAYMOND AND I WERE at the table eating bologna sandwiches when Maggie, Nancy, and Beth all walked in the house smelling like coconut sunscreen.

Nancy sat across from me and leaned forward, arms folded on the table. "I saw Mrs. Potter on the beach," she said. "She recognized me, and told me to tell you she said hello. That other woman was with her, the pretty one. Alice, I think?"

I finished chewing the bite I'd taken and wiped my mouth with a piece of paper towel. "I was actually planning to go over and see her, but we've had somewhat of a change in plans."

Maggie fixed the beach towel she had wrapped around her waist, covering her legs. She stood behind Nancy's chair, her hands resting on the back of it. "Is everything all right?"

"We just had a visit from the chief of police," Raymond said, his mouth half full of food.

Maggie said, "Chief Hanley was *here*?"

Raymond and I both nodded.

"He claims to be on our side," I said. "He actually asked for my help, because he believes Ron may be innocent."

"What?" Nancy said. "But he's the one who arrested him. How could he..."

"I don't know," I said. "He claims he had no choice, although he wasn't exactly clear about what he meant. He said he'd been digging into it, and started to realize he'd made a mistake. But now, his hands are somewhat tied."

"How can they be?" Nancy said. "He's the chief of police."

I said, "He doesn't have as much pull as you'd think. Especially once you cross over the town line."

Maggie looked confused, and maybe skeptical. "So, you're telling me Chief Hanley just came over here, decided to tell you he thinks Ron Tompkins is innocent? And why would he tell *you*?"

"He didn't come right out and say he was innocent."

Raymond said, "Just so you understand: the chief didn't just show up out of the blue. Officer Silva and Jake had a conversation about Hanley earlier."

I said, "I had a feeling Silva would run to his boss and tell him everything I told him," I said. "And that's exactly what he did."

Maggie pulled out a chair and sat between Nancy and Raymond. "You really think you can trust either one of them?"

I took another bite of the sandwich and swallowed what was in my mouth.

"You're eating bologna?" Nancy said, looking at my plate. "Do you know what that stuff's made of?"

I shrugged and took another bite. "One bologna sandwich isn't going to kill me." I wiped my mouth with the paper towel, looking at the spot of yellow mustard I'd collected. I said to Maggie, "Hanley was very convincing. And I'd say, at this point, I have to believe him.

If it's a mistake, then this'll no doubt come back to bite me. But maybe if he takes what I told him about Ralph Fuller..."

"Who's Ralph Fuller?" Maggie said.

"Maine's chief medical examiner."

"The one who oversaw both autopsies?"

I nodded, knowing Maggie and I were having the same thought. "Fuller's involved in all of this somehow. I just don't know why."

Nancy said, "What did the chief say about him?"

"Chief Hanley wasn't about to point fingers," Raymond said. "But he seemed to believe Jake."

"He was careful not to say too much," I said.

"So how'd you leave it with him?" Maggie said.

"First thing is figuring out who the man was who grabbed me. If we can get him to talk..."

Nancy said, "But if you saw this man, Ned O'Reilly, isn't that enough?"

"It's not going to be that easy," Raymond said. "Not if there are enough people involved, all making sure they have each other's backs."

Maggie had her eyes on the table. I could tell her wheels were turning.

"What is it?" I said, watching her.

She looked up at me and shook her head. "Oh, nothing. I was just thinking about Logan Reed."

"Anything you want to share?" I said.

She took a moment before she answered. "Well, I guess it's just... I can't help thinking about Ron driving up there to meet with him. He said Logan Reed called him, right? Then he gets in his sister's car and goes up there, only to find Logan's car surrounded by police and paramedics. So he leaves, rather than being seen, and goes to a bar?"

"It wasn't actually his car," I said. "Logan took the family car up there."

"He didn't have his own car?" Maggie said.

I had to think about it. "I don't know. I guess I'd have to ask Ron." I stood up from the table. "Is it all right I use the phone?"

"You really have to ask?" Raymond said.

I went into the kitchen and dialed the restaurant. I asked for Ron, but didn't say who it was.

After a couple of minutes, he came on the line.

"Hello?"

"Ron, it's Jake Horn."

"Oh, hi, Jake. Listen, I'm really busy in the kitchen right now."

I said, "I just have a quick question." I stood, leaning inside the doorway, everyone watching me.

"Uh, okay, is it about—"

"Ron, do you know why Logan wasn't driving his own car, up at the park?"

"I... I have no idea."

"Do you know what kind of car he owns?" I said.

"As far as I know, he still has... He owned an MG. Convertible. It might've been a gift from his parents, after he graduated from college."

"All right," I said. "Thanks."

"That's all you wanted?"

"For now," I said, and hung up the phone.

I went back to the table. "The night Logan was killed, he was driving the family's car."

"Family car?" Nancy said. "You mean, like his dad's car?"

"I don't know. I suppose so."

"What's the significance?" Raymond said.

I looked at him, thought for a moment, then shrugged. "I don't know that either."

Maggie walked to the window, staring outside for a moment before she turned. "Did you ask Ron if he had any feelings for Casey?"

"We've been through this," I said. "Why would he kill her if he did?"

Nobody responded.

I leaned on the table, my arms folded in front of me. "I'm done trying to come up with a motive for why Ron might've killed her," I said to Maggie, "Honestly, any sane person would have a hard time believing he's innocent. But that's why whoever is behind this... There's a lot to it and more than just a few people involved in pulling this off."

Maggie nodded, like she understood, but I could see it in her eyes she still wasn't convinced.

"The simple fact is, somebody threatened me," I said. "And I'm not the only one who's in danger." I looked at the others and made sure they understood what I meant.

Beth said, "How come you haven't mentioned this poor girl's family? I understand the parents were killed, but isn't there anyone else?"

"She has family in Ireland," I said. "But, after her parents, there was nobody, besides Logan. I guess you could include Ron as someone she'd kept in touch with, but..."

"No other friends?" Maggie said.

I shrugged. "I made some calls to a handful of names I dug up, with no luck. Her college roommate moved back to Florida. And a couple of others I spoke to hadn't been in touch with her in a long time."

We were all quiet, but I could see it in Maggie's eyes; she knew something didn't add up.

Beth headed for the stairs. "I'm going up to shower."

The phone rang and Raymond got up and walked into the kitchen to answer. "Hello?" He stood in the doorway with his back to us, nodding, listening to the caller. "Oh, yeah, sure." He was silent again. "Okay. Yes, he's right here. I'll let him know." Raymond hung the phone up on the wall and came back to the table. "That was Officer Silva. He said there's presently not an autopsy report available for Logan Reed."

"No autopsy report?" I said. "That doesn't make sense."

"No, it doesn't. He said there's some kind of holdup, and wasn't clear about why."

I said, "He wasn't clear why? Or he wasn't *being* clear about why?"

"He didn't know why," Raymond said.

I looked at Maggie, her arms folded, her eyes squinting like she was deep in thought. "Can you find out who might be holding it up?" she said.

I sat back down at the table. "My guess would have to be Ralph Fuller?"

"And you said he's the chief medical examiner?" she said.

I nodded and said to Raymond, "Did he say anything else?"

"That was it," he said. "He just wanted me to tell you."

I went back into the kitchen and grabbed the handset off the wall, taking a piece of paper from my pocket, then dialing the number written on it.

The first few tries only gave me a busy signal. But, by the fourth time I called, the phone rang at least seven times until she finally answered:

"Hello?"

"Mrs. Reed?"

"Yes?"

"I'm sorry to bother you. It's Jake Horn."

The line was quiet for a few seconds. "Oh, hello. What do you want?"

"Well, I'm sorry to have to ask you for a favor. I'm trying to get my hands on Logan's autopsy report. And I'm wondering if there's a chance you can help me get a copy?"

"For what?" she said. "You said you weren't involved in Logan's—"

"It's not that I'm not involved. I mean, I'm not directly involved in what happened to Logan. But, see, the thing is..."

"I'm sorry, Mr. Horn. But I've been advised not to speak to you."

"By who?" I said. "Your husband?"

There was a brief moment of silence.

"I'm sorry. But I can't help you," she said.

"Mrs. Reed, I know this is a very difficult time for you. But I'm just trying to get some answers."

"You're working to help clear the man who killed them. I can't help you."

"But you said it yourself. You weren't convinced he had anything to do with it."

"I'm sorry," she said. "Carl called me. He told me you showed up at the house where he's staying. He wanted to know how you knew. He was very upset."

"I'm sure he was," I said. "But you told me you didn't know where he was. So why would he be upset with you?"

Darlene Reed didn't answer.

I looked at the others talking, and said into the phone, "You said your husband knows a lot of people up here, in Maine. I'm curious if he happens to know Ralph Fuller? The state's chief medical examiner?"

There was no sound on the other end.

"Mrs. Reed?" I said. "Are you there?"

It took her a moment to answer. "Carl and Ralph have known each other since they were kids."

CHAPTER 32

I walked into Dr. Jason Strong's downtown Portland medical office, where he practiced as a family physician.

But he was also a part-time medical examiner for the State of Maine, and for some reason had been fired from the position less than a week after Casey Jilson's death.

The receptionist behind the desk gave me a subtle smile as I approached her and leaned on the counter. Barry Manilow's "Can't Smile Without You" played quietly in the background.

She said, "Do you have an appointment?"

"I'm here to meet with Dr. Strong."

"I'm sorry, unless it's an emergency, you'll have to make an appointment to see him." She smiled, although it seemed a bit forced, then flipped open the cover of the leather-bound book in front of her. "Would you like to schedule something? The doctor has openings next week."

I glanced behind me at the empty waiting room, where I could smell some kind of disinfectant. "I'm not here for medical reasons," I said. "But I do have something I need to discuss with him."

"I'm sorry, but the doctor is not available."

"How about if you tell him it's about Casey Jilson. Then you can see what he says."

"Casey *who*?" she said, a slight tilt to her head.

"Jilson. He'll know who she is," I said.

The woman held her gaze on me for a moment, like she was unsure how to respond, until she finally got up and walked through an open door behind the desk.

A moment later she came back and sat in the chair. "Dr. Strong can't talk to you right now. But he did say that you can leave your contact information, and he'll call you when he has a chance."

"I'm only asking for a few minutes of his time."

She smirked. "The doctor is a very busy man."

"You don't think I'm busy? I drove all the way up here to talk to him." I decided I wasn't going to get anywhere dealing with the young gatekeeper. So I walked around the back of the desk and through the door behind her.

"Sir!" she said, hurrying after me.

I stood in a hallway and looked left and right, unsure which way to turn. I called out, "Dr. Strong?"

The young woman followed and grabbed my arm, her voice raised. "Sir, you can't come back here!" I glanced at her as she looked to her left, somewhere down the hall. "Should I call the police?"

She clearly wasn't directing her question toward me, but I took a good guess where the doctor might've been when I saw a door close, gently, at the end of the hall.

I pulled my arm from the woman's weak grasp and headed for the closed door, pushing it open to see a small balding man in a white doctor's coat seated behind a desk. He was in the process of making a phone call, but I pressed down on the switch. "Dr. Strong?"

He placed the handset on the base, looking up at me from his desk. "What do you think you're doing?"

The woman repeated her earlier question: "Doctor? Do you want me to call the police?"

Strong glanced at her and shook his head.

"I'm not sure what you're hiding," I said.

The doctor said, "Who said I'm hiding anything?"

I sat down in the chair in front of his desk, across from him. "My name is Jake Horn. I'm a private investigator. I'm here to discuss a young woman whose body was found on Goose Rocks Beach: Casey Jilson."

The doctor gestured with his hand for the young woman behind me, out in the hall, to go away. "It's all right." He watched through the doorway as she turned and walked away.

I looked at the wall behind him, with a plaque hanging there from Tufts University. "I get the feeling you know why I'm here?"

"I'm sorry," he said, shaking his head. "I do not."

"But you *do* know who Casey Jilson is?" I said.

He cleared his throat, looking at the phone in front of him. "I'm sorry, I'm not at liberty to discuss anything with you."

"Did they tell you to lie?" I said. "But you wouldn't? Is that why you were fired from the medical examiner's office?"

The doctor shook his head. "I... I wasn't fired. I just didn't have the time to take on the work."

"Don't worry," I said. "You can be straight with me. Whatever you tell me doesn't leave this room."

"I told you," he said, his voice getting louder. "I'm not at liberty to discuss a pending case. It would put me in a lot of trouble, if I did discuss it. I could lose my practice."

"For telling the truth?"

"You don't understand. I'm not from around here. I've lived in Maine for ten years and I'm still considered an outsider. Especially compared to the people in charge of the state's medical establishment. They have a lot of power over what I can and can't do or say."

I said, "Why don't you just tell me what you know, and I'll be on my way. You won't hear from me again. Nobody will ever know we talked."

"You don't understand," the doctor said. "They probably already know you're here. They're watching me... my family."

I watched the nervous doctor fiddle with a paperclip, pulling it apart until it snapped in half.

"Did they want you to change the autopsy report?" I said.

He swallowed hard and closed his eyes, taking a deep breath as he let out a long sigh. "I can't discuss it. I won't. I'm sorry."

"Was Ralph Fuller behind covering up what really happened? Is he the one in charge?"

Doctor Strong held his gaze on me, but didn't answer. "I'm sorry. You have to leave."

"Was Casey Jilson killed by the impact of that pickup truck? Or was it something else that killed her? If you don't tell me what you know, an innocent man is going to prison for a long time for a murder he didn't commit."

The doctor stared back at me. "If you have questions, I suggest you take it up with Dr. Fuller."

"Is he the only one who knows?"

"I'm telling you I don't know. If you want to know more, then I'm merely suggesting you speak with Dr. Fuller."

I had a good feeling, by the look in the doctor's eyes, he was trying to tell me something without coming right out and saying it. But I was already certain Dr. Fuller was behind this alleged cover-up, and repeating my question wasn't going to get me very far.

"Okay, then. What about Logan Reed?" I said. "Were you the one who performed his autopsy?"

"Logan Reed?" He shook his head. "There was no autopsy."

I leaned forward on the chair. "What? Are you sure?"

"It wasn't required. They knew what happened."

"That he was shot and killed?" I said.

The doctor was still, staring back at me until he rose from his desk and stood by the door. "Please, I need you to leave. I told you who to talk to. I'm not saying another word."

***

I jumped into the back seat of Raymond's LeBaron. "Can we make it up to Augusta in an hour?"

"What's in Augusta?" Raymond said.

"Dr. Fuller's office."

Raymond pointed to the clock on the dash, the second hand ticking. "I can get us there by four. But how do you know he'll be there?"

"I was told Fuller often worked well past five, at least on the days he wasn't on the golf course."

"Shouldn't we call first?" Maggie said. "And make sure?"

Raymond had already started driving, and took a sharp right onto Forest Avenue, heading toward the highway.

"Stop if you see a pay phone," I said.

Raymond went another mile and pulled into Roy's Food & Fuel, driving toward the pay phone at the far left of the lot, under the gas station's sign.

"Dr. Strong wouldn't talk about Casey Jilson, but he hinted enough that Ralph Fuller's involved. I don't think he knows what or who else is involved with him, but he was scared to talk."

"Yeah?" Raymond said, turning with his arm up on the seat to look back at me, stopping next to the pay phone. "What else did he say?"

"He told me there was never an autopsy performed on Logan Reed."

"There had to have been an autopsy," Maggie said. "In a case like this…"

I got out of the car and reached into my empty pocket. "Anybody have any change?" I stood outside Maggie's open window and she reached into her own pocket. She handed me a dime.

Raymond dug into his ashtray and grabbed two nickels, reaching across Maggie to hand them to me through the window.

I hurried for the phone, knowing we were running out of time. I had a folded envelope in my back pocket with the number to the Kennebunkport police station and dropped the dime in the slot.

I recognized Thomas Silva's voice as soon as he answered, on the second ring. "Kennebunkport Police."

"Officer Silva," I said, showing him the respect he may have deserved. "It's Jake Horn."

"Jake?" he said. "I've been trying to reach you. Nobody knows where Chief Hanley is. He hasn't come into the station."

"Why not?"

"I don't know."

"You haven't heard from him?"

"No," Thomas said. "He didn't show up this morning. I called his house and he didn't answer, so I drove over. Nobody was there."

"Who else is at the station?" I said. "Somebody must know *something*?"

"The only other person who was here earlier, besides me, was Jim Shirley."

"Who's Jim Shirley?"

"He runs communications for the town, has a desk toward the back of the office. You might've seen him when you were here. He just left a little while ago."

I thought about the only other person in the station, besides the woman at the front desk, when I'd gone by the first time to talk to Chief Hanley. The man had kept his back to me for most of the time, although I had a feeling he was listening to most of what I'd said to the chief.

I covered the mouthpiece on the handset with the palm of my hand and poked my head out from the phone booth. "Thomas doesn't know where Chief Hanley is."

Raymond looked out at me from inside the car, then said to Maggie. "You hear that? Chief Hanley's missing."

I said, "I don't know if he's missing, or..." I put the phone back up to my ear and said to Silva, "Did you call anyone else? Maybe the state police, or..." As soon as the words left my mouth I thought, perhaps, that wouldn't be a very good idea.

Officer Silva said, "Last I spoke with Chief, before he left late in the evening, he told me not to trust anyone until we had some answers. Not even law enforcement from any other department."

I thought about the man in that station with Thomas, and the more I pictured his face the more suspicious he appeared in my mind. "Give me Chief Hanley's address; we'll meet you there in twenty minutes."

"Who's *we*?" Thomas said.

"I'm up in Portland with my cousin Raymond, and Maggie Donovan. She's an officer with the Boston Police."

I hung up the phone and dropped the two nickels Raymond gave me into the slot.

Raymond got out of the LeBaron. "Who are you calling now?" He leaned up against the driver's-side fender.

Maggie got out from the passenger side.

"I'm calling Beth," I said. "I just want to make sure Nancy—both of them—are all right."

I dialed the house and let it ring eight or nine times before hanging up. "There's no answer."

"They said they'd stay there," Maggie said. "You sure you dialed the right number?"

I nodded, reaching my finger into the coin return for the two nickels, dropping them back into the slot. I called the house again, whispering the number to myself as I turned the phone's dial.

It rang another five times before it stopped ringing. Somebody had picked it up, but didn't say a word on the other end.

I said, "Hello? Beth?"

Nothing.

"Nancy? Is that you?" I said.

After another couple of moments of silence coming through the phone, a male voice said, "I warned you, didn't I?"

CHAPTER 33

RAYMOND HAD THE LeBARON on two wheels when he hit the end of the driveway off King's Highway, turning toward Beth's family's house. He skidded around the Nova and just missed hitting Maggie's Scamp, slamming on the brakes as he skidded sideways.

The smell of burning rubber came off the tires as I jumped out, along with Maggie and Raymond, and we all ran onto the porch.

Raymond pushed me aside and ran ahead of me, yanking open the door so hard he almost tore it off the hinges. He rushed into the house screaming for Beth and Nancy.

I ran upstairs, yelling for Nancy and Beth.

There was no sign of either.

Maggie called out for us and I hurried down the stairs and onto the porch.

She had a note she handed to me.

Raymond came from outside after he'd run through the house and into the back, looking for Beth and Nancy, with no luck. "What is it?" he said.

There was a phone number on it. The note had a phone number, and under that was, *Call ASAP, if you want to see them alive!*

I ran for the kitchen, grabbing the phone off the wall and dialing the number.

A male voice answered on the first ring.

I yelled into the phone. "Where are they! I swear, you do anything to hurt them, I'll—"

"Calm down, Mr. Horn. They will not be harmed, unless you again decide to ignore my advice."

"What do you want?" I said, trying to remain calm.

"I already told you once, but you seem to be too thick-headed to want to listen. Maybe this time, you will."

I said, "You do anything to hurt them, I swear I'll..." I glanced at Maggie and Raymond standing by the table just outside the kitchen, watching me.

Raymond paced back and forth. "Where are they? Whatever they want, Jake. Don't play games with them." His eyes were filled with anger, but also tears.

The man on the other end of the phone said, "Meet me at the gas station in Saco in twenty minutes. Don's Texaco. Come alone." He hung up without another word.

"Don's Texaco in Saco," I said, running out the front door, onto the porch and into the driveway. I pulled my keys from my pocket to jump in the Nova, but Raymond was already behind the wheel of the LeBaron.

He yelled at me and Maggie, "Come on! Get In!"

We both followed and jumped in Raymond's car, and he was already halfway down the driveway before I'd even closed my door.

"It was him. The same guy," I said, pulling the handle and slamming the door as he skidded onto King's Highway, driving full speed toward Route 9.

"The cop?" Raymond said, his eyes on the road, the steering wheel within his tight two-handed grip.

Maggie leaned over the back of our seat from the rear. "Are you just going to do what he says?"

I nodded. "I should have listened the first time, instead of putting everyone in danger."

Raymond gave me a quick glance. I wasn't sure if he wanted to tell me I was right—that I should have walked away from the case, as per the threat I'd received initially—or if he was ready for a fight. I could see it in his eyes; he wasn't going to back down from anyone until Beth and Nancy were safe.

He'd gotten more careful about things since he'd retired. But backing down, especially when someone messed with our family, wasn't in his blood. Raymond reached under his seat and pulled his Smith & Wesson .38 out, resting it on the seat between us.

"I don't think we can just show up and start shooting," Maggie said, watching Raymond. She reached over, grabbed the gun, and released the cylinder to swing it out.

The gun was loaded and she placed it back down on the seat, a look of concern on her face. "I don't like this," she said. "I think it's time to get someone else involved here. From law enforcement. I'm a cop, you know how much trouble I'll be in?"

"We can't trust any of them," I said. "And don't forget, Chief Hanley's missing. There are people involved in this town... in this state."

Raymond got off Log Cabin Road and onto US Route 1. He said, "We get Beth and Nancy back safe. That's our priority. After that, we figure it out."

Maggie said, "Don't we need some kind of plan?"

I said to Raymond. "Drop me off a block away. You two can hang back and wait. Just make sure if I leave with him, you're right behind us. Don't lose me."

Raymond gave me a nod, breaking every speed limit on the way.

He pulled into the Saco Motel a block from the gas station and handed me the keys. "If you walk over there, he'll know you're not alone. Take the car, Maggie and I will walk over, go around and come in the back way. He'll probably take you in the car with him, so just leave the keys in the car." Raymond lifted his .38 from the middle seat between us. "Just give us time to get over there. Stall him."

"He knows who you are, and what you look like," I said. "Both of you."

Raymond got out and closed the door, looking in through the open window at me. "Like I said, just leave the keys in the car. We'll be right behind you."

"What if he tells me to follow him?" I said, sliding over behind the wheel.

Raymond looked from Maggie to me, shaking his head. He held up the .38. "Here's plan B."

Maggie came around to the driver's-side window, reached in and put her hand on my arm, looking me in the eye. "Be careful."

"You carrying?" Raymond said.

I shook my head. "No."

He rolled his eyes.

"I'm sure he'll search me either way," I said.

They both walked away from the car and headed down a side street, staying off the main road.

I looked at the clock and figured I'd give them five minutes to get situated behind the gas station, although waiting too long would put me past the twenty minutes I was given.

A white van drove by. I didn't catch the driver, but wondered if it was the short sidekick I'd shot. I guess that it was, as soon as I saw the blue Chrysler a few cars behind him. I slouched down in the seat and stayed low behind the wheel until both were past.

After waiting another couple of minutes, I pulled out onto the street and drove slowly until I got to the Texaco sign. I cut the wheel and continued across the lot.

I drove around the back of the building where the white van and Chrysler were parked, waiting.

The property was enclosed by a tall chain-link fence with a handful of leafy trees overhanging the top rail. I didn't see Raymond or Maggie anywhere, and hoped the two men didn't either.

I left the keys in the ignition and put the window down, stepped out and immediately raised my hands to show I wasn't armed. I could smell car exhaust, gasoline, and cigarette smoke.

Not a good combination.

The man sat in the Chrysler, elbow hanging out the open window, a cigarette in his hand. I saw his face in the side-view mirror, his car faced in the other direction. I walked past the white van and looked at my friend in the driver's seat.

He said something to me with a growl.

I continued toward the man in charge and he got out of his vehicle, the gun in his hand pointed toward me.

I said, "I just told you, I'm not armed."

The man, dressed in a suit like the last time I saw him, nodded with his chin toward the van. The door creaked when his short friend opened the door and stepped down. I glanced over my shoulder at him walking toward me with a bad limp.

Directing my gaze back to the man in front of me, I said, "Where are they?" It didn't exactly come in the form of a question, the way my teeth clenched.

The man from the van was right behind me and patted me down, running his hands up and around my legs, then around my waist. "Nothing," he said, then backed away.

"Good." The man with the gun gestured for me to get in his car. "Let's go for a ride."

I shook my head. "No."

"No?" The man laughed, but then the smile dropped from his face. "Get in the car."

I hesitated, then opened the back passenger door. But before I stepped in, the man reached past me and slammed it closed. "You're driving," he said, grabbing my arm. He took me around to the passenger side, holding the gun on me, and pushed me in. "Move over," he said, and I slid behind the steering wheel. "Pull out of the lot and take a left."

The car was already running. I said, "Are you going to tell me where we're going?"

"I just did." He wiggled the gun's muzzle. "Let's go."

I cut the wheel and looked in the rearview at the van, behind us. I took a subtle look back toward the building, but didn't see Raymond or Maggie.

I said, "So, you're a cop. What is this, some kind of side gig? Make some extra cash?"

"I'm not a cop," he said. "Not anymore. Good assumption on your part though."

"I know a lot of cops. Especially the crooked ones. You all smell the same... that cheap gas-station cologne." I glanced at him out of the corner of my eye, but kept looking toward the road. "Why don't you put that gun away," I said. "All I want is my daughter, and my cousin's wife. Whatever you want, I'll do it."

The man said, "Well, it's gotten a little more complicated since the last time we spoke."

I stopped at a red light. "What's that supposed to mean?"

"You met with Jason Strong. *Doctor* Strong. What did he tell you?"

I shook my head. "He didn't tell me a thing."

The man laughed. "Let's just be honest with each other here, okay?" He hadn't moved the gun.

"He was afraid," I said. "He wouldn't talk. I imagine that must've had something to do with you, and whoever else is threatening him to keep his mouth shut?"

The light turned green and I continued straight.

He pointed to the right. "Take this next turn."

"You'd better be taking me to them," I said, giving him a look so he knew I wasn't messing around.

"I told you not to worry. I just needed to get your attention, which I believe I have now. Sort of like with the pliers, although that obviously didn't work the way I'd intended." He let out a laugh, like he was having a good time. "Scare tactics like that usually work on most people."

I didn't respond, turning right, as he'd instructed me to do. I felt him watching me when I looked in the rearview.

There was no van or any other vehicle behind us. I wondered what happened to Raymond and Maggie.

"Oh, your cousin and your lady-cop friend won't be joining us."

I tried not to react, and thought maybe I should slam on the brakes and send the guy through the window.

But that wouldn't do me much good.

"Don't worry," he said. "They'll be fine. We're not in the business of hurting people. At least until it's absolutely necessary." He let out a sigh. "This isn't what I signed up for when I agreed to help."

"Agreed to help who?" I said. "Why won't you tell me what this is all about? Why is Ron Tompkins being set up?"

He pointed his gun at me. "Just keep driving."

CHAPTER 34

IT WAS NO SURPRISE when I was instructed to take a right turn into the driveway off of Simpson Road. I didn't say a word about what I knew, and continued up the steep driveway with woods on either side.

I put my foot on the brake and stopped behind the maroon Ford LTD parked in front of the three-car garage.

My friend in the passenger seat used his gun to gesture where I should go. "Over there," he said. "Park on the left."

I backed up, then cut the wheel, putting the car in park behind the door on the left, closest to the house.

"Don't try anything foolish," the man said. He got out of the passenger side with his gun pointed toward me. "Let's go. Get out."

I opened my door and raised my hands right away as soon as I got out. "I told you, you can put the gun away. I'm not going to do anything."

I glanced toward the front porch of the big yellow farmhouse when the front door opened. The older man with white hair walked out and down the steps carrying a black leather briefcase.

I knew it was Ned O'Reilly, although I hadn't gotten a good enough look at him the first time I was there.

The white-haired man walked right up to me and placed the briefcase at my feet. "There's twenty-five thousand dollars in there," he said. "Take it, and get out of Maine. Best thing you could do is to never come back here."

I glanced at the briefcase on the hot asphalt, then raised my gaze to the old man staring back at me. Taking a quick look over my shoulder, I saw the ex-cop with his gun still pointed at my back. "You really think you can buy me off?" I said, now facing the old man.

"We're not buying you off," he said. "We're asking for your assurance you'll go away for good, forget this whole thing. It's a simple gesture. A payment, for your troubles. I doubt Marilyn Bartlett's going to be paying you that much to get that loser brother of hers off the hook, so..."

"Where are they," I said, again without it being as much a question as a statement. I looked toward the front door of the house and around the property. Off in the distance, to my right, I could see a gray, square building with a flat roof.

The old man said, "Will you take the money? All we need is your word. You take it—it's all cash—and promise me you're done. You can leave with your daughter and your cousin's wife. Both unharmed, of course."

I looked the man in the eye, wanting to tell him where he could shove that briefcase. But I knew it would only put Nancy and Beth in more danger than they were already in. "Where are they?" I said, gritting my teeth, although I was doing my best to remain—or at least appear to be—calm.

The old man let out a sigh, shaking his head, and glanced past me at the ex-cop standing behind me. "You weren't kidding. He sure is a stubborn son of a..." He cleared his throat and nodded at the briefcase. "Go ahead. You want to count it first? You know what you could do with twenty-five grand? That's enough to cover your daughter's last few years of college. And then some."

"What if I don't want it?" I said.

"Then I'd say you're a fool."

"I can't let an innocent man go to prison," I said.

"You *claim* he's innocent," the older man said. "But I don't think you have enough proof."

I stared back at him. "I know that you, and whoever else you're wrapped up with, wouldn't go through all this trouble to stop me from finding the truth if he was guilty."

The man shrugged, nodding at the same time. "Well, all I'm saying is I believe it's in your best interest to walk away. Unless your daughter and..." He pulled at his chin. "The other one, your cousin's wife? She's a feisty one. Maybe I'd be doing him a favor... You sure he wants her back?"

The man behind me laughed.

I looked down at the briefcase. "All right," I said. "You win. I'll take the money." I crouched down, and grabbed the briefcase by the handle. "I *would* like to count it first."

"Go ahead," the old man said.

But before either one of the two had a chance to make another move, I spun around with the briefcase in my hand, swinging it at the ex-cop, striking him hard enough in the head, his eyes rolled back like a human slot machine. His body went limp and he dropped his gun, collapsing onto the ground.

I reached down and grabbed his gun, then trained it on the old man.

But he started to run from me, as fast as his old legs would take him. He climbed the stairs, tripping on the top step and falling with a crash on the porch and into the front door.

"Stop!" I yelled, running after him.

He sat up, covering his face with his arms up in front of him. "No! Please! Don't shoot me," he said. "Please! I'll give you all the money you want."

I grabbed him by the shirt with one hand and lifted him to his feet, turning him around to face me. I pressed the gun's muzzle into his turtle-like neck. "Where are they?" I yelled. "Take me there. Now!"

He nodded, shaking, opening the front door. I gave him a little shove and he stumbled, walking in ahead of me. His hands were raised. "Please, don't... Don't shoot me. I'll give you as much money as you want."

"I don't want your money," I said.

I prodded him down the hall, gripping his shirt, as I let him go ahead of me. He continued down the hall, and stopped at the open doorway to the kitchen, taking a key off a hook on a wooden key rack. He took another ten steps and stopped at a closed door, then slipped the key in the lock.

As soon as he opened it, a mildew-like odor escaped from the other side.

He flipped the light switch just inside the door and I looked down the stairs into the basement.

"Hurry!" I yelled, and he gripped the handrail going down the stairs ahead of me. "Speed it up!"

"Please, we didn't hurt them," he said, glancing at me over his shoulder as he stepped off the bottom stair. "I swear. We've done them no harm."

"Will you shut up?" I said, looking around the damp, cool, unfinished basement. "Where are they?"

I followed him around the corner and threw him out of my way and to the floor when I saw Nancy and Beth both tied to chairs, duct tape over their mouths. A single bulb hung from the ceiling over them.

"Untie them!" I said, lifting the old man to his feet, then tucked the gun into the back of my pants. "Are you both all right?" I said.

They both nodded, tears coming down their cheeks. I pulled the duct tape off each of their mouths.

"You son of a bitch," Beth said, staring at the whimpering old man as soon as the tape was off. "Wait until my husband gets a hold of you."

The old man was shaking, trying to remove the rope from her ankles. I was afraid she was going to kick him in the face once she was loose. "We may need him," I said. As soon as Nancy was free, I pushed the old man out of my way to help Beth.

Once the rope was removed and I helped them to their feet, I handed Beth the gun and used the same rope to tie the man to one of the chairs. I looked around for the duct tape, saw a roll on a wooden workbench on the other side of the basement, and covered his mouth.

Nancy waited until I was done, then came at me and wrapped me up in a hug. She was fighting back tears. "I knew you'd show up."

"You sure you're both all right?" I said.

They both nodded again and I took the gun back from Beth, picking up another couple pieces of rope before we headed up the stairs. "Be careful," I said. "I don't know if the other guy's waiting for us."

We walked outside and the ex-cop was gone, along with his car.

The briefcase was gone too.

I walked over to the garage and lifted the middle door. Inside was the hearse I saw the last time I was there. I opened the driver's-side door. This time, there was a key in the ignition.

Beth and Nancy followed me in and stood outside as I turned the key.

The engine started on the first try. "Get in," I said.

I glanced over at the other car in the garage, covered with a blue plastic tarp. At first, I thought nothing of it.

Beth and Nancy both got in front with me, and I backed the hearse out of the garage. I turned it around and started to head down the driveway, but stopped. "Hang on," I said, getting out of the vehicle.

I rushed into the garage and looked at the vehicle covered with the tarp. It was obvious the car underneath was small, especially compared to the hearse. I pulled the tarp off.

Underneath was a green convertible MG with a white vinyl top. But there wasn't much light in the garage, so I looked for the switch by the back door and flipped it on.

I went over to the front of the MG, where there was clear damage to the hood. It wasn't major damage, but it was dented. The left headlight was smashed.

I moved close enough my legs were up against the front bumper. Being six foot two, the hood above the grill came up to my thigh, just above my knee. I ran my hand over the dent, and a thought entered my mind. I yelled, "Nancy! Come in here."

Nancy and Beth ran into the garage.

"What's the matter?"

I said to Nancy, "Come here," then moved her to the front of the MG, looking to see where the bumper and hood aligned with her body.

Stepping back, I looked her over, compared to the height of the car. The hood came just below her hip. "You're five foot seven?"

She nodded. "Why?"

I didn't answer, but tried to open the driver's-side door. It was locked.

"Dad?" she said.

"Hold on." I ran out of the garage and into the house, toward the kitchen where there were other keys hanging from the rack on the wall. There was a single leather key chain with the metal MG emblem on it, a single key attached.

I grabbed it from the rack and ran outside to the garage. Nancy and Beth were standing outside.

"What's going on?" Beth said. "Aren't we getting out of here?"

"Give me a minute." I went back inside the garage and slipped the key into the driver's-side door's lock. The door opened and I ducked inside, reaching for the glove box. There was an envelope in there, and inside it was a Massachusetts vehicle registration. The car belonged to Logan Reed.

CHAPTER 35

I TURNED THE HEARSE toward Main Street in Saco and saw Raymond and Maggie leaning under the open hood of his LeBaron parked on the side of the road in front of a laundromat. I blew the horn and they both straightened up, staring back at us like they didn't know who we were.

I pulled into the laundromat parking lot and Beth jumped out, running toward him. He hurried toward her and she jumped into his arms, crying.

Maggie ran over to me and reached out for Nancy, wrapping her arms around her. "Are you okay?" she said.

Nancy nodded, but she was still upset, wiping the tears from her cheek.

"Thank God you're both all right," Raymond said, holding Beth's hand, walking with her toward us. "Why are you driving the hearse?"

"It's what was available," I said. "What happened to your car?"

"A white van stopped in front of us at the red light. The guy jumped out holding a gun. He first pointed it at us, then took six shots into the grill. Maggie wouldn't let me shoot him."

She glanced at me with a slight shrug.

"Where'd he go?" I said.

"The guy in the van?" Raymond said. "I don't know. Hopefully back to the zoo where he belongs. Is that the same guy you shot?"

"Most likely."

Raymond said, "I was going to walk back to the gas station, see if I could get a tow. But we decided to wait here. I knew you'd come back at some point."

I said to Raymond, "How can we get Nancy and Beth back to the house?"

"Where are you going?" Maggie said.

"I'd like you and Raymond to come with me. But it's not safe for everyone."

"Everyone?" Nancy said. "Why can't we all just go?"

"Go where?" Raymond said.

"Old Orchard Beach."

Beth looked out at the commercial buildings along the road. She put her arm over Nancy's shoulder, pointing toward a sign that said Jack's Diner. "How about we go get something to eat?" she said, turning to me and Raymond. "Do you want me to call the police?"

"Not yet," I said. "If we're not back in an hour, then it'll be our only choice. Call Thomas Silva, tell him we're at Chuck Johnson's place." I looked inside the hearse and came out with a business card for O'Reilly's Funeral Home and wrote the address to the house in Old Orchard Beach.

Beth took it from my hand and looked at her watch. "An hour? Isn't that a long time? What if he can't get there fast enough?"

"I'm not worried about it. But I'm not sure who else to trust up here," I said.

"You sure you can trust him?" Raymond said.

I nodded, hugged Nancy, and pulled a few dollars from my wallet, handing them to her. "Be careful," I said.

Nancy's tears had dried. "*You* be careful." Beth kissed Raymond, then put her arm around Nancy again and led her away, both heading toward Jack's Diner.

Maggie and Raymond stood outside the hearse, about to get in.

"Give me a minute," I said, and started walking toward the pay phone in front of the laundromat.

"Where are you going?" Raymond said.

"To make a call."

"To who?"

I glanced back at him over my shoulder. "Darlene Reed."

***

I expected to see the powder-blue LTD parked in front of the house in Old Orchard Beach, where Carl Reed had been staying. But it wasn't there. I assumed the ex-cop had headed straight over, once he took off from Ned O'Reilly's house. But the only vehicle at the house was Carl Reed's.

I parked on the street, opposite the house, and told Maggie to wait in the car. "I think it would be a bad career move if you come in with us," I said. "If you can wait here, keep an eye out?"

Maggie nodded, and slid behind the wheel as I got out.

Raymond got out the passenger side and Maggie stuck her head out the window. "If I hear anything I don't like, I'm coming in."

Raymond and I both walked around to the back of the house and up the steps to the screened-in porch. The door was unlocked, and slightly ajar. I pushed it open, walked onto the porch and knocked on the door to the house. It appeared as if the lights were on inside, but a curtain covered the door's panes of glass, making it hard to see.

I gave Raymond a quick glance behind me, then knocked on the door.

Nobody answered. But a voice from behind me said, "Open it. It's not locked."

Raymond and I both looked back at Carl Reed standing outside the screen door, a revolver in his hand pointed at us.

"Go ahead," he said. The screen door squeaked as he opened it. "Get inside."

I opened the door and walked in, Raymond following.

Carl Reed came in after us, gun raised, and closed the door behind him. The three of us stood in the kitchen. "Why couldn't you just walk away?"

"It's just not my nature," I said. "Not when someone else is set up to take the fall for something he had nothing to do with."

Carl yelled, "He's a worthless piece of—"

"I know all about your son," I said.

"You don't know anything," Carl said, the gun still raised, pointed at me and Raymond.

"I talked to your wife," I said. "She tried to make excuses for him. She said it was because of what happened... when his friend drowned in that boat. But I'm not sure why your son having a drug problem really matters at this point. The fact is, he killed his own fiancée with his car."

Carl Reed stared back at me without a response.

"I saw his MG," I said. "It was in the garage at Ned's house. I saw the damage. I know what injuries she sustained, all to her lower body. If she'd been hit by Ron's truck..."

"You have no idea what you're talking about," Carl said. "Her autopsy proved she was—"

"I saw the original report. The one from before you had your old buddies tear it up. You've got this whole state in the palm of your hand, huh? Doing whatever they can to cover up what happened?"

"You son of a bitch," Carl said. "You're making a big mistake."

He looked like he was about to crack. "Logan told your wife what really happened to Casey."

Carl swallowed hard, shaking his head. Tears filled his eyes. "He... he told her?"

"He told her it was an accident. But that he killed her."

Carl was wavering, on the edge of admitting what really happened, but still hanging on to his own denial. "My wife's nothing but a drunk," he said. "She makes things up. She doesn't know what she's saying."

"It's time for the truth," I said. "I believe Logan took his own life. Is that what happened?"

Carl took a moment, gently nodded, and lowered his gun. He took a step back, his free hand reaching behind him for the chair he pulled from the round kitchen table in the corner. He sat and leaned forward with his elbows on his knees, head lowered. He let out a long sigh before he raised his gaze to me and Raymond.

His eyes were filled with tears, and I wondered if it would be a good time to make a move toward him. But he still had the gun in his hand, and I wanted him to talk.

"All I wanted to do was protect him. I told him nobody would ever find out what happened. He didn't deserve to have to deal with something like this again. He... He was a good kid. He really was. And he loved Casey, but..." He stood, the gun raised.

"Was Casey's death really an accident?" I said.

"He stared back at me, eyes narrowed. "He loved her."

"Then why?" I said. "Why would you go through all this trouble to cover it up?"

"I told you. All I wanted to do was protect my son." He wiped a tear with the back of the same hand holding the gun.

"We need the truth, Carl. It's the best thing now. For Logan. And for everyone else involved."

He sat, silent. Waiting, as if he still wasn't sure how much to say. But after a few moments, he finally cleared his throat. "They—Logan and Casey—were on their way to Swan Lake, up in Searsport. I'm not even sure why they were going up there. I never asked. He came here to see me, at this house. He borrowed some money, said they wanted to spend the night. They were both broke. They never had money. But I always gave him what he needed. He was my only son, you know?" He glanced at me and Raymond, taking his time, like he was thinking it through. He shifted his gaze to the window over the sink, the warm sunlight shining through the glass onto my back. "I guess they'd stopped at a bar on the way up and had a few drinks." He shrugged. "Who knows what else they were on."

"Drugs?" I said.

He took a deep breath, shoulders raised until he slowly exhaled. "We always did all we could to help him. We sent him to the best doctors, the best rehab facilities. But nothing ever worked. Not with the way the two of them would pull each other back into the same old habits." He looked me in the eye. "I don't know the last time I saw my own son sober. And Casey... she had her own problems."

It was quiet in the house, other than the hum from the refrigerator behind me and Raymond.

"Your wife believes it was an accident," I said. "Is that true?"

Carl took another deep breath, nodding as if preparing himself to let out all he'd been holding in.

"It was late when he called me. Almost midnight. I was asleep, so it took me a minute when he called, but I knew something was wrong. He told me he was at a pay phone in Lewiston."

I glanced at Raymond and he turned to me, a look on his face like he wasn't sure what was coming next.

Carl said, "I'd had a few drinks myself that night. But Logan..." Carl just shook his head.

I tried to prod the guy along. "But Logan what?" I said.

Carl shrugged. "I could hardly understand him. He was drunk... high, or... whatever those two were doing. He was crying into the phone. And, you know what?" He shook his head. "My son never cried. It was like he couldn't anymore. Because, back when he lost his friend, the boy who drowned... It was so long ago, but I remember it like it was yesterday. Logan cried for days. Weeks. They were just little boys. He didn't understand what happened to his best friend. And it... it broke him. That boy drowned in that lake. His parents lost their child. But, you know what? We lost ours, too. He never got over it."

The tears flowed down Carl's face. I could see his pain. But I wasn't going to excuse him for what he'd done to Ron Tompkins. Or for what he did to me.

Carl cleared his throat, again wiping his face with the back of his hand. "I remember the drive up. It took me an hour to get there, and at least another one trying to find him." He closed his eyes, shaking his head. "Casey might've survived, if he'd only taken her to a hospital instead of... He should've called someone else for help. But it was my fault. I was the one who told him to wait for me. I was more worried he'd get in trouble."

"So you already knew what had happened before you got there? I thought you said—"

"Logan could barely string two sentences together. But he told me enough. I knew the deal. I knew it was bad." Carl appeared like he was doing all he could to choke back the tears. "They went to some bar in Lewiston, on Lisbon Street where all those social clubs and pawnshops are. It's not a good place to go. Not unless you're looking for trouble. Or drugs. I don't know if you've ever been up there at night, but people park their cars on Lisbon Street just to watch the drunks coming out of the bars, stumbling into the streets... fights left and right... drugs... the police taking half the people in the streets into custody."

"Carl," I said. "Can you tell me what happened to Casey?"

I had my eye on his gun as he ran his free hand through his hair, holding it there for a moment and closing his eyes.

"Turns out I found him at a place up there called Hank's Food and Fuel. Like I said, it took me a good hour to locate him." He let out another long sigh, got up and grabbed a glass from the cabinet and filled it with water from the tap. He guzzled the whole thing, turning his back to us for a moment. I was tempted to try to grab the gun from his hand, but thought better of it.

"I pulled into the parking lot, and they were both in the car... white as ghosts. I wasn't sure either was alive at that point."

I pictured Casey Jilson's body, not in the front seat of Logan Reed's car, but the way I saw it on the beach that morning. "Was Casey already dead?"

He paused, then nodded. "I told you, it was just an accident. He didn't mean for any of it to happen."

The exterior screen door slammed closed on the porch, the three of us turning to the doorway from the kitchen to see who it was. I thought, for a moment, it might've been Maggie. But she wouldn't have let the door slam that way.

A woman called out, "Carl?"

I watched Carl hide the gun behind his back.

A much younger woman, the one I'd met the first time I was at that house, walked into the kitchen with a bikini top and a towel wrapped around her waist.

"Oh," she said, gazing at the three of us. "What's going on?"

"Nothing," Carl said. "We're just talking. Maybe you should go back to the beach. I'll come down and get you when we're done."

"She doesn't know?" I said, glancing at Carl.

"I don't know *what*?" the woman said.

"Nothing," Carl said. "Please, hon. Just go back to the beach so we can finish up."

She didn't move, but looked over her shoulder when the screen door outside creaked.

We all heard it.

And in walked the man I was almost expecting.

The ex-cop had his gun raised. He had a pretty good gash on his head where I'd hit him with the briefcase full of money, blood dried on his cheek and around his neck. His neat, well-dressed appearance was gone: the way his white dress shirt hung, untucked, dirty, and soaked with sweat and bloodstains.

The younger woman had her eyes open wide, looking across the kitchen at Carl. "Cuh... Carl? What's... What's going on here?"

"I told you to go back to the beach!" he said, his voice raised this time. "Listen to me, will you? Please. Just get out of here. And don't come back."

"No," the ex-cop said. "Nobody's going anywhere."

Carl shook his head. "Frank, no. It's over. I told them everything."

"Frank?" I said, looking at the man. "You never did tell me your name."

Frank gave me a quick look, but shifted his gaze back to Carl. "I knew it was a mistake helping you. You're too weak. Look at you. After all we did for you? Now you're going to—"

"It's gone too far," Carl said, shaking his head. "It was a mistake. All of it."

"I'm not going down for you, Carl. Just because you couldn't keep your mouth shut? I did you a favor to keep that drug-addict kid of yours out of jail. We all helped you. And now what? You think I'm going to pay for any of this?" Frank shoved the woman across the kitchen and she stumbled, falling into Carl's arms. Frank used his gun and gestured for me and Raymond to step over with the other two.

Raymond's .38 was tucked into the back of his pants, but I wasn't sure I wanted him to bring it out.

Carl had his own ideas.

He reached behind his back and pulled the revolver he had tucked in his pants. But before he could get it raised past his belt, two shots rang out. Carl fell onto the table behind him, then rolled off to the floor, taking the chair down with him.

The woman screamed and ducked under the table, trying to slide Carl under with her.

Raymond had his gun pulled.

But Frank, the ex-cop, had dropped to the floor, facedown. Blood soaked through the back of his white dress shirt.

Raymond and I looked at each other, and I reached for the gun Carl had dropped on the floor. I knew he wasn't the one who shot his buddy Frank.

Officer Thomas Silva walked in from the porch, gun in hand. Chief Hanley came in behind him, battered, bloodied, and beaten. One eye was half shut.

Officer Silva tucked his gun into his holster and knelt next to the ex-cop, feeling for a pulse. "He's still alive," he said, looking up at Chief Hanley.

Maggie came onto the porch from outside with two Maine state troopers.

Sirens screamed in the distance.

CHAPTER 36

DARLENE REED WAS LOOKING out at me, waiting on her porch at her Cambridge home. She had a coffee mug in her hand, taking a sip as I walked from the Nova parked on the street in front of her house.

"Thanks for meeting with me," I said, stopping at the bottom step.

"I didn't mean for anyone to get hurt," she said.

I nodded. "I know."

She looked down at me from the top step, shaking her head. "But, like I told the police, I had no idea what Carl was doing. I hope you believe me."

"He made it clear you had nothing to do with any of it. I can't say the same for all his friends."

"I'm glad Rick Hanley was cleared of any wrongdoing," she said.

"I can't say for sure they won't be looking for a new chief in Kennebunkport, but I'm sure he's happy to be alive. They beat him up pretty good, when he confronted them. All he wanted was for the

278

truth to finally come out, going all the way back to what happened at that college."

"I hope you know, I didn't know about that either," she said. "I mean, I never knew if Rick was the one who put those drugs in Ron Tompkins' car or not. I guess I believed him, the way he denied it."

"Well, he was telling the truth the whole time," I said. "Little did he know a cop in his own department was behind making it appear Ron was the one dealing those drugs. And not your son."

"Carl and I had our secrets. But, I'm embarrassed... He loved Logan so much. Spent his whole life trying to keep him out of trouble."

"You mean, to keep him from paying the price, like most kids without your husband's money and connections usually do," I said. "I guess I don't understand why Ron Tompkins had to be the scape-goat."

"You're asking me like I was involved in any of it. I just told you, Carl and I had our secrets. Anytime I asked him questions, he'd tell me not to worry. He'd take care of everything."

"I guess by having his old buddy, Frank Richards, pulling the strings from the inside," I said. "Frank Richards was the one who decided to put Hanley out front, to lead the investigation, because he knew he wasn't much of a cop. All they had to do was put enough evidence in Hanley's lap for him to go after Tompkins. That's why they knew they could do it again, and Hanley would be more than happy to go after Ron a second time, for a much more serious offense."

Mrs. Reed lowered her chin, her eyes toward the porch floor. "Who was the other man involved? I know most of them, but I'd never heard the name... I think he works for the police. Or maybe the town."

"You mean Jim Shirley? He was head of communications for the town, and worked dispatch for the police. He was the one who received multiple reports there was a truck on the beach, but kept it quiet until everything was ready." I looked up at her. "You weren't kidding when you said your husband knows a lot of people in Maine."

"He's related to half of them," she said, a small grin on her face. "Even still, I'm surprised so many were willing to help him."

I ran my hand over my rough, unshaven face. "Well, people were always suspicious of Ron. I don't think he's ever been very well liked up there. So he didn't have many people on his side." I glanced at her big house, in one of the most expensive areas of Massachusetts.

Mrs. Reed lifted her mug and sipped from it, staring into it before raising her gaze. "Do you know what happened that night? With Logan and Casey?"

I wasn't sure if she was putting me on, or what she actually knew had happened. She told the police she knew nothing.

I said, "Your husband never had a chance to finish telling me. They rushed him off to the hospital after he was shot, then took him right into custody once they knew he'd be all right." I looked out at the Nova on the street.

"Can you tell me what you know?" she said.

"Well, like I said, he never finished the story. But I got my hands on the report, and his confession."

"I want to know everything," she said.

I didn't think she had plans to go visit Carl at Maine State Prison, otherwise I would've told her to get the whole story from him if she wanted it.

Or if she really didn't know.

"But I thought Logan told you?" I said.

She shook her head. "Not everything."

At that point, I realized she was telling me all she could. She knew some of what happened that night, but apparently only enough to know her son was going to need her husband's help.

I cleared my throat and told her what I could.

"After they left Lewiston," I said, "They ended up in a fight."

"With each other?" she said.

"Apparently."

She closed her eyes with a sigh. "That's all they did. They'd fight all the time."

"From what I understand, Logan pulled into a church parking lot and Casey got out of the car."

Darlene glanced out into the street.

I turned to look, seeing a neighbor outside in her yard across the road. The woman waved, and Darlene waved back, although barely lifting her hand.

Her eyes had glossed over. "It was really an accident, wasn't it?"

I wasn't sure of the answer. I'm not sure anybody was, with any certainty. All we had was what Logan had told his father, and what his father had told the police.

"It was," I said. It was the only way for me to answer.

She wiped a tear from her cheek. "But he still would have paid a price, maybe spend the rest of his life behind bars."

"I don't know about that," I said. "But keeping it a secret is rarely the best option. The truth always comes out in the end."

She closed her eyes and lowered her head. "Logan didn't want any more secrets. That's what he told me, the last time I saw him. But I... I didn't know what he meant, or what he'd planned to do." She burst into tears and fell into my arms, crying and resting her head on my chest. Her tears soaked through my shirt.

***

I drove the Nova across the border into New Hampshire, Nancy squeezed in the middle seat between me and Maggie.

Those two were talking, the radio loud with some kind of disco music I didn't like. But I wasn't listening to the song, or what Maggie and Nancy were saying. With the windows down, the wind blew around inside the car.

I hadn't said much for most of the ride, thinking about not only the way the summer had ended so fast and about my latest case... but also how much I hated having to drop Nancy off at school.

It had come too soon.

Dropping her off at college hadn't gotten any easier for me, even though everyone said it would. But not everyone had been through what Nancy and I had together.

I had my elbow out the window, wind in my face, thinking about her first day of kindergarten, like it was yesterday. I remember I'd spent the morning at the kitchen table, wondering at the time how fast five years had gone by. My wife, Barbara, laughed at me, although I think she was just better at holding it all in.

Nancy reached for the radio and changed the station, then lowered the volume. "Did you hear what I said?"

I turned to her, like I'd snapped out of a daze. "Huh?"

"I was asking about that creepy guy from the party. Are you going to do anything?"

"You mean, the one who sliced my tires?" I rolled the window halfway up so I could hear her. "I don't know. Maybe not."

"We think you should just let it go," Maggie said, leaning forward, looking past Nancy at me.

"Don't you think I should at least get him to pay for them?" I said. "You know how much I paid for those tires?"

"Thirty-nine dollars each," Maggie said. "You told us five times."

Nancy and Maggie both laughed.

Nancy said, "Besides, there's no real proof he did it. You still have his knife."

"I'm sure he had another one. I'm sure it was him," I said.

Nancy gave me a questioning look. "You're sure? Without any real evidence? Aren't you the one who always says—"

"All right, all right," I said. "That's enough. I don't like the way you two always gang up on me like that." I laughed.

I couldn't have been happier to have Maggie with us for the ride back to Nancy's school. I know Nancy was happy she came for the ride. It was like she'd become part of our family again, the same way she was after Barbara was killed.

Nancy raised the radio's volume, this time for a new song, "My Sharona," by a band called The Knack.

The three of us didn't say a word for the next couple of miles. I felt the lump in my throat when I saw the sign for the main entrance to Plymouth College.

I glanced at Nancy, and she looked happy to be back. As much as we wanted our kids to stick around, sometimes maybe it was better—at least for them—if they didn't. At least for a little while...

I pulled up to the sidewalk in front of her dorm, where there were at least another dozen or so cars, some parents outside hugging their kids, others doing a drop-off without much more than a quick wave goodbye.

I got out and opened the trunk and pulled out Nancy's suitcase. Her bedding was stuffed into a garbage bag, with a duffel bag filled with more of her things. I wasn't sure if she wanted us to help her carry everything up, and was afraid to ask.

Nancy reached out for Maggie and gave her a hug. "I'll miss you guys." She held on to Maggie for a long few seconds.

There was no denying it; I was fighting back tears.

Two female voices yelled from across the parking lot, "Nancy!"

She turned and two girls—young women—ran toward her.

I watched, and a smile filled my face. The three hugged and screamed with excitement, like the little girls they once were.

Maggie put her hand on my arm, watching me stare at Nancy and her friends. "I don't know if I can say the same about you," she said. "But she'll be all right."

***

Thank you for reading *The Silence of the Sand*. I appreciate it more than you know.

If you enjoyed the mystery, I'd love to stay in touch. Head over to GregoryPayette.com to sign up for my newsletter — you'll get some fun free stories just for joining.

And if you have a minute, an honest review on the store where you purchased *The Silence of the Sand* makes a real difference for an author. Even a line or two helps other readers find the series.

Jake is back in *When the Smoke Clears* — the third book in the series.

Learn more at GregoryPayette.com

Visit GregoryPayette.com for more stories

HENRY WALSH MYSTERIES

Dead at Third

The Last Ride

The Crystal Pelican

The Night the Music Died

Dead Men Don't Smile

Dead in the Creek

Dropped Dead

Dead Luck

A Shot in the Dark

Dead or a Lie

JAKE HORN MYSTERIES

A Ring and a Prayer (Series prequel)

A Good Time for Goodbye

The Silence of the Sand

When the Smoke Clears

U.S. MARSHAL CHARLIE HARLOW

Shake the Trees

Trackdown

Half Moon Rising

JOE SHELDON SERIES

Play It Cool

Play It Again

Play It Down

STANDALONES

Bicayne Boogie

Drag the Man Down

Half Cocked

GREGORY PAYETTE

Danny's Womack's .38
We're Not Down (summer 2026)

www.ingramcontent.com/pod-product-compliance
Lightning Source LLC
Chambersburg PA
CBHW050031120726
47903CB00006B/1988